A. M. S'IIKEL

BAD MAGIC

WOMBACH PRESS

For Ailsa

ISBN: 978-1-9161601-0-1 (paperback)
978-1-9161601-1-8 (eBook)

WOMBACH PRESS
wombachpress@gmail.com

About the Author

A. M. Stirling has had a varied career as a freelance photographer, an artist with several national and international exhibitions to his name, and an academic. After harbouring an ambition to write fiction for far too long, he completed an MA in Creative Writing at Newcastle University in 2012.

Bad Magic is his first published novel. He lives in Newcastle upon Tyne.

1

Richard had his eye to the peephole, watching the woman on the other side of the door. He was enjoying making her wait. It proved he was a different person now; that he wouldn't stand for the way she used to treat him.

She knocked again, more insistently this time, and he steadied himself against the door. But it shifted under his weight and the lock clicked. The woman's face came closer. Distorted by the wide-angle lens, it ballooned up at him. Closing one eye, she cocked her head to one side, as if she could see him squinting at her through the peephole.

He opened the door. Her face was not quite as he remembered it. But as he stared, embarrassed at being caught out, he began to recognise the features of the girl he used to know; the dark eyes, the upturned nose. And her smile. That bloody smirk of a smile.

"Hello, Amanda," he said.

"You took your time, Dickie."

"No one calls me that anymore."

"All grown up now, are you?" She pushed passed him and dropped her handbag on to the sofa.

"You caught me having a snooze. It was a long flight."

"Really?" She noticed his drink on the coffee table. "Aren't you going to offer me one?"

"I brought gin but there's no tonic in the mini-bar. And there's no ice."

She picked up his glass and took a sip. "It needs ice."

"There's an ice machine on another floor. I couldn't be bothered."

"You haven't changed, Dickie. Give me a neat gin. It'll have to do. I need a bloody drink."

At the kitchenette, a counter with a sink and a microwave, he opened the bottle of Beefeater he'd brought from Heathrow, poured a good measure into a clean tumbler, and topped up his own glass. She went through the sliding double doors into the bedroom. He followed and stood in the doorway holding their drinks. There was a laminated notice on the window-sill and she picked it up. It warned guests not to open the windows because there was a plague of lake flies in Toronto.

"You can't open the window?" she said, bending to look at the tiny black flies gathering on the other side of the glass. "Persistent little fuckers, aren't they?"

Richard didn't know why she had come into the bedroom, and stayed where he was, leaning against the doorframe. As he watched her, she turned, showing off the way her black leather skirt hugged her figure.

He had rested after the flight and the bed covers were pulled back. Amanda kicked off her shoes and laid full length on the rumpled sheets, her head on the pillow. She bent her knees and her skirt rode up to show her thighs. He knew she was testing him.

"I have terrible insomnia at the moment," she said. "I'm always so bloody tired."

"I'm sorry about Aunt Emily," he said, and he meant it because his aunt had been kind to him all those years ago.

"I'm an orphan now, just like you," said Amanda. "Can I have my drink, please?"

"It's here," he said, holding up the glass.

She put her shoes back on, got up from the bed and came towards him.

"Let's have them in here." He turned and went back into the sitting room.

"Aren't you going to give me a hug?" she said, raising her arms as she came towards him.

Of course, she knew he would. Hadn't she always known these things about him? He put the glasses on the coffee table and embraced her. Touching her bra strap through her blouse made him feel furtive and confused. The last time he had seen her she had been sixteen, two years older than him, and he'd wanted her to be kind to him after the death of his parents. But she had bullied him, just as she had when they were children.

And then that night, after the business on the island with Lisa McKee, she had come across the landing into his room, and into his bed. They tussled and twisted up the sheets. He couldn't stop her; she did what she wanted to do.

Now, she held him by the shoulders and looked at him in a peculiar way. Thinking she might try to kiss him on the lips, he pulled back even though he knew he wanted her to. That was why he'd elected to stay in a hotel; he hadn't wanted to be alone with her in an empty house.

"You don't seem very sympathetic." She had a slight Canadian accent, but the North East of England was still there in her intonations. "You should know what a difficult time I'm having," she said. "You of all people. Are you annoyed I didn't meet you at the airport? Or is it something else?"

"It was just a long flight, that's all," he said. "We should go down to the bar and get a decent drink."

Amanda wanted a cigarette first and they went out and stood under the portico of the hotel where the taxis came in.

"Do you want a cigarette?" she said. "Or don't you smoke?"

He laughed and took one from the packet she offered.

"You taught me how to smoke," he said. "Don't you remember?"

He didn't mention that she'd taught him how to kiss as well, had insisted on giving him 'kissing lessons', and showing him the thing with tongues. But she must have sensed it, or remembered it too, because she mentioned Lisa.

"She'll be there tomorrow. I wonder if you'll still like her."

They sat at a table in the hotel bar and drank gin and tonics.

"So, no Nana?" said Amanda. "She really fell down some stairs and broke her hip?"

"On one of her cruises. I think she was pissed, but she insists that she'd only had a glass of Muscadet as an apero. She's still getting over the operation. She wanted to come, but a transatlantic flight is beyond her."

His grandmother had made Richard come, and paid his expenses, but the cruises were a sore point. They were just one of the ways she seemed determined to spend her fortune before she died. She flaunted her excessive spending, even as he was always crawling to her for handouts.

"I feel abandoned," said Amanda.

"Well, I'm here," he said, hearing the whine in his own voice.

"Yes, but you don't want to be, do you?"

He was angry with her, but he couldn't show it; angry at the way she was playing the injured party, trying to force him to give her sympathy. She always twisted things to get the upper hand, even when she was in the wrong. Especially when she was in the wrong. She'd never had to face the consequences of her actions. He'd never known how to deal with it, and changed the subject; how did Aunt Emily die?

"It was an accident. Or at least I like to think it was an accident. Mom had rheumatoid arthritis. She was in a lot of pain and her mobility was...well, she was housebound. I knew she was depressed. She was addicted to the painkillers. Opioids. And I think she was drinking in secret. These things don't mix very well, do they? Sometimes she was confused. I like to think that's why she took the overdose. That it was just a mistake. I can't bear to think it was deliberate. Of course, I blame myself. I'd come home to look after her, and look what happened."

Amanda told the story with little actions, clutching at her hands and pulling along her fingers as she spoke. She closed her eyes and pulled her mouth down to show how sad she was. It all looked too considered, but Richard felt compelled to reach out and squeeze her hand. If he were kind to her, if he could help her, she might be kinder to him in return. The thought was an old feeling, a fantasy he used to have about her when they were children. The memory of it made him feel pathetic and he loosened his grip.

Twenty years ago he'd had his own story to tell, embellishing the details of the accident, exaggerating the things that didn't really matter. He hadn't cared that the trivial details were boring; they took attention away from the bloody thing itself.

He used to talk about the family car, a BMW 5 Series, the car his father had always wanted. 'The ultimate driving machine,' he called it, repeating the advertising slogan. He dwelled on the fact that it was his birthday; that they'd been to see 'Jurassic Park' and then gone to Pizza Hut, even though his mother abhorred fast food.

In the story Richard told, they'd been driving back to the village when something appeared in the road. A roe deer. His father swerved and lost control of the car. They came off the road, the BMW turning over and over, metal groaning as it crumpled, glass cracking, until it came to rest against a tree. It lay on its side, the engine still running and the headlights shining out into the darkness. His mother's head was at a strange angle, silhouetted against the crazed white of the shattered windscreen, but he couldn't see his father, who was slumped in deep shadow. Richard lay awkwardly in the back of the car, trapped by his seatbelt, and called out.

In telling the story he left out the bit about being frightened when they didn't answer. Instead he tried to explain how he knew that the worst had happened. "You can feel it," he would say. "Suddenly there's a big empty space where something used to be." He was never able to stop himself crying when he told that part, which was the end of his story and the truest thing about it.

Amanda had booked them into a faux Italian restaurant, which served handmade pasta, across the street from the hotel. It had bare brick walls and the sound of other people's conversations was hard and brittle. He ordered bruschetta to start, and the veal ragu, and they agreed on a bottle of Chianti. The waitress brought the wine and poured a little for Richard to taste. She was pretty, and when she commented on his accent, he flirted a little with her while she poured the wine.

"Do you want to sleep with her?" said Amanda after the waitress had gone. "I wouldn't have thought she was your type."

"How do you know what my type is?"

"Well, she's too young for a start. Too innocent for you, surely?"

Richard looked across the table. Amanda's dark hair fell to her shoulders and her lips curled into a smile. That smile, come back so soon to haunt him. It was a cruel thing, and the moment he'd opened the door to her he realised that he'd never forgotten it. She was beautiful, he had to admit that, but there was something more. Something he didn't want to think about.

She wanted to know if he was married. And did he have kids?

"Divorced," he said. "And no kids."

Richard took a sip of his wine. Amanda had made his own childhood difficult, and he wondered if that was why he'd never wanted to be a father. There was too much responsibility involved in making other people happy. And he wasn't able to face up to that. But Sarah had wanted children. It was one of the reasons they'd split up. Perhaps it was the reason.

"And you?"

"Plenty of men," she said. "No kids."

"We're at the end of the line," he said, raising his glass. "The Waverleys are doomed to extinction."

"I'm going to change my name to Waverley," she said. "I don't want Ray's name anymore. Mom always went by Waverley after the divorce."

"What on earth for?"

"It's the family name, isn't it?"

She was curious about what he did and he told her about the gallery, building it up, not mentioning the trouble he was having making it pay, or the fact that their grandmother was keeping it going with the cheques he wheedled out of her. Instead he talked about the art fairs he was planning to go to, Miami, Basel, London, because he thought they sounded glamorous. Despite himself, and his feelings about her, he wanted to impress her, to make her think he'd made it.

The waitress brought their starters and topped up their glasses.

"I hate the way they do that," said Amanda, when she'd gone. "Will you tell her not to?"

Richard sensed she was trying to get him to be rude to the waitress, but he wouldn't rise to it. What did Amanda do? That's what he wanted to know.

"I did drama at college and went to Vancouver to get into acting. But it's tough so I kind of fell into modelling," she said, concentrating on running her finger up and down the stem of her wine glass.

"What kind of modelling?"

"Oh, you know. Fashion. Hostess work. At trade fairs, things like that."

"Was that interesting?" he said, although he didn't think it could have been.

"Really, it's just acting. I know what men are like, you see. And I know what they like. But you know that, don't you?"

When the waitress brought their main courses, she picked up the bottle of wine and began to top up their glasses.

"Dickie," said Amanda, kicking him under the table. "Tell her."

The waitress froze. "Is there something wrong?"

"Everything's fine," said Richard. Amanda started kicking him again and again, the sharp toe of her shoe pecking at his shinbone. He gripped both sides of the table because of the pain and smiled up at the waitress. "Everything's fine. Really."

"You're playing the fool," said Amanda, raising her voice. "It's my mother's funeral in the morning and I've no time for your nonsense. Come to the house at ten if you can be bothered."

She'd stood up. She was going outside to call a cab. People

at the other tables looked over, and Richard felt his face flush. Now she was trying to make him look bad. But she was drunk and unsteady on her feet, knocking against the chairs of the other diners as she made her way to the door, and someone shouted, "Hey! Watch out!" The waitress was still standing with the bottle of wine in her hand, her mouth open.

"Please forgive my cousin," said Richard. "She's a little upset, that's all." He had a view of Amanda through the plate glass window, pacing backwards and forwards on the pavement outside. She was smoking a cigarette and holding her phone to her ear. "Her mother, my aunt, has just died, and the funeral's tomorrow."

"I'm sorry for your loss," said the waitress.

Richard smiled to himself. It was what they said on American cop shows. It was what the Bangladeshi taxi driver and Joshua, the handsome young desk clerk at the hotel had said to him. After the death of his own parents no one knew what to say. He was to live with his grandparents, but his grandmother was unable to cope with his numb presence.

His aunt Emily, Amanda and her stepfather, Ray, had come over from Toronto for the funeral. Later it was agreed that he would go and visit them later in the year, and stay for the whole summer. It was hoped that new experiences would bring him out of himself. He was quiet and sullen when they picked him up at the airport, and showed no interest in the things his uncle pointed out to him as they drove towards the city: the CN tower, the lakeshore, and the fast food restaurants with bright signs and unfamiliar names. His aunt said that he should think of their house as his home.

Amanda had come up to his room to help him unpack. She wore denim shorts with boots and stomped about the room, opening the drawers and the closet to show him where to put his clothes. She was sixteen now and he didn't know what to say to her. He noticed that she had breasts and he could see the shape of a bra, the straps and everything, under her t-shirt.

She noticed him looking. Did he want her to pull her t-shirt up? He'd nodded, half nodded anyway, still numb from his journey, and not sure what the right answer was. She laughed at him and called him a pervert.

He turned away from her, embarrassed, and she caught him by surprise. Grabbing his arm, she twisted it up behind his back and pushed him down onto the bed, squashing his face into the pillow. He struggled, panicking because he couldn't breathe. He'd hoped that the death of his parents guaranteed him immunity from the way she used to treat him. But he was wrong; she laughed when she let him up. Said he whimpered like a sick puppy.

Now as he waited for the waitress to bring the bill he looked out of the window. Amanda was getting into a taxi. It drove off and he was glad. She hadn't changed at all. He would go to the funeral to keep up appearances, which, after all, was the only reason he was here. And that would be an end to it.

2

In Richard's memory the house was a mansion in a street of mansions. But when he got out of the taxi he saw that it was just an ordinary suburban house with a lawn and a driveway leading to a garage. The grass was yellowed and bare in patches. And it had just been mown; loose clippings were scattered all along the path. Up on the porch were a white plastic chair and a matching table. He noticed the glass ashtray full of cigarette stubs and rang the doorbell.

Earlier that morning he'd gone out to the Tim Hortons on Dundas. He'd bought a large filter coffee and a blueberry muffin, and taken them back to his suite in a brown paper bag. The sun was shining and he sat at the table by the window. Sipping his coffee, he looked out from the fourteenth floor. In the office block opposite workers were arriving at their desks, and tiny black specks showed against the pale blue sky; the lake flies gathering on the other side of the glass.

Last night he'd been pleased that he'd put Amanda's nose out of joint. It proved he couldn't be pushed around anymore. But now he knew he'd been cocky because he'd had a few drinks. And there were always consequences where Amanda was concerned; he remembered that well enough.

Standing on the porch, listening to what he imagined were high heeled shoes on a polished wooden floor, he was prepared to apologise, ready to blame the booze mixed up with jet lag. But when Amanda opened the door she kissed him on the cheek. Her dark hair was swept up into a chignon, she wore a black fitted dress and a pearl necklace glistened at her throat. A woman with a clipboard stood behind her in the hallway.

"I'm busy with the caterers," said Amanda. "Ray's hiding from me in the kitchen. Go and get a coffee. The hearse and the limo will be here in about twenty minutes."

Richard went into the kitchen. A man in his sixties was sitting at the breakfast bar, clutching a mug of coffee. He looked up nervously, and then he smiled.

"Richard," he said, standing up. "Is it really you?"

"Uncle Ray," said Richard, and they shook hands and hugged.

"I came too early. I'm not even sure she wants me here."

Ray was Amanda's stepfather, long divorced from Emily. His thick grey hair needed a trim and he wore a dark blue suit he wasn't used to wearing, and the cut was out of date.

Richard's grandmother had insisted he wore an expensive suit. And she'd paid for it. If she wasn't able to come herself, it was important he made a good impression on her behalf. And even though she wasn't going to be at the funeral, she had predicted what it would be like.

"A Humanist ceremony?" she'd said when she'd read Amanda's email. "How wretched." She thought that without evoking God or the afterlife the ceremony was just a way of getting rid of the body. No one would make an effort; they'd turn up wearing any old thing, including anoraks. "I've seen it happen," she said. If she believed in nothing else, and Richard wasn't even sure his grandmother believed in God, it was in keeping up appearances.

In the back of the stretch Mercedes Amanda took a small mirror from her handbag. She refreshed her lipstick, adjusted the black chiffon scarf that covered her head and put on a pair of sunglasses. She slipped her arm through Richard's and pulled him closer. He thought they must look like a fairy-tale couple; Prince and Princess Charming in a gleaming black limousine.

At the crematorium the chauffeur held the rear door of

the Mercedes open for Amanda. As she stepped out of the car, Richard realised how carefully she had considered her appearance. Everything she wore: the headscarf, the oversized sunglasses with the gold logo, the long gloves, the bright gash of red lipstick with all that black, created an effect. She looked magnificent, mythic even, as if a stylist had primped her for a fashion shoot on funereal glamour.

The casket was carried into the crematorium. Amanda and Richard followed it down the aisle. She took his arm, sagging against him as if grief made walking difficult. The congregation turned to watch. Richard knew that was the point; she was directing a piece of theatre in which he was forced to play the part of a grieving and supportive cousin.

And when the time came for her to deliver her eulogy he had to help her to her feet, and guide her to the lectern. She fumbled for a piece of folded paper in her handbag. Her hand was shaking as she read from it, her voice cracking as she talked about her wonderful mother, how close they were, how the shock of her sudden death had knocked her down.

She was still wearing her sunglasses. Richard thought that this was for dramatic effect or to cover the emotional gaps in her performance. But he was surprised when she took them off. Tears, black with mascara, streaked down her cheeks. Had he misjudged her? Or, like all actors, was she able to cry on demand?

As they walked back up the aisle, he got a clear look at the congregation. In the rows of pews were about fifty or sixty people, most of them dressed in a way his grandmother would have considered unsuitable; leather jackets, bright coats and scarves. A woman caught his eye, a bespectacled blonde in a black coat who smiled at him. He smiled back. It wasn't an automatic response; he recognised her.

Back at the house young men and women in waistcoats and bow ties stood behind the buffet table in the sitting room, or moved about with trays of drinks. Richard squeezed through the crowd and grabbed a glass of wine. He stood at the edge of the room and watched Amanda. She had freshened her make up, and was now a bright and capable hostess, charming her mother's friends and neighbours.

"She puts on a good show, doesn't she?" It was the woman who had smiled at him in the crematorium. Richard was pleased; he'd been about to search her out.

"Hello, Lisa," he said.

"I didn't think you'd recognise me. It's been a long time."

She looked down at her glass. It was empty. Richard signalled to a passing waiter, took another two glasses of wine and handed one to Lisa.

"I was a slip of a thing back then, wasn't I?"

"And you had braces, didn't you?"

"Oh, yes. Mom wanted to make sure I had 'lovely' teeth," she said.

"Well, it worked," he said.

She laughed and Richard recognised the face of the pretty teenage girl he'd had a crush on all those years ago. Lisa had liked him too, but Amanda had ruined it. She'd provoked another boy. Wound him up into a jealous frenzy to attack Richard and there'd been a fight. Lisa had been Amanda's best friend then, and had lived just a few streets away.

"I still live in my Mom's house," she said. "I couldn't face selling it after she died. When I moved back after the divorce, I used to visit Emily. She was a lovely woman. A real friend after Mom died. And then Amanda came back from Vancouver. She made it clear I wasn't welcome. We were never really friends again after that summer you were here. She's a real piece of work."

Lisa wanted to know how long he was going to be in Toronto. He knew she wanted to see him, and they exchanged phone numbers, tapping them into their smart phones as if they were teenagers again. He gave her his card as well, to show off about the gallery.

"This is me," he said.

"The Waverley Gallery. That sounds glamorous."

"It will be when it's properly established. It's hard work at the moment," he said.

Something made him look up; Amanda was watching them. Lisa turned to see what had caught his attention.

"Is she coming over?"

"No," he said. "Too busy playing the grieving daughter."

"Can we go somewhere else? There's something I need to tell you. In private."

He followed her into the kitchen, but there were people looking for drinks or snacks and the caterers were in and out with trays. Too crowded, said Lisa. She picked up another glass of wine and led him through the sliding glass doors out onto the deck.

Lisa took one of Richard's cigarettes, and touched his hand as he gave her a light. He smoked and looked out over the garden. He'd remembered it as well tended, with a lawn and shrubs and garden seats. Now it was overgrown with tall weeds amongst the long grass.

"Emily loved gardening," said Lisa. "She saw it as a way to keep going. She had to hire a gardener for the heavy stuff, but it gave her a purpose. It was only after Amanda came back that she became withdrawn. She stopped gardening, visiting friends. It was kind of unnatural, if you knew her."

"She just got worse, I suppose. The pain became too much. Wasn't that it?"

"Nah, she was a fighter. Listen, Richard…" Lisa took a deep breath. "I don't think Emily's death was an accident. After Amanda came back, Emily changed. I mean she really changed. She became confused and forgetful. At first, I thought she was drinking because she was depressed, and mixing it with her painkillers. But that didn't feel right, she used to be a nurse and knew her way around this stuff. When I was still allowed to visit, Amanda was always encouraging her to have a glass of wine or a gin and tonic."

"Wasn't there an autopsy?"

"There was. But it just showed an overdose of painkillers.

Opioids. It was recorded as an accidental death by the coroner. Sure, it could have been suicide, but nobody wanted to say so. There's nothing to say it wasn't, but the whole thing felt wrong. I think she was being fed something else, something to confuse her, to get her brain all mushy. Her decline seemed managed. Engineered."

"You mean Amanda, don't you? But why? What for?"

"Money. What else? You watch what happens. She'll sell the house. It's worth about a million dollars."

"Why didn't you go to the police?"

"With what? All I have is a feeling. And you can't show that to the cops. I'm a thirty-five year old divorcee with no kids and too much time on my hands. How's that going to play? I watch TV mystery movies if I'm at home in the afternoons and I drink too much. Something's wrong, that's all I know. And you know what's she's like. You remember, don't you?"

"I know how bad she is, how bad she can be. I really do," he said. "But murder?"

There was a knocking on the window, knuckles rapping hard against the glass. It was Amanda. She came out onto the deck.

"You two are getting pretty cosy out here," she said, taking Richard's cigarette from his hand and drawing on it. "Are you making up for lost time? Lisa's divorced now, Richard. She's Lisa McKee again. Single and fancy free."

"I was just telling Lisa about the gallery, Amanda."

"I think it sounds very glamorous," said Lisa.

"You're family, Richard, I need you to mingle. Ray doesn't count. Anyway he's hopeless. I can tell he can't wait to get away."

They went back inside. Richard picked up a glass of wine and went around introducing himself. Everyone was older than he was, and there was no-one he remembered from his visit twenty years before. He mentioned it though, saying how kind his Aunt Emily had been to him. They commented on his English accent and he talked up the gallery, saying the same thing over and over, until he thought he'd done his duty.

He saw Lisa alone by the drinks table and went over.

"Look who came," she said. "All the way from England."

Richard realised how drunk she was because she took his hand and squeezed it. He looked around to see if Amanda was watching them. Lisa pulled him closer.

"Don't be frightened of her," she said.

"Not here," he said, because he thought she was going to kiss him.

"I should go," she said, dropping his hand. "I've had too much to drink. I do stupid things."

Richard watched her go into the hall and put on her coat. He followed her out on to the front porch. She was halfway down the steps when he called her name. She turned and came back up. She kissed him on the lips. He kissed her back and she put her arms around him.

"You always were a good kisser," she said. "I remember."

"Not here, Lisa. It's not a good idea," he said, taking her hands from round his neck. "You've got my number. Call me tomorrow if you want to meet," he said, because that meant it was up to her.

It was early in the afternoon, and the sun was still shining. Richard watched Lisa walk down the path, her head bowed, something melancholy in her slow, deliberate, drunken steps.

Ray came out and said he was going to make a break for it. He started to ramble on about the weather. What a nice day it had been for the funeral. "But winter's coming. I heard about the winters before we came, you know? I heard they were cold. But nothing prepares you for it. I'm too old to take it. I'm heading down to Florida soon. Renting an apartment for the duration. I just can't take the cold anymore."

"It was good to see you again, Ray," said Richard and they shook hands.

Ray started down the steps. He stopped and turned at the bottom.

"It's all a bloody shame," he said. "Amanda and I never got on. She blames me for bringing her and Emily here. I did it for the best, you know? But she never wanted to come."

"What do you mean?" said Richard.

But Ray acted as if he didn't hear him, or didn't want to talk about it, and went on down the path.

And then everyone seemed to be leaving. Richard stood at the front door to see them off. They said goodbye to Amanda in the hall. He shook their hands, saying over and over how much they both appreciated them coming.

Afterwards he sat on the porch and watched the caterers loading their van. He thought about what Lisa had said about him being a good kisser, and remembered Amanda's kissing lessons, and then the other things he wished he could forget. He went inside to say goodbye. Like Ray, he needed to make his escape.

Amanda had changed into jeans and a plaid shirt and was kneeling in front of the fireplace in the living room, burning papers in the grate. She looked up at him when he came in.

"You've been a long time. I thought you'd run off. That you and Lisa were up to something."

"What do you mean?"

"You looked pretty cosy. And then she was holding your hand. I thought you were in the throes of something. Seriously. You liked her once, didn't you?"

"That was a long time ago."

"She got fat, didn't she?" said Amanda, tossing another sheaf of paper onto the fire and watching the flames flare up. "You should do some tourist stuff while you're here. It's a shame to come all this way just for a funeral. You could get Lisa McKee to show you round. I bet you'd like that."

"I'll manage," he said. "What are you burning?"

"Mom's old papers. Junk mostly. I'm going to have a drink. Do you want a drink?"

He said he would have a gin and tonic and she told him to mind the fire while she went to fix the drinks. He squatted down, picked up the poker and pushed the papers back into the flames, watching them catch alight. Something that hadn't caught dropped through the grate and onto the hearth. He pulled it towards him with the poker. It was a piece of white card from a small package, with a lozenge shaped logo and some text printed on it. Roche. And there was another word: Rohypnol. He picked it up and slipped it into his pocket. Was this what Lisa had suspected, the thing that had been fed to Aunt Emily to make her brain all mushy?

Amanda came in with the drinks on a tray. She put it on the coffee table, picked up a packet of cigarettes and took one out.

"Mom never liked me smoking, you know. Wouldn't let me smoke in the house. Even in the bloody winter. I had to put a parka on and sit outside. Then, today I just realised. Fuck it. It's my house now." She lit the cigarette. "What do you think of that?" she said, blowing out a plume of smoke.

"Are you going to sell it?"

"Maybe," she said, talking with her cigarette between her lips, and sitting back in her chair with her drink in her hand. "It's worth about a million dollars."

"That's about half a million pounds," he said. "That's a lot of money."

"Well, it is and it isn't," she said, blowing smoke across the room towards him. "You haven't touched your drink."

"I don't think I want it now. I've had too much already."

"Well, you asked for it," she said. "And I made it for you."

"I'm sorry," he said. "I just don't think it would do me any good right now."

Richard went over to the window and fumbled in his jacket pocket for the card the taxi driver had given him that morning.

3

Richard sat on the sofa in his hotel room, drinking a glass of wine and looking at the fragment of charred card he'd rescued from Amanda's fireplace. The word Rohypnol shocked him; it belonged in the tabloid press. They delighted in calling it The Date Rape Drug, which should have sounded like something from a world that had nothing to do with his own.

Except that it did. Amanda had tried to drug him, hadn't she? He remembered the drink she'd offered him, how she'd put the tray down on the coffee table so that one of the glasses was nearer to him than the other. And how annoyed she was that he didn't want it.

It dawned on him that Amanda might have spiked Lisa's drink, and he imagined her in a stupor, collapsed on the floor of her house, or worse, in the street. He thought he should call her to see if she was all right. But she might think he was being needy, or God forbid, creepy because he'd left it up to her to call him.

Their teenage romance, if it could even be called that, had been a long time ago. But he was still attracted to her; she had an air of melancholy that echoed his own. He remembered the way she'd taken his hand and squeezed it that afternoon. And how she'd kissed him on the porch. It was a weakness of his, the need to be wanted. If she was in trouble, he could be in a taxi in ten minutes, riding to the rescue. And after more than one glass of wine the idea of playing the hero appealed to him.

Lisa's phone rang for a long time. Richard thought it might go to voicemail, and then he would have to get a taxi over and embarrass himself by banging on the door, just to make sure she was all right. But then she answered, sounding sleepy and distracted. He heard other voices punctuated by music; a television set in the background.

"I was asleep," she said. "I couldn't find my phone."

"I was worried about you," he said.

Richard told her about finding the remains of the Rohypnol packet; how he had been worried that Amanda might have drugged her. How he was sure that she'd tried to drug him too.

"I know what she's capable of," said Lisa. "But I'm okay. I just had too much to drink. I fell asleep in front of the TV. That's what I usually do." She must have switched the television off because he couldn't hear the voices or the music anymore. "I know I drink too much. Mom went through all that trouble to bring me up right and see how I turned out?"

"Sometimes it helps to have a drink," he said. "I know that."

"I meant to kiss you, Richard. It wasn't just because I was drunk."

"I was glad you did. I liked it."

"You're sweet," she said. "Or you're drunk. We should stop now before we make real fools of ourselves. I'm going to get an early night. I'll call you tomorrow. We could meet up. That is if you really want to see me."

"Of course I do," he said.

When she hung up, he finished the glass of wine he'd been drinking and poured himself another.

In the morning he had breakfast in the Tim Hortons near the hotel, sitting at the counter by the window as young office workers passed by in the morning sun, the formality of their dark suits at odds with their bright backpacks. Everyone was on the move. Connected to the modern world by thin white cables and ear-buds, they all appeared to be talking to themselves.

Some of them came in from the street, opening their laptops, staring at the screens as they sipped their coffee and ate muffins or bagels. Richard flicked through a listings magazine he'd found on the counter, looking for an exhibition to fill his time until Lisa called. The Art Gallery of Ontario were showing a Chardin they'd recently restored; he would go and see that.

It was another bright hot day. That morning Joshua, the desk clerk, had told him that it was unseasonably warm for September, which was why the lake flies were lingering in the city, clinging to the glass of tall buildings warmed by the sun. Richard had made a comment about not being able to open the windows in his room, how air-conditioning was no substitute for cold night air. Really, he was complaining. But the young man, immaculate in his slim fitting suit, had just shrugged. There was nothing anyone could do. It was just the weather.

Richard took a streetcar across the city. He was soothed by a cool breeze coming through an open window and the lazy rhythm of the wheels knocking against the rails. Looking out at the people on the sunlit pavements, the Chinese restaurants with their bright signs as the car passed through Chinatown, he fell into a reverie; what would life be like here? Such thoughts were because of Lisa, because he wanted to see her again. But what future did they have? It was the tail end of a fantasy he'd had when he was fourteen, because she'd held his hand when he was sad. The car jolted and he came back to himself, and started checking his map, looking out for the street names at the intersections, so as not to miss the stop.

There was a room dedicated to the Chardin, but Richard had to wait to look at it. A large man was taking photographs of the painting, oblivious to the fact that he was preventing anyone else from seeing it. Richard wanted to say something but he didn't. Instead he pretended to be interested in the information panels that described the restoration, but he was chewing the inside of his mouth in frustration. Why didn't the fat bastard just go? He was taking too much time, checking every photograph he'd taken on the screen of his camera before taking another. He didn't appear to be looking at the painting at all, nor was he aware of the middle-aged couple waiting patiently behind him, which only increased Richard's irritation.

Eventually he was alone with the small oval painting. *Jar of Apricots* was exquisite. Light glistened on the jar itself, on the wet fruit inside it, and on the handle of a knife. These and the other things depicted; the loaf of bread, the glass of wine, all of them had a physical substance. They were tangible enough to touch; the ordinary had been transformed into the extraordinary. But it was more than that. Richard felt as if he was experiencing something profound; a moment that had existed in Chardin's studio over two hundred years ago, and it calmed him.

He found solace in art. That was what had saved him twenty years ago when, thanks to his grandfather's encouragement, he had discovered an enthusiasm for it. After his expulsion from school he'd realised his mistake. He took his 'A' levels at a sixth form college and managed to get a place to study art history at UEA.

Afterwards he'd worked in an auction house in London for a couple of years, and then a contemporary gallery in the East End. He had a talent for explaining art to people, and for making sales. It was that that inspired him to go home, back to the North East where property was cheap, and set up his own gallery. Not such a good idea in retrospect perhaps, but it was his lack of business acumen, rather than his faith in art, that let him down.

The Art Gallery of Ontario, like all public galleries, had a shop. Richard, still waiting for Lisa's call, browsed the cases of Inuit sculptures, depictions of animals, which were on sale to tourists. He bought a six-inch tall standing bear made of black basalt as a present for Catherine. He felt guilty; he was sure he was going to be unfaithful to her. Then, as the assistant handed him his receipt, he wondered if their relationship was enough of a 'thing' for him to worry about. But he knew he was being disingenuous, because it was obvious that she was in love with him.

Richard waited for Lisa in the hotel bar. He had been having lunch in the gallery café when she'd called. It was best that they meet at his hotel, she'd said. It would make things easier for her. He ordered a coffee because it was too early for a drink and sat by the window to watch for her. Taxis came and went, guests pulled their wheelie cases across the paving, or strutted about under the portico as they smoked and talked on their mobile phones. And all the time, as his coffee grew cold, he wondered why she had wanted to meet him here.

He had first met her that summer after his parents' death. His Aunt Emily had wanted Amanda to take him under her wing. And she had reluctantly taken him to meet Lisa at her parents' house. "She's my best friend, so don't show me up," she'd said. And she'd made a big thing of calling him Dickie all the time. That had been his baby name, and if it kept him small for her, it made him feel like a child again too. The true nature of Richard and Amanda's relationship was invisible to everyone else. She'd bullied and tormented him when they were children in Newcastle. Until he'd been born, she'd been the pretty little girl everyone indulged. But he became the new favourite and she punished him for it. And his visit to Toronto offered her new opportunities to abuse him.

It started that afternoon, after they'd sat on the porch of Lisa's house, drinking ice-cold bottles of Coke that her mother had brought out on a tray. Lisa was kind to him from the beginning and he was attracted to her. Perhaps it was just a crush, but she made him feel something, something that was a relief from the confusion of his grief.

It must have shown on his face, enough of it for Amanda to make fun of him when they got back to the house. "You like Lisa, don't you?" she'd said, bursting into his room, and the blood had rushed to his face and given him away. That was when she'd proposed the kissing lessons. "You want to be able to do it properly, don't you?"

Amanda had pushed him down onto the bed and lay on top of him. She'd kissed him, and showed him the thing with tongues that she called French kissing. His heart was beating fast, he had an erection, and he couldn't help but touch one of her breasts. She smacked his hand away and jumped up, laughing.

Lisa got out of a taxi. She was carrying a small bag, an overnight case, and Richard felt a tremor of anticipation. When she came into the bar he stood up and called out her name. She walked over to his table and kissed him.

"It's not too early for a drink, is it?" she said when the waitress came over.

"I don't think so," said Richard, and he ordered two gin and tonics.

While they waited for their drinks, he showed her the fragment of the Rohypnol packet.

"Put it away," she said. "I don't want to think about it now. Anyway, it doesn't prove anything. Legally, I mean."

"I know it doesn't," he said.

He'd made a mistake. The piece of burnt card meant Amanda was there with them, because to think about the Rohypnol was to think about her, and he put it back in his pocket. When the waitress brought their drinks, they touched glasses. She asked him what he had been doing, and he told her that he'd been to see the Chardin. He told her about the fat man with the camera who had annoyed him so much. Lisa laughed.

"Oh, poor you," she said. "Hasn't he got as much right to stand in front of it with his camera as you've got to look at it? You think you're more sophisticated, and that people like him don't know how to look at art. But you do, so you think you've got more of a right."

"I admit it," he said. "I'm a snob. But it's become a hobbyhorse of mine. I know people are curious about the world and they want to travel. But they don't know what to do when they get there. They go to museums to look at art because it's what the guidebooks tell them to do. So the galleries are packed with people who take photographs of every painting and then the label of every painting. And then move on. They don't actually look at the art, so they miss the point."

24

"Art intimidates some people, you know," she said.

"All you can do is look. Sometimes a painting gives itself to you. But what you're feeling comes into it. And sometimes you have to give a little of yourself."

"You're an expert, so you've got an unfair advantage."

"I know about the history of it. Well, some of it. You can study it, but in the end, it really is just you and what you feel. I don't like Modigliani or Monet, for instance, but plenty of other people do. And there's plenty of contemporary art I could cheerfully throw on the fire."

"We should go to an art gallery together," she said. "And we can argue about what I like and what you don't like."

"We should go to London, or Paris or Rome," he said, thinking about how easy it would be to get away and leave Catherine to mind the gallery. "We could actually meet in Rome."

They'd finished their drinks and their fingers were touching on the table.

"We should go up," said Lisa.

Richard picked up her bag without saying anything. As they walked across the hotel lobby a silence had fallen between them. They didn't speak to each other in the lift. It was if they were holding their breath in the stiff hot air of a humid day, waiting for a storm to break. As soon as they were through the door of Richard's room, they were at each other. Somehow, they crossed the floor of the sitting area towards the bedroom in a confusion of fumbling, kissing and a frantic struggling with each other's clothes, until they fell on the bed.

It was strange that he'd kissed her lips before, in long teenage kissing sessions twenty years ago. He had a memory of it. But her naked body was new to him. It was a woman's body now, with curves and soft smooth skin. Beneath the smell of soap and shampoo and perfume there was something else. He tasted it as he kissed her neck and shoulders. And when he sensed that she'd abandoned herself to him, that she was giving herself so freely, he took great care to give her pleasure in return.

Afterwards they lay together under the sheets. The afternoon sun cast long shadows from the window frames across the bed. Lisa pulled back the covers to look at him.

"I was worried it was too late for us," she said, stroking his chest. "Perhaps it is."

Richard didn't say anything and as she dozed off, he wondered if there was any future for them. Lisa was lonely and damaged, and he knew from personal experience how sex often substituted for affection. But he was genuinely attracted to her; perhaps it was because there was a comfort in the company of fellow travellers.

Struggling to keep his eyelids open, he began to fall asleep himself. He heard sounds at the door of the room; someone turning the handle, testing to see whether or not the door was locked. Lisa mentioned it when they were getting ready to go out for dinner. "I'm sure I heard something," she said. He lied and said it was someone going into a room across the corridor. And perhaps it was nothing, just a befuddled guest who'd forgotten their room number.

4

Lisa was sitting on the bed lacing up her sneakers.

"We should go to the islands," she said without looking up.

Richard thought she was being too casual and offhand about it, as if she was pretending it didn't bother her.

"Really?" he said. "You think that's a good idea?"

"I've never been back since," she said, brushing her hair from her face and looking at him. "But it still bothers me if I think about it. Or when anyone says that they had a lovely picnic on the islands. Or went to a concert, or something like that. It's like it's haunted and I can't go back there."

"You can't change what happened."

"No. But we could create another memory of the place. Just for us."

"Like an exorcism?"

"It's the only chance we have to go there together, isn't it? Only being there with you would change anything. Change how I feel about it, I mean."

It was another bright day and they walked down to the ferry terminal. When the boat came in, they went up on to the deck and leaned against the railing, looking out towards the islands. Lisa was wearing a short denim skirt with her white sneakers and her bare legs glowed in the sunshine. She reached out and touched his hand. Richard turned to look at her and thought of the way she'd been twenty years ago. Were their feelings for each other really the same as they were then? Or perhaps that was just wishful thinking on his part.

As the ferry crossed to the islands, he knew they were

playing a game; pretending that this was their first time here. Mingling with the other tourists they walked along the jetty holding hands. They had landed on Centre Island and made their way to the north shore. The lake was as long and wide as a sea, and the sky looked bigger than a sky ought to look so close to a city. Waves crashed against the beach wall, throwing up white plumes of spray.

The physical details, the wooden houses and the lanes, were not what had stayed with him. There were other things to remember; a gang of them had come over. Ten or twelve, he thought, including him and Lisa. They were too wrapped up in each other to pay much attention to the others. Amanda had been there, and a boy called Tony, and these were the only details that had mattered. It had amazed him, another thing he'd forgotten, that it was possible to walk from one island to the other without crossing water. They went onto Ward Island, walking past more cottages towards the south shore. Another lane led them towards a concrete pier with a chain link fence across its width, and then round to a small beach, which looked across to the city, its towers of gold and turquoise glass bathed in bright sunlight.

Richard remembered the beach. And when he looked at her, he knew Lisa did too. There was driftwood on the sand, including a large tree trunk that made a good place to sit and look across the bay. In front of it a ring of large blackened stones and charred wood showed where fires had been set.

Twenty years ago there had been the remains of a fire, and a tree trunk too. And this was where it had happened. It was easy to think that Tony had started it; he had a thing about Lisa. He'd seemed to think she should be his girlfriend. But when Richard came, Lisa gave all her attention to him. If the gang went anywhere together, on a bus or a streetcar, to the movies or for a burger, she would sit next to him.

On the beach that afternoon they had all stood at the water's edge, skimming stones. But Lisa and Richard drifted away and sat in the sand together. Her legs were across his lap and her arms around his neck. They kissed. The others shouted out, laughing, and teasing them. Calling them lovebirds.

Tony didn't like it. He came and stood over them with a stick he'd picked up from the beach. He started shouting; Richard should leave Lisa alone; he should fuck off back to where he came from. And he should stop trying to make everyone feel sorry for him. Everyone was sick of hearing the stupid story about the car crash. Lisa jumped up and started yelling, telling Tony to stop being so stupid. But Tony didn't take any notice; he started to hit Richard with the stick.

Richard felt the blows on his head, knocking hard against his skull. Wailing, roaring with anger, he forced himself to his feet, knocked Tony to the ground and straddled him, hands on his throat, strangling him. Meaning to kill him.

Richard remembered that the girls were screaming as he was pulled off Tony. Someone told him to fuck off and pushed him.

"We need to go," said Amanda, leading him away. He followed her back to the southern shore in a daze and back along the path to the ferry.

Later that night, when the house was asleep, she had come into his room, and into his bed. She was naked, and she lay on top of him, kissing him and putting her hand down inside his pyjamas. It surprised him that he had an erection, but she'd seemed to expect it. She grabbed his cock and straddled him. He felt himself inside her and realised that they were having sex. The feeling overwhelmed him and he shuddered as he came.

"That was your first time," she said. "I wanted to be your first. Just think, I'll always be your first. Doesn't that make you feel special?"

"Aren't you worried you'll have babies?" he said.

"Don't be stupid. Do you think I'm new to this?"

This was the first of Amanda's 'sex lessons' that summer. If he showed any reluctance, she would punch him, or knock him down; she had a way of kicking his legs out from under him so that he fell to the floor. And anyway, he always had an erection, which proved he really wanted her to do what she did, didn't it?

"It was all Amanda's fault," said Lisa, holding Richard's hand as they looked across the bay to the city. "She kept whispering into Tony's ear that he should be with me. Not you. Got him all wound up. And all the boys thought I was easy after that. Tony put that around with a little help from Amanda. And the two of us were never friends after that."

Lisa led Richard off the beach, back along the path. They came to a playing field and she took him behind the building that housed the changing rooms. She kissed him and they had sex standing up, her legs wrapped around his waist. It had been so spontaneous that Richard felt there really was still something between them.

When they boarded the ferry and stood out on the deck, she put her arm through his. He thought that they didn't look out of place amongst the other couples leaning on the rail; she in her denim skirt with a hooded top, he in a pink Oxford shirt worn outside his Levi's with the sleeves rolled, and a sweater tied around his neck. Perhaps the memory of that awful day had been vanquished, and he pulled Lisa closer to him and kissed her on the lips.

From the landing they walked up to the Old Distillery District. Richard was interested in seeing the galleries in the old brick buildings. They wandered around from one to the other. Lisa pointed out a painting she liked in one of the small studio galleries, but it was too decorative for him, and he grunted in response. She laughed at him.

He told her that the art world was a series of parallel universes, infinite enough to include everything from watercolours for tourists to dead animals sawn in half for the crème de la crème. But the bottom line was whether it sold or not.

"Is that the only way to know if something's any good?" said Lisa. "Isn't it about talent and ideas?"

"Probably not," he said.

"Isn't the Waverley Gallery going to make lots of money?"

"You're asking me to be logical and face up to reality," he said, wrinkling his nose at a large abstract painting she was looking at. "If I was to think that through, I might come to the conclusion that I'm on a hiding to nothing. I'm a dreamer, like these artists. We all dream our dreams. The rest is down to luck."

They walked around the St Lawrence Market arm in arm, eating pea bacon sandwiches for lunch as they looked around the stalls. Lisa wanted to buy food, to cook dinner for him at her house. Would he stay the night? Of course, he said.

"I'll have to go to back to the hotel and pack a bag."

"Why don't you check out? Stay with me until you have to go. I'll drive you to the airport."

"I'd like that," he said.

He was holding both her hands, and they were gazing at each other like lovesick teenagers. He didn't care. But he knew he would have to buy another present for Catherine to mollify his guilt, perhaps one for each betrayal of her trust.

When he got back to the hotel Amanda was waiting for him. She called his name as he crossed the foyer. Perhaps she'd known he'd been with Lisa and had been lying in wait for him. But that seemed impossible, as if she had powers that he couldn't understand. No, he thought, it's just bad luck.

"I think I've upset you," she said. "I didn't mean to. It's just this business with Mom. It's had me on edge. I hoped you'd understand that."

"What do you want, Mandy?"

"Mandy?" she laughed. "It's been a long time since anyone called me that. Will you have a drink with me?"

"I've got things to do."

"Oh, it's Lisa McKee, isn't it?" said Amanda. "That's so sweet."

She touched his arm. Couldn't he come and sit down with her, just for a few minutes? And then she said they might as well go into the hotel bar because she needed a drink. He could have a coffee, couldn't he?

Richard felt helpless. And then there was the way she looked. Something about her eyes and her lips and the swell of her cleavage. Perhaps he had wanted her to do the things she did to him. Even when they were kids, and later, even after she'd had sex with him, he knew he'd wanted to please her because that meant she might be kind to him. He'd always wanted that, and had always hated himself for it.

It was almost as if she led him into the bar and made him sit at the table by the window. He thought he would humour her, have a quick coffee and go. But when the waitress came for their order and Amanda ordered a gin and tonic, he asked for one too.

"I was so glad when I knew you were coming to the funeral," she said. "Because I knew you'd understand. And I know you do, but we've got off on the wrong foot somehow. We should be friends, shouldn't we? Nana would like that, wouldn't she?"

The mention of his grandmother made Richard nervous. What was Amanda getting at? It was as if she was implying something. A threat to spill the beans that he was less than sympathetic to his bereaved cousin?

When the waitress brought the drinks, Amanda picked up one of the glasses from the table and poured a small splash of tonic into it. She said something about preferring the gin to the tonic. Richard picked up the other small bottle of Schweppes and emptied it into his glass. He drank quickly, nervously, in an attempt to cover his unease, to hurry the whole thing along.

"What will you do now?" he said.

"I don't know," she said. "What do people do all day if they don't have to work and they've got a little money?"

"I don't know. Perhaps you could travel."

For a moment Richard wondered what he would do if he didn't have the gallery to worry about. Perhaps he'd travel and look at paintings. Perhaps he would fall into drinking too much. Well, more than he did now.

Amanda had finished her drink.

"I'm drinking a little too much at the moment," she said.

"Sometimes it helps."

Hadn't he said something like that to Lisa? The thought of her made him want to go. He picked up his glass to drain it.

"Here," said Amanda, pouring the remains of her tonic into his glass before he could stop her. "You're drinking too quickly. And we haven't finished, have we?"

The waitress came over and asked if they wanted the same again.

Richard slumped against the back of his chair and nodded. One more drink and he would go. He could arrange a meeting with Amanda before he left, and use that as an excuse to get rid of her. The drinks came and the waitress took away the empty glasses and bottles.

"Don't you like me just a little bit?" she said, leaning across the low table towards him.

Her lips were moist, a glistening, vivid red. The buttons of her blouse strained against the swell of her breasts. Her presence excited him and he felt the stirrings of an erection, proof that he had always wanted her; that her attentions weren't unwanted. That he'd always been to blame, and so had always deserved what he got.

He didn't know how long they stayed in the bar, or how many drinks they had. Or even what they talked about. But when he was in the lift going up to his room, Amanda was with him. She helped him with the key card. They were in the bedroom, and then on the bed. She was above him. He remembered he was naked and that he wanted her.

"How do you feel?" she'd said, smiling at him as if she already knew.

Richard woke up and made it to the bathroom before he vomited. He was shocked by his reflection in the mirror above the sink; his dull eyes and grey skin. And the love bites on his neck. His first thought was how to hide them from Catherine.

He looked in the sitting room for clues to what had happened and saw two empty wine bottles on the coffee table in front of the sofa.

When he went back into the bedroom a fresh breeze cooled his torso because the window was open, but he didn't think anything of it because he'd started looking for signs of sex on the sheets. He found the stains easily enough, but there was something else; tiny black specks. They were on the pale walls as well, and on his white shirt lying on the chair. They were moving slowly and he thought he was hallucinating. Then he realised what they were; lake flies.

He phoned Lisa and told her what had happened; that Amanda had drugged him. She said she would come over, but she didn't arrive for over an hour. When he opened the door to her, he expected her to kiss him but she just pushed past him into the room. It looked as if she'd spent some time getting ready; she'd done something to her hair and she was wearing too much make up. Richard thought she'd been crying, or that she'd a hangover to cover up, because it showed in her eyes. She looked around the room.

"I thought you'd stood me up," she said, staring at the two empty wine bottles. "That you'd changed your mind about us."

"It was Amanda," he said. "She'd planned it. She wanted you to think that."

Lisa saw the love bites and grabbed his neck. "I think you had sex with her." She went into the bedroom and looked at the bed. The sheets were a crumpled mess, the covers still on the floor. "What's all this about?" she said.

"I told you. It was Rohypnol. She wanted me to have a drink with her. She was pushy about it. I don't know how she got it into my glass. We had drinks in the bar downstairs. I thought they'd be safe."

"Is there something between you?"

"I can't talk about it. It's not that I don't want to, Lisa. I can't. Words can't make any sense of it." Tears came into his eyes and he sat down on the bed.

"A bit more than kissing cousins, then?" said Lisa.

Richard didn't reply. Instead he pointed out the lake flies still crawling over the pillows.

"She must have opened the window to let them in. At first, I thought I was hallucinating. That they weren't really there."

"Oh, they're there alright," said Lisa.

5

The flight from Heathrow to Newcastle was on time. Water streaked across the window as the aircraft banked to make its approach. Richard peered out at the sprawl of housing estates below. Tyneside was a blur of thick grey drizzle.

In the taxi from the airport the driver was jolly, stoical about the weather.

"It's been like this for a week," he said. "I think I'm growing webbed feet." His Geordie accent, the pop music on the radio, and the other sounds that went with driving through the city in the rain; the beat of windscreen wipers and the hiss of tyres over wet tarmac; all of it was familiar to Richard. He was home.

But it had been a difficult journey. On the flight from Toronto to Heathrow he'd been unable to stop thinking about Amanda. He tried to watch a movie on the plane about a rogue CIA agent hell-bent on revenge. But he kept dwelling on what she'd done to him, and during the scenes of violence he fantasised about hurting her.

Not just because of the business with the Rohypnol, or because of the sex lessons when he was fourteen. But because of the way she was when they were children. It was as if he could remember all the things she'd ever done to him, and the fact that on every occasion he'd been unable to stop her. It was the way it had always been; he was still not good enough or strong enough to stop her. It was what defined him. Now and forever.

When he got to his house it was obvious that Catherine had been living there while he was away. In the kitchen there were no dirty dishes; her breakfast things were neatly stacked on the draining board; the sitting room was clear of the usual clutter of empty wine bottles, newspapers and art magazines. He knew that the bed in his room would be neatly made, and his clothes would be hanging in the wardrobe instead of dumped on a chair. She brought a calm order into his life, and today it unsettled him.

He phoned her at the gallery and told her he would call by later. He heard the pleasure in her voice, her expectation of what would happen when she saw him. Then he went out on to the street, sheltering under an umbrella while he cleared fallen leaves from the windscreen of the Saab, and drove to his grandmother's house.

Peter Morgan was on his hands and knees under the table by the window in the sitting room. He was wearing red corduroy trousers and wiggling his bottom. Jane Waverley was sitting on the settee prodding him with her walking stick and laughing.

"Why the floorshow?" said Richard, kissing his grandmother on the cheek.

"New router," said Peter, coming out from under the table, and holding up the black plastic console. He set it down and the three of them watched the lights blinking, and then change colour from red to green.

"Now let's get online," he said, picking up Jane's iPad.

"We're planning trips," she said to Richard. "We're thinking of a river cruise. The boats don't rock, apparently."

"Or Madeira in a few weeks," said Peter. "Get away from this bloody weather for a while."

"When I can travel," said Richard's grandmother.

Richard gave her the bottle of gin he'd bought in duty free.

"Oh, is it time for a drink?" She looked at her watch. "Close enough, don't you think?"

"Well, we could celebrate the new router," said Peter, picking up the bottle of Tanqueray and going off to mix the drinks in the kitchen.

Peter Morgan was Jane's boyfriend. A retired accountant, he

was always keen to prove himself useful. He had a grasp of the modern world, a world that often confused the other members of Jane's social circle. As such, he was in demand for advice about computers or smart phones. He also claimed to know about the stock market and was always giving Richard tips for buying shares.

"Tell me about poor Emily's funeral," said his grandmother.

Richard told her how upset Amanda had been, how she had looked in her mourning outfit, how moving her eulogy had been. He was on safer ground when he said how many people had been there and how badly dressed most of them had been. He told her about the grand buffet afterwards, the waiters and waitresses with their trays of drinks. And what an awfully good show it was.

"Uncle Ray was there."

"Ray? Is he still as awful as ever?"

"Was he awful?"

"I never knew what Emily saw in him. It was his idea to take them all to Canada, you know. And he was never very keen to let her keep in touch with her family. And poor Amanda. I should have been there. I really should. How do you get on with her now?"

"What do you mean?"

"I've lost both my children. You and Amanda are all I've got left," she said, taking Richard's hand. "Promise me you were nice to her."

"Of course I was. Why wouldn't I be?"

"You never liked her when you were children."

"What do you mean?"

"Oh, it was a funny time for all of us, I suppose. And now it's too late."

Jane allowed herself to be distracted. Peter had brought the gin and tonics in on a tray and passed them round, and the thread of something, something that Richard felt he ought to grasp, was lost.

"Did you get any of those shares I told you about?" said

Peter, patting him on the arm to get his attention. "You know, the Chinese tech company?"

"No."

"They've gone up twenty five percent in the last week. You could still get in; I could help you with that."

"You should listen to Peter, Richard. Might help keep that gallery of yours afloat."

"Oh, how's that doing?" said Peter.

"It washes its face," said Richard, which was a lie. It didn't even do that.

"You'd be better off in London, wouldn't you?"

Peter was not the first to say it, but Richard didn't have the money to make a go of it in London. Right now he was having trouble keeping the gallery going. For this he needed his grandmother's money. But with Peter Morgan here it was impossible to ask her to get out her chequebook; he'd known that when he'd seen the Mercedes in the drive. He would have to come back later, tomorrow or the next day, and wheedle and fawn to get round her.

He drove into the city centre. It was late on Friday afternoon and the hen parties were out despite the rain. A group of women in pink tutus were gathered at the traffic lights near the Cathedral, drinking Red Bull from cans and passing round a bottle of vodka.

He parked the car across the street from the gallery and turned off the engine. There was a new exhibition opening at the end of next week. Through the plate glass window he saw the bubble wrapped paintings leaning against the walls, and an aluminium stepladder in the middle of the floor. On Monday the technicians would come and start hanging the show; a series of new paintings by James Heath, an artist Richard was keen to promote.

He could see all the way into the gallery because the lights were on. A floor to ceiling window separated the office from the exhibition space. The blinds were open and he saw Catherine sitting at her desk. He stayed in the car and watched her.

Three years ago, when he was in the middle of the divorce, she had come to the gallery looking for a job, or anything she said that would help her get into the business. After finishing her M.A. she was anxious to find a start in the art world. He had exploited her with an unpaid internship, and then seeing how capable she was, he had made her his assistant and then gallery manager. That she was pretty and emotionally insecure made her attractive. They started sleeping together and, in Catherine's eyes at least, they were in a relationship.

Eventually Richard got out of the car and crossed the road, calling out as he walked into the gallery. Catherine came out of the office and leaned against the doorframe with her arms folded. She was smiling as he walked towards her. She wore blue jeans, sneakers and a cream blouse with a bow at the neck. There was nothing provocative about her; she was very pretty without being beautiful, and she was a natural blonde, a rarity in a world full of blonde women. Her cheeks always had a flush of red because she liked walking in the hills.

"Welcome home," she said.

As he went into the office, she closed the door and twisted the rod that closed the blinds. She wrapped her arms around him, kissed him all over his face and then on his lips.

"I've been keeping your bed warm," she said. "It's such a big bed and so empty without you."

"It is a big bed," he said, kissing her nose. "I'm very tired, you know. Jet lag or something."

"Poor you," she said.

Richard dropped down on to the office sofa. Catherine got a bottle of Muscadet out of the fridge in the small kitchen area that opened off the office, the en-suite she called it, and poured them both a glass.

"Any bad news?" he said.

"A few overdue bills need to be paid. Two artists who want money for paintings sold. And James Heath has been calling. He's desperate to talk to you about the show. Pre-exhibition nerves, I think. Haven't you been looking at your emails?"

"I resisted the temptation."

"Was it really awful in Toronto?"

"Family stuff," he said, making a circular motion with his forefinger at the side of his head. "Things get churned up."

"I thought we could stay in tonight."

"That would be nice. I am very tired."

"I've been shopping. I got steaks, so you won't have to do a thing."

His house was too big for him to live in alone. He knew that, but he liked it too much. He'd bought Sarah out, rather than sell it when they got divorced. It was a three storey Victorian terrace on a crescent by the Metro, and he had to pay someone to keep on top of the gardens. There was one at the front, a small lawn with shrubs, and another at the back, with a bigger lawn and fruit trees.

Catherine had been more or less living with him for the past few months. She had a flat of her own across the city in Heaton, and he was disappointed that she hadn't gone there while he was away. It was getting too late to object to the arrangement; she was already thinking of renting her own place out because she was rarely there.

That evening they sat in the kitchen at the old pine table that he'd bought in France. Sarah had been with him on that trip, but he always thought of it as his table. Her taste had always been more contemporary. She liked flashy expensive stuff, which he thought too brash and bourgeois.

Catherine mixed him a gin and tonic and he brought one of his bags in from the hall and unpacked her presents. Besides the Inuit bear, which made her shriek with delight, he'd bought her other things during his stopover at Heathrow; a bottle of Chanel No. 5 and a pair of Dolce e Gabbana sunglasses from Sunglass Hut. She tried them on and went and looked at herself in the mirror in the hall. "They're so cool," she said, and Richard realised, seeing them on her, that they were like the ones Amanda had worn at the funeral.

Later when they went up to bed Catherine was amorous,

kissing him too fiercely and touching him through his Levi's in an attempt to excite him. He feigned tiredness and made another comment about jet lag. When he knew she was asleep, he disentangled himself from her arms, found his jeans and a sweatshirt and went downstairs. It was still raining. He put on an anorak and stood out on the patio to smoke a cigarette. He was still thinking about what had happened in Toronto.

Lisa had rescued him from the hotel, made him pack his bags and check out without mentioning the lake flies. Back at her house she'd nursed him through the after effects of the Rohypnol and made up ice packs to reduce the love bites Amanda had marked him with. Then she gave him a bottle of concealer that had a roller ball applicator like a deodorant. She showed him how to use it to keep the marks hidden while they faded.

"It's best to call them hickeys," she'd said. "Love had nothing to do with it."

Then two days later Lisa had driven him to the airport in her bright blue Hyundai coupe. Their farewell at Pearson International had been drawn out with one final kiss after another. When she asked if there was anyone at home, he hadn't lied to her. He'd shrugged and said it wasn't anything serious.

"Will I see you again?"

"Could you come to Rome?" he said, because he knew he could get away on his own. "It would be romantic."

"Call me," she said and kissed him again. And then he'd had to go into the queue for security, and when he turned to give her one final wave, she'd gone.

Had sleeping with her been a mistake? He wasn't really sure why it had happened. Was it just the fulfilment of a teenage fantasy, an antidote to Amanda's power, or was there more to it? And what was the reason for his relationship with Catherine? He knew his judgement was flawed. Quite simply, he never knew what he wanted, or what he needed, where women were concerned.

When he'd first met Sarah she had come across as someone

who was eager to please, and he'd liked that. He'd missed the signs when she started planning the wedding. She had very fixed ideas about how it should be, and the main thing it had to be was expensive. After they were married it was clear that her prime survival skill was in getting her own way. And she did like to spend money.

He felt trapped in the marriage and this pushed him back into his old habit of sleeping around. Like sex masquerading as affection, this was adultery pretending to be freedom. Sarah wouldn't put up with it. She pushed for a divorce and she had very clear ideas about that too; she made him pay for it. She had told him that he was an absolute shit where women were concerned and persuaded him to have some therapy. He had chosen a female therapist and Sarah thought that said something about him.

Later he'd asked the therapist if that might mean 'something'. She asked him if he thought it meant anything. That was the point. Of course, he talked about Amanda, but he was surprised at his own reticence when it came to describing their sexual encounters. He struggled to say that she had 'interfered' with him when he was fourteen. Although it had been more than that, and much more frequent than he admitted to. The therapist said that Amanda sounded like a very disturbing person, but he knew that already.

In all the sessions he never mentioned the fact that he found something about Amanda compelling, an attraction that existed despite, or more likely because of, her cruelty. It was a sexual thing and he knew he didn't understand it. Standing out on the dark patio in the rain Richard lit another cigarette. It came to him that the reason that he really resented her drugging him with Rohypnol was not because she'd had sex with him, or abused him or whatever it was she'd done, against his will, but because he wasn't able to remember it.

6

Jane Waverley sat at the bureau in the sitting room and unscrewed the top of her fountain pen. Richard stood over her, waiting for her to write out the cheque and for the final flourish of her signature. But she hesitated, holding the nib just above the surface of the paper.

Richard didn't understand; he'd done what he'd always done, fawned and made a face. The gallery was going through a rough patch, he'd said. It needed to keep going, to make its presence felt at art fairs. It just needed a little more money. This was the game they always played; only Nana could make things better.

When they were children Amanda used to taunt him about his 'sick puppy face'. She would kick his shins and punch him because he got his own way. And now, instead of writing out his cheque, his grandmother was talking about *her*, about giving her money. Richard bit the inside of his mouth and tasted blood.

"I think I should probably settle something on her," she said. "I give you money for the gallery. But I've given her nothing over the years."

"Amanda has money," he said. "Aunt Emily left her the house. She'll sell that. For millions of dollars. She took great delight in telling me that."

"You never liked her when you were children, did you?"

That again! "Why do you think that?"

"Tell me you were kind to her when you were in Toronto."

"Of course I was," he said, putting his hand on her shoulder.

"You of all people must know how it feels to lose your parents."

She looked up at him, and he saw that she was crying. Something had changed since yesterday. She'd obviously been drinking. There was a glass on the coffee table with ice and a slice of lemon in it. God knows how many she'd had before he'd arrived. And then she must have sat alone, brooding over things, feeling sorry for herself. Richard thought it must be difficult for her to see any point about the future at her age; since her fall the scope of her life had suddenly diminished.

"It's a cruel thing for a mother to lose her children," she said, squeezing his hand. "You and Amanda are all I've got left now. I should have gone to Emily's funeral, you know. First your father. Now her. Both my children gone. I should have made the effort."

"And it's some effort," said Richard.

"Peter encourages me to get out of the house. He takes me out for lunch in the country. You need a look out, Jane, he says. Now he's trying to get me to Madeira because of the weather. Says it would be easy if we used a wheelchair."

"You deserve a holiday. And it would be something to look forward to."

"That's what Peter says, but I can't help feeling so wretched about it. If I can get into a car and go to a country pub for lunch, I could have managed a flight. Couldn't I?"

"It's eight hours, and that's just from Heathrow, Nana. It's exhausting. Take my word for it."

"I couldn't have done it, could I? That's why I didn't go, isn't it?"

"That's right, Nana. It would have been too much for you."

She nodded and looked down at the open cheque-book again.

"What's the date?" she said. "I've forgotten."

Lately, he'd had to watch her carefully when she filled out the cheques she gave him. Once she'd written the wrong year, which had embarrassed him at the bank. She signed the cheque, tore it out of the book and passed it to him. He waved it in the air to dry the ink.

"It was all a silly misunderstanding," she said. "Really, that's all it was."

"What was?" he said, distracted as he folded up the cheque and put it in the breast pocket of his shirt.

"Isn't that why families fall out about things? If Ray hadn't taken them off to Canada everything would have come right in the end."

He wanted to know more but he heard a car coming up the gravel drive. Peter had arrived; he came every morning for coffee, and Richard went into the kitchen to make it.

On the breakfast bar he saw the bottle of Tanqueray he'd brought yesterday. The level was well down. Next to it was a bowl of half-melted ice and a cut lemon on a small chopping board. So he was right; she had been drinking, getting maudlin about something. This misunderstanding, whatever it was, had obviously been playing on her mind. He scooped some of the remaining ice into a glass with his fingers and poured a good measure of gin in after it. A misunderstanding, she'd said, but what kind of misunderstanding?

As the coffee gurgled through the filter machine, he knocked back the gin. It was cool, but the alcohol was warming and stung the inside of his cheek where he'd bitten it. Fuck, he thought, he hadn't seen Amanda for twenty years and now she was all anyone could talk about. Settle some money on her indeed!

Catherine was applying vinyl lettering to the window when he got back to the gallery, and he called out to her as he came through the door. The place was in disarray; the exhibition of James Heath's work was opening in two days' time. The large aluminium stepladder still stood in the middle of the main room. Wolfgang and John, the two freelance technicians, had finished preparing the walls, and were getting ready to hang the paintings.

Catherine followed him into his office.

"Well?" she said, shutting the door behind her.

"Bingo!" said Richard, holding up the cheque between the thumb and forefinger of each hand so that she could see it. Catherine yelped and snatched it from him.

"All of it?" she said, her face brightening as she read the amount.

"All of it," said Richard.

"Clever boy." Catherine leaned back against the desk, her hands gripping the edge, and pushed her chest out. "I have a little bit of good news too, Mr Waverley," she said.

"Don't be coy."

"Johnny C. Robson called."

Richard stopped noticing how Catherine's t-shirt was pulling across her breasts, and grabbed her by the shoulders. "Tell me," he said.

Johnny C. Robson was a property developer who turned old warehouses and factories into apartments or office blocks. He also had an interest in art, and thought of himself as something of a collector. Richard had cultivated him at openings, hoping he would eventually buy something, and lately he'd been talking up James Heath's large gestural paintings. He had even taken the trouble to show Robson some of the individual pieces that were held in the gallery store.

"He wants a private, private view before our official opening."

"He wants first dibs, does he?"

Richard picked up his grandmother's cheque and looked at it again. Money gets money, he thought. Isn't that what they say? He would get the technicians to work overtime, have James' pictures hung by the end of play tomorrow. He could even invite Robson to dinner after the opening.

"Bingo," he said.

Robson parked his Porsche Carrera right outside the gallery.

"It's a loading bay," said Richard. "You'll probably get a ticket."

"It's only money," said Robson. "And anyway, I wanted to show off my new motor."

Richard walked over to the window and looked out. He wondered if he should be really obsequious, and indulge Robson by going out onto the pavement to admire the bright red Porsche. But that would make him look weak and far too desperate.

Robson was a large man with a shaved head and oversized black spectacles. He always wore a black suit, and a white shirt with no tie, the cuffs studded with a pair of gold cufflinks, each set with a large ruby. Somehow, he also managed to show off a large gold wristwatch. Richard didn't know what make it was, but Robson told him. A Panerai.

Catherine went to make coffee, and Richard walked around the gallery with Robson, looking at each of the paintings in turn. Along the main wall were hung five very large canvasses, almost abstract images of the sky, swirling masses of paint to represent the vagaries of weather over the River Tyne.

"They're very expressive," said Robson.

"Yes, they are very emotional. But they're still very masculine," said Richard. "There's nothing shy about that brushwork."

"Do you think, though…" said Robson, hesitating. "Do you think that they're too Northern?"

Richard hadn't anticipated a question like that. Robson had obviously paid for elocution lessons to try and erase his Geordie accent. But it was still there; breaking out from under all the tricks he'd learnt, the lilt rising up in particular words and phrases. He couldn't hide where he came from. Were the paintings too Northern? Richard knew that there was no doubting the fact. James Heath had grown up in Wallsend, worked in the shipyards as a young man, and poured his experience of the region's post-industrial decline into his work, without apology.

"Too Northern?" he said. "That's their strength, Johnny."

Richard told Robson about James' history, about how he saw his painting as work, hard physical work, which was why he made the paintings so large, and used the paint so thick.

"I like them," said Robson, stepping back for a wider view. "I really do like them."

"Enough?" said Richard, meaning enough to buy them.

"Oh yes."

They went into the office to discuss money and complete the paperwork. Catherine brought the coffee in on a tray. Robson looked at the list of paintings with the prices next to the titles. He didn't say anything for a moment, and then started talking about the building where he was planning to hang them, new offices converted from an old factory behind the Central Station. They should come and see the space, he said.

Richard knew that even if Robson had softened, become less brash in front of the paintings, he would harden up in negotiating a price. His singular avoidance of talking about money was a strategy, trying to get Richard to mention the price first and then beat him down. It was obvious he would want a discount for the suite of five pictures. But how much would he ask for? And how much, Richard wondered, was he willing to give him? He asked Catherine to pull out a copy of the standard contract. Robson looked at the list, waiting.

"Will you pay now?" said Richard, a pen in his hand. "Or shall we invoice you?"

"Hang on, Bonny Lad," he said, suddenly laughing. "Just listen to me, a Geordie born and bred." He sat up in his chair. "We haven't talked money yet. How much is this going to cost me?"

Richard made a thing of picking up the list, looking at it, and then pretending to do the sum in his head. He told Robson.

"How about twenty percent off that?"

"So, you pay for four paintings, and get one free?" said Richard. "It's not that kind of business. You know that, Johnny. That's the sort of thing that hurts everyone, the gallery, the artist, and ultimately you, because the value of the work's degraded."

"Come on," said Robson. "You've got to sweeten the deal. That's how any business works."

"Perhaps this isn't the right deal for you," said Richard, looking at Catherine and noticing her pained expression.

"Fifteen per cent."

"I can give you five."

"Ten,' said Robson, quickly, like a kid playing a game.

"That hurts me too much. It eats into my commission; I can't pass it on to the artist. Every collector knows that."

Robson shook his head and began to stand up.

"Seven and you've got a deal," said Richard.

"Deal." The big man grinned and reached his hand out across the desk.

As Richard shook it, Catherine picked up the calculator to work out the final price, and wrote it into the contract.

"An invoice,' said Robson, as he signed the paper. "Send me an invoice after you've delivered the paintings."

"I thought you'd blown it," said Catherine after Robson had left.

"I didn't want to let him get away with it. We might be desperate, but I really don't like being pushed around."

Richard walked over to the paintings and stuck a red dot on the wall next to each one to show they'd been sold. He stood back to look at them, this symbol of good fortune. Finally, the gallery was coming out of the doldrums, and he would be proved right.

That evening he and Catherine went for a meal together to celebrate the sale. He was caught up in the rush of success, but he realised she would see it as further evidence that their relationship was on a firm footing. He regretted that he didn't have the courage to burst her bubble. It was too difficult now; they were on what felt like an unalterable course to be an actual couple. And he knew that everyone thought they were.

They had got drunk in the restaurant and in the morning, seeing Catherine in his bed, in his house, rattled him. His hangover was, as usual, tinged with guilt, and the dreadful feeling of powerlessness that always followed his moments of wild buoyancy.

He didn't cheer up until late afternoon. It was then that the four young women, the Fine Art students he employed to serve wine at openings, arrived. They wore pretty dresses and Richard enjoyed their company. They weren't deferential because of his age or the fact that he owned the gallery, but they did as he asked. They carried the folding table out of the store, covered it with a fresh white tablecloth, set the wine glasses in neat rows, and put snacks out in bowls. It was as if gallery life was second nature to them.

Everyone's mood shifted down at about a quarter to six, when James Heath arrived. A bag of nerves in a suit he wasn't used to wearing, he grabbed a glass of red wine from the table. It was obvious that he couldn't look at his own work on the walls, too fearful of seeing the faults in it, and his gaze was fixed on the floor or the ceiling as he stood awkwardly, drinking too quickly. Richard knew it was stage fright; he had it too. Everyone did; Catherine was pacing around the office and even the young women had ceased their bright chatter.

Richard led James by the arm to stand in front of the five sky paintings and told him to look very carefully, not at the paintings, but at the wall itself.

"What the fuck am I meant to be looking at then?"

"Each painting has a red dot next to it, Jimmy," said Richard. "And I'm sure even you know what that means."

"You're kidding me. When?"

"Yesterday afternoon. So get your face out of that glass and cheer up. And be very nice to Johnny C. Robson. He is our benefactor."

Richard wore the same black suit he'd worn to the funeral and a crisp white shirt, open at the neck. Just before six he went out onto the pavement and lit a cigarette. For him the first great fear was that no one would turn up, and then that there would be no buzz, or that everybody would just drink his wine and pay no attention to the work on the walls. But he'd sold five paintings to Johnny C. Robson, so perhaps nothing else really mattered tonight.

He dropped his cigarette to the ground, twisted it under his foot, and turned to go into the gallery. A horn beeped and Peter Morgan's glossy black Mercedes pulled up to the kerb. Peter got out and opened the rear door. Richard went to help his grandmother out of the car.

"I'll get the wheelchair out of the boot," said Peter.

"No, no," said Jane Waverley. "I don't need the bloody thing."

"Are you sure, Nana?"

"Richard, I've got wonderful news. I was so glum yesterday, wasn't I? Feeling sorry for myself. I don't know why I didn't do it before, I really don't."

"Do what?" said Richard.

"Why, telephone Amanda of course. It was so wonderful to talk to her. She understood why I didn't go to the funeral. She really did. And she said how lovely it was to see you. Oh, it's just so..."

"What is it?" said Richard, as a hollow feeling crept into his stomach. He looked at Peter Morgan, who stood at the open boot, smiling. Inscrutable.

"I asked her to come and visit and she said yes. Isn't that wonderful? Give me a kiss, darling. I'm so happy."

Richard kissed her and she took his arm. The thing that had started in his gut turned again. The gallery was filling up, full of bright chatter. The opening was going to be a success, but all he could think about were the lake flies in Toronto. He wanted a drink. He needed a bloody drink. And then he heard, inside his head, a single word running on a loop. A single word that summed up everything, "Fuck! Fuck! Fuck!"

7

"Can I get a picture, Mr Waverley?" It was the photographer he'd hired.

The young woman, a blonde in a black leather jacket, wanted him to stand in front of one of the paintings. He put his hands in his trouser pockets, pushed his shoulders back, and looked directly into the lens as she worked the camera. At each sound of the shutter he renewed his smile. Eyes, tits, teeth, he thought, that would be his mantra for tonight. This was show business after all; it wouldn't do to let anyone know what was actually going on inside his head.

He surveyed the crowd, the artists and academics, the art students with their studied eccentric cool, and the dull arts administrators who'd come to network. The people from Arts Council were no good to him; they refused to fund the gallery and he despised them for it. Curiously, it was the business people, the ones with real money who stood out: the men in suits, or out-of-office preppy clothes, and the women in designer dresses.

Of course, the free booze brought them, but they also came because it was a social event, a part of the cultural life of the city. He'd made that happen. This was his gallery. He was the master of ceremonies. And Amanda couldn't take that away from him.

He took his grandmother a glass of prosecco, and showed her the five paintings on the long wall, pointing out the bright red dots next to each one. Her mood had lifted since the day she'd given him the cheque, but her enthusiasm was all for

Amanda's visit, and how wonderful it would be. He knew the scale of his own achievement was lost on her, but he gave her his best bright smile.

James Heath still looked lost amongst the crowd. He'd made an effort, had his wild hair and beard trimmed, and wore cowboy boots with his suit. Consumed by nerves, he didn't know where to stand, or who to talk to, and was still drinking his wine in long, nervous gulps. Richard went and rescued him. Could James give his grandmother a tour of the exhibition?

As Richard slipped off, wanting to work the room, he heard Jane babbling the words 'Canada' and 'grand-daughter'. He took a deep breath, grabbed a glass of wine as he passed the drinks table and asked the photographer to get a few shots of James with his grandmother, and then of James alone with one of his paintings; a portrait for the press release.

He was halfway across the room when he was ambushed by Peter Morgan.

"It's good news about your cousin," he said, sipping his glass of orange juice.

"Really?" Richard thought that Peter was bored because he wasn't drinking, and that he'd come fishing for information about Amanda.

"Well, it's had a terrific effect on Jane," said Peter. "Emily's death really knocked her down, you know. And not being able to go to the funeral, well that was just the final straw."

"I thought you were going to cheer her up with some foreign travel."

"Perhaps your cousin...Amanda, isn't it? Perhaps she could come with us."

"She's not going to be here that long."

"Oh, I thought she was coming back here to live."

"What gave you that idea?"

"Jane told me. She's coming home. That's why Jane's so excited."

Richard clapped Peter on the shoulder and said he had people to see. Robson for one; he'd just seen him talking to two other men in suits who might be persuaded to buy art for their offices. Turning away, he made his way through the crowd, smiling at all the familiar faces, and stopping here and there to chat or make a witty comment as he crossed the room. Yes, he knew how to perform, how to pretend that everything was all right; he'd been doing that all his life.

"Here he is," said Robson, shaking his hand and introducing him to his friends. Richard felt as if he belonged in the company of men like these. He knew they respected him because he knew about art and culture; the very things they were unsure of themselves. And he knew Robson wanted him to talk up the paintings, to make his new acquisitions seem desirable, to show he had good taste.

Catherine came over to say hello, and said she would send one of the girls over with a tray of drinks. Richard noticed the way one of the men watched her walk away. She wore a simple fitted dress that showed off her figure as she moved.

"Pretty girl," said one of the men. "Is she taken?"

"I suppose you could say she's my girlfriend," said Richard. "And she manages the gallery for me."

"How can you keep your mind on the job?" said the man, laughing.

"You're a brave man," said Robson. "I wouldn't bring my wife into the office every day."

Richard realised that he hadn't met Robson's wife and used the fact to change the subject.

"Come and meet her," said Robson. "Talk to her about the paintings, could you? And introduce her to the artist? You know, make her feel special?"

They walked over to a group of women in their thirties, all dressed similarly; dresses, high heels and large handbags. They reminded Richard of the well-dressed women he'd seen in Rome, but brasher, their make-up more garish. New money, he thought, as he shook Rhiannon Robson's hand. She had dyed blonde hair and a tan and wore a red fitted dress, tighter and more revealing than Catherine's. And much more expensive, too. It had a low neckline and her cleavage distracted Richard for a moment. She was about Amanda's age, but for some reason, probably her generous figure, she reminded him of Lisa McKee and the memory surprised him.

Unlike Robson, Rhiannon hadn't tried to disguise her regional accent. When Richard introduced her to James, they realised that they were both from Wallsend, and that they'd known each other slightly when they were teenagers. They seemed to hit it off, laughing about people they both knew.

Peter came and told him that his grandmother was tired and had gone to sit down in his office. Jane, he said, was ready to go home and he was going to get the wheelchair out of his car.

Richard grabbed another glass of wine from the drinks table and went to see her. The office blinds were always closed during openings, to allow for a moment of privacy should it be needed. His grandmother was sitting on the sofa by the far wall.

"You're tired?" he said, closing the door behind him.

"Too much excitement for one day," she said. "But it's such good news about Amanda, isn't it?"

"Peter said that she's coming here to live. Is that true?"

"You two are the only family I've got left. It will be wonderful to have us all together. I haven't got that long left, you know."

"Are you going to give her money?"

"You're drunk, Richard," she said, sitting up. "I'm tired and won't put up with this. I never understood why you always had a problem with Amanda. She adored you as a baby, you know. Always fussing over you. This is just childish jealousy and it's time you got over it." She tried to push herself to her feet with her walking stick, but slumped back down. "Is this just about money? You'll both inherit my estate when I die if that's what you mean. Or did you think it was all for you?"

Peter came in with the wheelchair, and Richard tried to help her into it, but she hit him around the ankles with her stick.

"You're drunk and I don't want you sucking up to me now," she said. "Go away."

She let Peter help her into the chair, and as he wheeled her out through the office door, Catherine came in. She'd heard raised voices.

"Just a family squabble," said Richard. "A misunderstanding, that's all."

The opening was winding down; the young women had stopped serving drinks and were collecting glasses, a clear hint for the crowd to clear out. Richard told the photographer to call it a night. He was taking James out for dinner, and invited Robson and his wife to join them.

Their small party gathered in the office as the gallery was closed up. Richard fetched a bottle of champagne from the fridge and Rhiannon cheered as he popped the cork. Robson took a clear plastic packet with white powder in it out of his jacket pocket, and waved it in the air.

"Who's for some Charlie?' he said.

Catherine wasn't happy. She is such an innocent, thought Richard. He took a framed print off the wall, wiping his hand across it to remove any dust, and put it on the desk. Robson chopped out the lines with his credit card on the glass, swishing the white powder around and dividing it up into five fat lines.

Richard knew that one of his depressions was coming. The cocaine would take the edge off it tonight, but would only make it worse tomorrow. The whole evening had been a performance. Now he felt apart from the others and details of the moment stood out, sharp and clear; Catherine's look of disapproval, Rhiannon's long pink fingernails as she held a rolled up twenty-pound note to her nostril, the way James' eyes lingered on her cleavage as she leaned forward to snort her line. The way Robson noticed it too.

Rhiannon passed Richard the banknote. He bent forward to take his turn, seeing not the picture under the glass but his own dim reflection amongst the grains of loose powder and smears of finger grease. He snorted the coke, felt it irritate the membrane at the top of his nose. He stood up and passed the banknote to Catherine. She hesitated, but Rhiannon was insistent.

"Come on, Babes!" she said.

The taxis came and took them to the restaurant on the Quayside. Richard said the bill was on him, on the gallery. Rhiannon was drunk and loud. Robson went to the toilet, and when he came back, he passed the little plastic packet to Richard under the table. He and James should get themselves a line. Richard laughed and went first; James waited for thirty seconds and followed him.

Richard went into one of the cubicles and chopped out two lines of coke on the cistern, and snorted one. James hovered outside, and then took his turn. They made a thing of washing their hands. Richard looked at James in the mirror above the sinks, and then at his own reflection. He practised his smile so that his teeth showed back at him in the fluorescent light.

"It's all make believe," he said.

"I'm actually off my head," said James. "And I've no idea what you're on about."

"It's all a game, a performance. Everything. Johnny's just showing off by handing out coke. It's how he does business. You've got to show you can handle it, or you'll lose face."

"That Rhiannon likes to party," said James, watching himself in the mirror as he made a dance move. "Had a bit of a rep as a wild one back in the day."

"Leave it alone, will you?

"Oh, come on Richard. She just likes a laugh."

"If this was the Renaissance, Johnny C. Robson would be our patron. Think of the Medicis and keep your hands to yourself. Chat up Catherine, will you? She's in a foul mood, and you'd be doing me a favour."

"You two have been ages," said Rhiannon when they got back to the table. "James and Richard, Richard and James. Johnny? Does that sound gay?"

Robson just laughed.

"You're not a James," said Rhiannon, poking James in the

chest. "You're a Jimmy. And you," she turned to Richard. "What shall we call you? What do you call him, Catherine?"

"I call him Richard," she said.

Rhiannon shrieked and Richard looked at Robson, smiling as if everything was just as it was meant to be.

When they got home Richard had the urge for another drink. He took a bottle of red wine from the rack, one with a screw cap, and opened it. Catherine said she didn't want any. He went out of the kitchen door on to the patio, sat on the bench and lit a cigarette. There wasn't much light from the house, or from the streetlamp in the back lane. The fruit trees, the low shrubs and the garage block at the far end of the garden were vague, dark shapes.

Catherine came out with a glass in her hand. "I will have a drink with you," she said, taking the cigarette from his hand. She took a draw and let the smoke drift out into the darkness. "It all got a bit wild tonight, didn't it?"

"It's just Johnny Robson showing off. You know, he thinks he's a bit of a bad lad, and that it's sophisticated to snort the odd line of coke."

"Rhiannon's a handful, isn't she? It made me wonder if they're both reliable. Do you think the sale will be alright?"

"He's signed a contract, hasn't he?"

"I suppose so."

When she went up to bed Richard fetched the bottle from the kitchen and took it outside. He sat and lit another cigarette, and wished he'd had the courage to tell Catherine that he wanted her to stay at her own place for a while. He should have got the taxi to drop her off. The feeling that he was about to have one of his depressions came back to him. It would start with the hangover and build from there. It would mix with the thought that he had upset his grandmother, and the awful fact that Amanda was coming home.

It was one o'clock in the morning and he had drunk too much wine on top of the cocaine. A car alarm went off in another street. It stopped and he took out his phone and called Lisa McKee in Toronto.

"What time is it there?" she said. "It must be the middle of the night."

"Amanda's coming home," he said. "Did you know?"

"Are you drunk?"

"Yes," he said. "I'm drunk. It's been an eyes, teeth, tits kind of a night."

"I don't know what that means."

Richard wanted to tell her what it meant, but he was too wired. He couldn't get his thoughts into words. "I can't explain," he said.

"I'm flattered that when you call me up after all this time, you're too drunk to actually speak."

"I thought about you tonight, that's all," he said. "Amanda's coming home. To live."

"I heard. She's sold the house and she's already moved out. It's good riddance as far as I'm concerned."

"Was I a good kisser?" he said. "When we first met?"

"What? Why ask that now?"

"There were things that happened then. Things no one knows anything about."

"What things?"

He didn't say anything.

"Isn't there anyone you can talk to about these things?"

"No," he said. "There's no one."

"You were a good kisser," she said. "For all the difference it makes."

Amanda hadn't wanted to introduce him to Lisa; his Aunt Emily had insisted on it. If he was staying for the summer then he had to meet her friends in the neighbourhood. He remembered that when he'd told Lisa the story about the car crash, she'd held his hand and squeezed it.

That was when Amanda said he needed kissing lessons. At first it was just on the lips, but the next day she slipped her tongue into his mouth. It was moist and wriggling, like another living thing inside him. He tasted her, something almost sweet, different from the smell of her.

After the first time she'd had sex with him, she started to come into his room every night and force her hand into his pyjama bottoms, always finding him erect. And every night he was helpless as she took him inside her. The kissing lessons had become 'sex lessons'. She said that she was in charge of his sex education from now on and that he had a lot to learn if he wanted to be a real man.

Had he wanted it to happen? Yes, he did. And no, he didn't. He was always frightened of displeasing her. How could he explain the confusion? The feeling of violation mixed with desire. But desire was not the right word. It was a sort of a need that he had learned to live without. No, there was no one he could talk to about that.

Thinking about it now, looking out across the garden in the dark, he felt unworthy. It was the past, but it was still inside him like a worm. It twisted up the idea of his life into something that was off. Rotten even. Later, when the wine had taken the edge off the cocaine he slipped into bed beside Catherine. Lying next to her warm body and inhaling the fragrance of her smooth skin, he felt tainted.

Sex with Amanda had been different from sex with anyone else. Perhaps she was right. The fact that she was his first meant she had some kind of claim on him, forever. He'd wanted sex with Lisa to be like his first time, to be like finding another place to begin from. But was that even possible? None of it made any sense. He was still too jittery to fall asleep and the car alarm went off again, wailing in the darkness.

8

Richard was in the gallery, trying not to think about Amanda. He was trying to keep his mind on other things by tidying the storeroom, wrapping odd paintings in bubble wrap, and re-organising the storage racks. He came across a catalogue from an exhibition of still life paintings that reminded him of the Chardin he'd seen in Toronto. And then he thought about her, just like that.

He remembered her in his hotel room, just before the Rohypnol took effect. She'd smiled at him. And it was the memory of that smile that shocked him. It reached back in time; it was his defining image of her. And here it was again, charging around his brain. He knew its meaning. It meant I know something you don't know, which is what I'm going to do to you. It meant watch out. That funny little smile was a bloody threat.

His phone rang and he pulled it out of his pocket.

"She's here," said his grandmother.

Jane Waverley sounded happy. She'd sent Peter out for some champagne and now she was busy in the kitchen.

"Just a few nibbles," she said. "To go with the drinks. Come at six."

"Who's going to be there?"

"Peter will be here and you must bring your friend."

"You mean Catherine?"

"Yes, that's right. I'd forgotten her name. But she must come."

Catherine stood on the drive and looked up at the house while

Richard paid off the taxi. She was carrying a large bouquet of red, white and yellow roses. It had been her idea to get the driver to stop off at the florists on the High Street, and she had chosen the flowers, because he couldn't be bothered. She heard his footsteps behind her on the gravel, and turned.

"Take these,' she said, thrusting the bouquet into his chest.

"You give them to her."

Richard pushed them away and fumbled in his pocket. Catherine was surprised to see that he had a set of keys to the house.

"I lived here on and off after my parents died," he said. "And before that, we were always here for family things. I suppose I still think of it as my home."

Opening the front door, he called out a hello and led Catherine into the sitting room. He barely glanced at Peter Morgan, standing by the sideboard, or his grandmother sitting in her armchair. He'd braced himself to see Amanda again; she was at the French window looking out into the garden, and turned as he came into the room. She wore wide black trousers, and a white shirt unbuttoned to reveal her cleavage. Her hair was tied back to show her face; her sparkling eyes and her full red lips.

Richard froze as Amanda walked towards him with open arms. She embraced him. He kissed her automatically on the cheek, because she offered it to him, and then tried to pull away, but she held him by the shoulders. The smell of her perfume lingered in the air between them, and she smiled at him.

"He was such a help at the funeral, Nana. Did I tell you? I couldn't have managed without him," she said.

He felt everyone's attention on him, so that he had to stand there with a smile on his face like an embarrassed schoolboy, while Amanda kissed him hard on the cheek.

"It's a beautiful house, isn't it?" she said to Catherine. "We had a lot of lovely times here when we were kids. Didn't we, Richard?"

Catherine handed Amanda the flowers.

"Oh, that's so kind. Nana? What should I do with them?"

"They need to go in water, or they'll die," said Richard.

"He's very overdramatic, isn't he, Nana?" said Amanda.

"He always was," said Jane, trying to get to her feet, wanting to deal with the flowers.

But Peter said he would find a vase, and took the flowers out to the kitchen and came back with a bottle of champagne and flutes on a tray. When he popped the cork, Jane gave out a girlish whoop. She proposed a toast, and using her stick to help herself up, she stood and raised her glass.

"To Amanda," she said.

"To Amanda," they echoed.

Richard looked at himself in the mirror over the fireplace. Amanda had left a lipstick print on his cheek and he smudged it with the back of his hand.

"Oh, I'm sorry," said Amanda. "I've left a mark." She turned to Catherine. "I think he wants to wipe it off. Have you got a Kleenex?"

Catherine handed Richard a tissue from her handbag, but Amanda snatched it away.

"Let me. After all, it's my fault," she said, and began to scrub at Richard's face. "This reminds me of when we were children, Catherine. I was always helping him out of scrapes. Do you remember, Nana? What he was like? We used to call him Dickie, didn't we?"

"Dickie?" said Jane, laughing. "Oh, yes we did."

"He doesn't like being called it now, though. Do you?"

He took the tissue from her, looked at his reflection in the mirror again, and began to wipe the last trace of lipstick from his face. Amanda laughed at him and so did his grandmother. Even Peter chuckled. Richard pretended to ignore them, and took Catherine on a tour of the house.

He was keen to show her not just the house, but the antiques, sculptures and paintings that his grandfather had collected throughout his life. They came at last to the dining room and what he thought was the best painting in the house: a still life of flowers: roses, irises, and a parrot tulip. The flowers emerged from a dark background, their beauty undercut by the browning of the leaves and the cool melancholy of the light.

"Seventeenth century Dutch. By Simon Verelst," said Richard, and pointed out the discoloured leaves and the butterfly that hovered, almost too real, at the edge of the bouquet. "It's this juxtaposition that gives the picture its moral sense. Don't you think?" He moved closer and studied it for a moment as he'd done so many times before.

"It is very beautiful," said Catherine. "And quite sobering."

They were both distracted by the painting, but Richard sensed that someone had come into the room behind them, and turned. It was Amanda.

"I've been sent to find you," she said. "Time for more champagne, and a special cake."

"We were just looking at the Verelst. Do you remember it?"

"That old painting? I remember granddad always made a fuss about it when people came. It's always been very dark, hasn't it? It's quite dull."

"It's a real work of art, for God's sake," he said. "Granddad bought it at auction in the sixties. He paid quite a lot for it."

"So how much is it worth now?"

"About fifty, maybe sixty, thousand pounds. Maybe more."

"What are you all doing in here?" said his grandmother. She was standing in the doorway leaning on her stick. "Peter's about to open another bottle."

"Richard's just telling us how much this old painting's worth," said Amanda.

"What? He's talking about money again?" she said, thumping her stick down on the floor. "It's all he seems to think about these days, Amanda. Come on, all of you."

As they followed her, Amanda caught Catherine by the arm.

"Why did you say that the picture was sobering?"

"Because of what it's about," said Catherine, turning to look back at the painting. "That the moment won't last. The butterfly will die and the flowers will wither and die."

65

"So it means we should just live for the moment, right?"

"Its moral, if you want to think about it like that, is to remind good Christians that a secular life is just a passing fancy."

"I can see why he likes you," said Amanda. "You're a sentimental girl."

They went and drank more champagne. Richard watched his grandmother. He had fallen into her bad books and he was desperate to catch a smile from her. But she was ignoring him and making a fuss over Amanda. Going on about how happy she was.

Because she was drunk and the audience was really too small for her, and because there was no one else to give the good news to, she ended up repeating herself, and demanding that Peter or Richard fill her glass. She said the champagne would help her sleep; the pain in her hip made it difficult. So what was wrong with having a little drink sometimes? They had something to celebrate, didn't they?

Amanda went into the kitchen and came back with the bouquet that Catherine had brought her in a glass vase, and set it on one of the lamp tables. Richard's grandmother was impressed.

"I love fresh flowers," she said.

"What do you think, Catherine?" said Amanda. "It's a bit more cheerful than that sad old painting, isn't it?"

"It's not the same thing at all," said Catherine.

"Are you still talking about that old painting?" said Jane Waverley. "I never knew what your grandfather saw in it. I don't like it at all, and never have."

"Richard says it's quite valuable," said Amanda.

"Well, perhaps I'll sell it."

"No," said Richard.

"Why not. It's mine, isn't it?"

Richard walked out of the room before he lost his temper, and went into the garden so that he could have a cigarette. A wind was getting up, animating the trees and shrubs, and rustling the leaves. He wanted to be alone and collect his thoughts. There was a place, behind the shrubbery down by the side of the garage, where he couldn't be seen from the house. He'd hidden there when he was a child, and later, when he'd lived in the house as a teenager, he'd gone there to smoke.

Before he slipped out of sight, he looked up across the lawn towards the back of the house. It had been built in the 1930s, and as a boy it had seemed to him like a castle, full of rooms crammed with treasure. Even from this distance he could see movement through the windows of the sitting room. Someone had switched on a table lamp and it glowed with a warm light, bright against the gathering dusk. The party, such as it was, was in full swing.

There was a bench, sheltered from the wind, which the gardener used sometimes. Richard brushed his hand across it to clear away some dry leaves. He sat and lit a cigarette. But he'd had too much to drink; his head dropped and he looked at the ground between his feet as he smoked.

If his grandmother was in a bad mood with him, it was Amanda's fault. She had brought up the value of the painting, but he'd been made to look venal. It was as if she'd played a trick on him. The annoying thing was that if it were up to him, if the painting was his, he would never sell it; what it was worth was just a point of idle curiosity.

He'd always thought the house, and the art collection, would come to him, but now he wasn't so sure. It would depend on what kind of settlement his grandmother was going to make on Amanda and himself. It was stupid, he knew, to have ever thought he would be the sole heir. His grandfather had encouraged the idea, just as he had encouraged him to love art, and so he assumed that he was secure in his expectations. Now, here was Amanda beginning to ask what things were worth, perhaps even beginning to put together an inventory so she could reckon up her share of the estate.

Richard lit another cigarette. He knew he should go back up to the house and put a brave face on it. But his grandmother's attitude to him seemed to have changed, and Amanda, so long in exile, would become the favourite now.

The wind dropped and he heard something, footsteps on the path, and then the soft sound of someone walking on the grass. He sat still, hoping to remain undisturbed, but the person was coming down between the wall and the shrubbery towards him.

"Who's there?" he said. There was no answer but he knew who it was.

"I thought I'd find you here," said Amanda, standing over him. She was wearing a leather jacket around her shoulders against the chill. "You used to hide down here when you were a kid. But I always found you, didn't I?"

"What do you want?"

"Give me that cigarette, will you? Nana said she hoped you weren't sulking somewhere. I told her you'd gone out for a smoke, but she didn't like that much either. You're wanted back inside." Amanda took a long draw on the cigarette, and threw it to the ground. "Come on," she said and reached out to touch Richard's hair.

He jerked his head away, and stood up.

"You drugged me in Toronto."

"I needed you," said Amanda, clutching at his lapel, and pulling him towards her. "It was the only way, wasn't it?" She smiled at him. That bloody smile. "You might not remember much about it. In fact, I don't suppose you do, but you wanted it, Dickie. You were very, very horny."

"What was it? Rohypnol?"

"It was a witches' brew," she said, tilting her head and bringing her mouth close to his. "I cast a spell on you. That's all you need to know."

Looking down he saw the smooth skin in the valley of her cleavage, and almost kissed her. But he turned his face away and walked out onto the lawn. She laughed and followed him.

"Is she drunk?" he said, looking up towards the house.

"She is. And Peter is opening bottles on demand. Who is he, anyway?"

"He's Nana's boyfriend as far as I can tell. And he sorts things out for the old ladies of the bridge club. Computers, broadband, internet stuff. That sort of thing."

"What's he after?"

"I've never really thought about it. I think he just likes to be useful."

"He gets you off the hook, you mean. Running about after Nana, so you don't have to. We should keep an eye on him."

They were walking side by side and she took his arm. He didn't mind; he wanted his grandmother to come to the window and see them walking towards the house together. That would make her happy, to think that the two of them really were friends.

9

Jane Waverley held what she called 'a proper party' to celebrate Amanda's homecoming. "It'll be just like the old days," she said to Richard. "We always had lovely parties then."

About twenty people came. The guests, Jane's friends from the bridge circle and her book group, were an elderly bunch. It was the fashion amongst the men to wear pastel coloured merino sweaters that clung to their paunches. The women were better dressed; hiding the truth of their ageing bodies under shift dresses, or long tops over wide legged trousers.

Jane sat in her chair. She was playing hostess. But Peter looked lost. His usual role, making sure everyone had a drink, was being played by Amanda. Richard watched her moving around the room with a tray of drinks: glasses of fizz, and red and white wine.

He took a glass of red from her, but Catherine asked if she could have a gin and tonic. Peter jumped up and said that he'd take care of it. Amanda put the tray down on the coffee table, and said everyone should help themselves now, as if she was suddenly bored with the whole thing.

"So you and Richard are like girlfriend, boyfriend, are you?" said Amanda, smiling at Catherine. "And you work together? Is that really okay for you?"

"What do you mean?"

"Well, an employer having a relationship with his assistant. That's what you are, isn't it, his assistant? I mean, God forbid you're just an intern and he's exploiting you."

"She's the gallery manager," said Richard.

"So what is it you do then, Dickie? Look at pictures all day?" said Amanda.

"The real question is what are you going to do all day, Amanda?" he said. "Now that you're here?"

"Something you've neglected to do," she said. "I'm going to support Nana. She needs looking after."

He wanted to say something but he couldn't think what. Instead he sneered at her. It was the best he could do, but she just smiled at him. That bloody smile! He said he was going outside for a cigarette.

Smoking, once frowned upon by his grandmother, had become acceptable since Amanda's arrival. A large glass ashtray had appeared on the wrought iron table on the patio. Richard sat on the bench and lit a cigarette.

He remembered another party, more than twenty years ago; what his grandmother had meant by 'the old days'. The good old fucking days, he thought. It was a summer party and the house was full of adults drinking too much and spilling out on to the patio and across the lawn. Amanda had made herself look grown up by wearing make-up. When his father had said how pretty she looked, Richard had been jealous. He'd gone down to his hiding place and sulked. Wasn't that what he was doing now?

Catherine came out through the French doors looking for him.

"She's asked me if there was something between us before I started working for you," she said. "Or, she wanted to know, did I wait until after I'd got the job? You know what she's implying, don't you?"

Richard took a long draw on his cigarette. What did she expect him to do about it? When he didn't react, Catherine walked over to the top of the wide steps that led down to the lawn. She stood with her back to him and her arms folded. A space was opening up between them. He was letting it grow; he knew she was crying and waiting for him to go over and put his arm around her.

"She's just drunk. Don't let her get to you," he said, leaning forward to stub his cigarette out in the ashtray.

"I have to go," said Catherine, turning so that he saw her tears. "I can't stay. Will you take me home?"

"I'll have to make an excuse."

He knew that Amanda would keep on needling Catherine, trying to wear her down. Then there would be more and more reasons for her not to come to the drinks parties, or the Sunday lunches, or whatever other events his grandmother was going to expect him to attend. And then Catherine would be forced back on her old friends, and their relationship would unravel even more. Perhaps it would be best to get it over with.

"Go in through the kitchen door and wash your face in the cloakroom," he said, looking up at her, his face impassive. "I'll call a cab."

He thought she was going to cry again, but she walked down the patio towards the other set of doors that led into the kitchen. He pulled out his phone and ordered a taxi. Amanda came out with a bottle of wine. She filled his glass and sat next to him. Richard lit another cigarette.

"Is Catherine alright?" she said, reaching for his cigarettes and lighter.

"She's got a migraine. I'm going to take her home."

"What a shame," she said, taking a cigarette out of the packet and lighting it.

"You didn't think to be nice to her?"

"She's too young, isn't she? And too sensitive," said Amanda. "I wouldn't have thought she was your type. Nana agrees with me on that."

She smiled at him, that irritating, inscrutable smile. Richard looked down and focussed on crushing his cigarette out in the ashtray. He wanted to storm off the patio, back into the house where he could hear laughter, the sound of people getting drunk. But Amanda held him here, talking about how she wanted to come and see this illustrious gallery of his. He told her to come tomorrow. Having given way to her on something, he was finally able to push himself to his feet and go into the house.

Jane Waverley was drunk. She called Richard over, making a show of affection by grabbing his hand, and pulling on it, demanding that he lean down to give her a kiss. Under his lips her skin had the smooth texture of dried parchment. He caught the taste of her by accident; something perfumed like a cream or a powder, and beneath that the taste of ageing flesh. He pulled away in disgust.

"I have to go," he said. "Catherine's got a migraine."

The taxi would be twenty minutes or more, and he wanted another drink. He went into the kitchen and poured himself a glass of red wine. Catherine came to find him. He knew that she wanted to go straight away because she was wearing her jacket; she'd been standing and waiting for him by the front door.

"The cab's coming. Twenty minutes," he said. "Do you want a drink?"

"Did you make an excuse for me?" she said, taking the glass he offered her.

"I said you had a migraine."

"Here's to little white lies," she said.

She said she didn't want to stay in the house any longer, so they walked down the drive to wait for the taxi at the gate. Richard leaned against the gatepost and lit a cigarette as Catherine paced about.

"Look," she said. "She's watching us."

"What do you mean?" he said, following her gaze up towards the house.

Amanda was standing at the front door, looking down the drive towards them.

"Did something happen in Toronto?" said Catherine. "I mean with her?"

"What are you getting at?"

"It's as if there's something between you."

"Here's the taxi," said Richard, dropping his cigarette to the ground, and raising his arm as a signal to the driver.

The gallery was empty until the buzzer on the street door sounded and Amanda walked in. Richard felt compelled to watch her through the open office door. After all, she was performing just for him. He knew that from the way she wore her tight black leather skirt with a short denim jacket, in the way she'd undone the top buttons of her silk blouse. And in the way she moved her body as she walked towards him, her high heels clacking on the polished concrete floor.

Catherine ignored her as she came into the office. But Richard stood up. Amanda offered him her cheek and as he kissed it, she put her arm around him, pulled him towards her, and kissed him on the mouth.

"More lipstick, I'm afraid," she said, smiling.

She looked over his shoulder at Catherine, who sighed and tossed a box of tissues across her desk. As Richard wiped at his mouth, Amanda began to walk around his desk, running her hand around the edge, touching his computer and his desk diary as if marking out the ground.

"So why don't you show me around this gallery of yours?"

Catherine followed them out into the gallery, as if she was keeping an eye on them, and Richard worried that Amanda might be tempted to torment her. She had an extra confidence about her since she'd arrived. It was as if she knew not only what she wanted, but that she was going to get it. The only way he knew how to behave towards her was to mask his anxiety by pretending to be calm. It was what he had always done. To enter into battle with Amanda only meant that whatever she was planning would come with more force. There had always been a payback for resistance.

James Heath's exhibition was still on the walls and he walked her around the show, giving the spiel he usually used on collectors and visitors alike, selling not the paintings, but the idea of them. Amanda had the same bored look in her eye as when he'd talked about the Verelst. She knew nothing about art, and in fact had no interest in it at all. So, he wondered, why was she here?

Amanda wanted to see everything in the gallery, opening a cupboard door, as if she were an estate agent valuing a property. The little kitchen interested her, and she was curious about the large fridge they used to chill wine for openings, looking inside it as if she was gauging the capacity. Then, coming across the door to the storeroom, she wanted to see that too.

Richard switched on the lights. The fluorescent tubes flickered and then clicked, coming on bright to reveal the room. Amanda examined everything: the floor to ceiling racks used to store paintings vertically, the large table in the middle for viewing and wrapping work, the small workbench with tools in the rack above, the rolls of tape and a box of surgical gloves. She tried the handle of the door that led into the back lane.

"What's on the other side of this?"

Richard told her that there were a couple of parking places for the gallery. Amanda wanted to know if she could park there sometimes.

"I suppose so," said Richard. "If you've got a car."

"Nana's letting me use hers until I get one of my own," she said.

Catherine leaned on the door-frame with her arms crossed, as if she were keeping an eye on them both. Amanda stood with her back against the table facing Richard. She smiled at him.

"Oh, Catherine?" she said. "I forgot to ask. How's your headache this morning?"

"It's much better, thank you. I'm fine now."

"Really?"

"Really," said Catherine, but she seemed hesitant.

"A migraine is much more useful than an ordinary headache, isn't it?" said Amanda. "I mean a headache. That seems such a trivial thing. Just a couple of painkillers from the drug store, and grit your teeth until it goes. Not that much of an excuse if you want to get out of things. But a migraine is something else. Nobody can argue with a migraine. They're so difficult to challenge. And they can be so convenient, can't they? I've had a few in my time, I can tell you. Very useful for getting your own way."

Amanda laughed and Catherine looked embarrassed. It was not in her nature to fight back and Richard thought she might cry. But she turned and walked away. He heard her footsteps half running across the gallery floor and the office door slamming.

"What was that for?" he said.

"There was no migraine. I wanted her to know that I knew that," said Amanda, moving towards him. "Anyway we're alone at last."

She was too close to him; he could smell her. Then she kissed him and her tongue was in his mouth and he tasted her. She pushed her thigh between his legs and he was caught up in a rush of memories and the old confusion. True, he wanted her; he had an erection, didn't he? But then she always made him hard, despite himself. It was as if his desire wasn't his choice, it was hers.

He pushed her away so that she fell back against the table.

"I don't want this," he said. "You've no right."

"No?" She came up to him again, cupped her hand around his groin and squeezed. "Don't you think I know what goes on down here?" she said. "I own that part of you."

"Fuck off," he said.

"Fuck off?" She was still smiling at him. "We'll see about that, won't we, Dickie?"

And then he was watching her walk across the gallery to the front door. Her heels sounded on the floor again and he saw the way her hips moved, the shape of her buttocks under the tight leather skirt. He went into the office. Catherine was pretending to be busy at her computer but he could see that she'd been crying.

"We had a bit of a falling out," he said.

"I doubt it was about me. I'll ask you again, Richard. Is there something between you?"

"It's just family stuff", he said. "It's hard to explain."

"Try me."

He shook his head and she stood up and came around the desk. She reached out for his sleeve as if to pull him towards her, but he didn't respond and she let her hand drop. She wanted to hold him, or have him hold her, but they both knew that she couldn't have what she wanted; he didn't have it to give.

"You know you've got her lipstick all over your face," said Catherine. He didn't react; he just sat there staring at something on his desk. "I've got another migraine coming on. I'm going to stay at my place for a while."

"Okay," he said.

"Okay? Is that it? You're not going to try and stop me?"

Richard shrugged. "You know your own mind, don't you?"

Catherine put on her jacket. As she picked up her bag, he knew that he ought to say something to stop her. But he didn't want to. He watched her, head down, shoulders sagging, as she walked through the gallery towards the front door. She was having some difficulty moving her legs. She looked pathetic. He hated her for being weak and enjoyed the feeling. That he could be so cruel shocked him. Was this the same kind of pleasure that Amanda took from provoking him? The thought that he might be like her repulsed him.

No one came into the gallery that afternoon which was not unusual. Nor did he do any work; he just sat at his desk until it was time to put the alarm on, power down the shutters and close up.

When he got home, he went from room to room as if he was testing the edges of the house. He kept finding things that belonged to Catherine; the book she was reading, the pop CD he hated, but which she sang along to when she was drunk, and her dressing gown sprawled over his bed. He'd always been ambivalent about their relationship, and now he'd let this rift open between them.

Richard drank a bottle of wine, but he still couldn't sleep. At about two o'clock in the morning he heard the doorbell. It rang more than once and he put on his dressing gown and went down to answer it. It couldn't be Amanda; she didn't know he was alone tonight. Perhaps it was Catherine, drunk and distraught and anxious to patch things up, but she had a key.

The bell stopped ringing as he came down the stairs. He heard hard banging and a man's voice calling out his name. At first, he thought it might be the police, but when he turned the lock James Heath pushed his way into the house. Leaving the door wide open he leaned against the wall, eyes wide and red rimmed. His face was pale, tinged yellow by the electric light, and a film of sweat glistened on his forehead. His hands were moving and he couldn't stand still.

"Have you got any stuff, Richard?"

"What stuff, Jimmy?"

"Coke. You got any coke, for fuck's sake?"

"What's going on?" said Richard, going to close the front door. There was a car in the street with the engine running. "Is that a taxi?" But he saw that it was a Range Rover. "Who is that, Jimmy?"

"It's her."

"Who's 'her'?"

"Rhiannon," said James.

"Rhiannon Robson?"

James nodded and slid down the wall to the floor. Pulling his knees up to his chest he began to weep. Richard went to the door and looked out into the street. The interior light was on in the Range Rover and the woman in the driving seat reached across to pull the passenger door shut. She revved the engine hard, too hard, and drove off.

Richard slammed the front door shut. He stood over James and started batting him around the head.

"You fucking idiot," he said. "If Johnny finds out you've been shagging his wife, we can all say goodbye to our money."

10

Richard was surprised to see Catherine; he'd expected her to be too upset and too angry to come to work after yesterday. But there she was, at her desk in the office, talking on the phone. He attempted a smile and she gave him a quick, cool look.

He retreated behind his own desk. Sitting in his swivel chair, he swung the seat slowly from side to side and looked through the plate glass window that formed the wall of the office, listening to her arrange the delivery of the two paintings she'd sold last week. When she'd finished the call, she wrote something in the gallery diary and started working on her computer. Richard knew Catherine was doing her best to be professional, pretending that that was the limit of their relationship. And she was ignoring him.

He was trying to think of something to say, anything to break the tension in the room, when Peter Morgan phoned. He was always too avuncular, which annoyed Richard, calling him 'my dear boy' as if they were friends or even, because of Peter's relationship with his grandmother, actually related. It was obvious that he wanted something, but as usual he took his time getting to the point.

"I forgot to mention it last week," he said. "I've got an appointment at the hospital this afternoon. The old slippery snake." Richard didn't understand. "A gastroscopy. Camera down the throat. Looking for signs of wear and tear in the old digestive tract. It's giving me a bit of gip at the moment. Trouble is, it's Jane's turn to host the bridge session this afternoon. I usually help out. Drinks, nibbles, setting up the tables, that sort of thing. Could you step into the breach, my dear boy?"

"Amanda's there, isn't she?"

"I'm sure she will be. But, shouldn't you…? Sorry, it's none of my business, dear boy."

"What isn't?"

"I'm overstepping the mark. None of my business."

"For God's sake, Peter. Say whatever it is you've got to say."

"Well, Jane's been a lot brighter since your cousin arrived. Obviously, that's a good thing. Really good. But there's something…"

She's causing him problems, thought Richard. He's being pushed out.

"I just think if you were there more often," said Peter. "Perhaps you could see if anything's going on. It might just be me. Feeling left out, feeling sorry for myself."

"What do you mean?" said Richard, knowing there must be something. It was Amanda, for God's sake. "It doesn't matter, Peter. I'll go."

He put the phone down and looked across at Catherine. She was intent on staring at her computer screen, looking at her emails or at least pretending to.

"I need a coffee, do you want one?" he said, and went into the kitchen to set up the filter machine. As the coffee gurgled through, he leaned on the doorjamb.

"You look tired," she said. "Another late night?"

"It's not what you're thinking."

"How do you know what I'm thinking?" said Catherine.

She'd clenched her jaw and narrowed her eyes. Trying to look tough, but really trying not to cry, he thought.

"I mean, you'll never guess what happened," he said.

And he told her about James and Rhiannon and the bender they'd been on while Robson was away on business. How he'd left James on the sofa with a duvet over him that morning. "Three days they've been at it, clubbing, staying at the Malmaison. I was listening to his gibberish until four this morning. He thinks he's in love. He thinks she thinks she's in love. But if Johnny finds out, we're fucked."

"Obviously," she said. "You wouldn't want to own paintings by the man who was sleeping with your wife."

"You certainly wouldn't want to pay for them."

"Can't you get James to keep his hands to himself, at least until the money's in the bank. That would be in his interest, wouldn't it?"

"I just hope they haven't left too much of a trail. You know how gossip can spread."

That was what worried Richard the most. One of Rhiannon's friends they'd met in a club, the hotel receptionist, or whoever it was who had sold them the coke; one of them would talk to someone else. And then, because Johnny was a local celebrity, the news would spread around town.

"We need to get the paintings out to him as soon as the show comes down and then invoice him," he said.

"Offer to have them delivered and installed on site," said Catherine. "That might speed things up."

"He still might dither over paying the invoice. It's what people like him do."

The filter machine hissed as the last of the water steamed through and Richard went to pour the coffee. He put a mug down on Catherine's desk and she smiled up at him. She was on the phone now, to Wolfgang, sounding out the idea of installing the paintings in Robson's building as soon as they came off the gallery wall next week.

Richard sat at his own desk and sipped his coffee, pretending to check his emails as Catherine laughed and made jokes over the phone. The hint of a crisis had enlivened her, changed her mood. She saw that she could be useful to him, supportive in his hour of need, and that was important to her. But if she came to him expecting love and affection, what would he do then?

They'd crossed a line when she walked out of the gallery yesterday, and he didn't want to cross back over it. He wanted to ask her to pick her things up from the house. He would have to make out it was temporary to soften the blow. Until his head was straight, he'd say, blaming Amanda. "You can see she's trouble," he'd say. "And I don't want you getting hurt."

After lunch, a sandwich at Di Marco's, he drove the Saab to his grandmother's house and wondered at the advantages of spending the afternoon mixing gin and tonics for Jane's friends. It would certainly keep him out of the range of Catherine's mooning looks, but the reason was more self-serving. It was obvious that if the deal with Robson went tits up, he would need more cash. And he only had one other source. But he remembered the last time he had asked his grandmother for money, the way her pen had hovered over the chequebook. Peter was probably right; he needed to show his face more often, and now was as good a time as any to start. The longer Amanda stayed, the more influence she might begin to have over the writing of cheques.

The autumn sun was bright on the house as he drove up the drive. He parked so as not to block in the gardener's Toyota pickup. The lawn was being mowed, the last cut of the year, and a little late at that. Standing on the wide steps that led up to the front door, he watched the sit-on lawnmower, like a toy tractor, moving across the grass. The driver waved at him and Richard waved back. The chugging of the engine and the faint whiff of petrol reminded him of days long ago, when he was a boy.

Putting his key into the lock, he opened the front door and called out. Amanda came into the hall as he stepped inside.

"You needn't have come," she said, standing in the doorway to the sitting room with her arms crossed. "I'm sure we could have managed without you."

"Richard! Is that you?"

"I'm here, Nana," he said, and brushed past Amanda.

Their grandmother, wearing a patterned silk top with a mandarin collar, was trying to get up from the settee, pushing down on the arm and trying to use her stick to help her stand, but she fell back and gasped.

"Painkillers," she said. "Would someone get me my fucking painkillers?"

It was Amanda who brought them; a small box and a glass of water, and it was she who pushed two tablets from the blister strip into the palm of Jane's hand.

"Is it getting much worse?" said Richard.

"Well it's not getting any better, that's for sure," said his grandmother, swallowing the painkillers, with a quick, expert flick of her head. Richard caught sight of what was printed on the box as it lay on the coffee table. The tablets were Tramadol; something he ought to look up on the internet.

"Perhaps you should have cancelled today," he said. "If it's going to be too much for you."

"I'm not going to start giving in to it," she said. "That would be the end of things. I've seen it happen to too many other people. Seen them shrink away from the world." Jane lay back on the sofa, and closed her eyes, waiting for the painkillers to take effect.

Richard told Amanda that it was time they set up the card tables, which were kept in the large cupboard under the stairs. She followed him out into the hall, and he opened the door in the oak panelling. Before he could find the pull switch for the light, she had pushed him inside, and pulled the door shut behind them. He felt a faint thrill as he inhaled her smell, and then she punched his arm.

"I used to bring you in here. Do you remember?" she said, punching him again and again, on his arms and on his torso. Then she pinched his nipple through his shirt. "We used to play this game, didn't we?"

"Fuck off!" he said, and pulled the light cord. The fluorescent tube flickered like a strobe, and he saw flashes of Amanda's smile before the light came on full, and then he saw it in all its enigmatic glory.

"Fuck off?" she said, laughing at him. "Did you really just tell me to fuck off?"

"Why have you come back?" he said.

"Perhaps I missed you. We used to have such fun together, didn't we?"

She pushed against him, forcing him back by jostling her breasts and her thighs against his body. He felt confused; he had an erection, a ridiculous feeling of desire. If she tried to kiss him, and he wanted her to, then he knew he was lost.

"We need to get these tables out," he said, and pushed the door open, feeling relief as cool air rushed into the cupboard.

They set up three card tables in the sitting room, carried in chairs from the dining room, and arranged occasional tables for drinks and snacks. At three o'clock Richard went into the kitchen, filled the ice bucket and sliced a lemon. He uncorked some wine, two bottles of white that he stowed in the fridge, and a couple of bottles of red. Amanda hovered, watching him fuss. Did she know how much he'd wanted her to kiss him?

The guests started to arrive. Twelve had come to play bridge, and a few others had come to watch and chat. All of them had been at the Friday drinks party. They all came by taxi because they were expecting to spend the afternoon drinking. Richard was ready to mix gin and tonics to order, pour wine into glasses and deliver them on a tray as they settled around the tables. His grandmother was shuffling a pack of cards and called him over.

"You haven't asked me what I want to drink, Richard," she said, putting down the cards and reaching for his arm. "I'd like a gin and tonic."

"Should you?" he said, keeping his voice low.

"Should I?"

"I mean, because of the painkillers."

"Don't tell me what I can and can't do, Richard," she said, still holding on to his arm and pulling him close. "I'm eighty-four years old, and I want a bloody gin and tonic. And make it so I can taste the fucking gin."

Richard found the afternoon tedious. He wasn't drinking, because he had the car and he didn't trust himself to stay sober, and slipped out on to the terrace every now and again to have a cigarette. Amanda, on the other hand, appeared to show great interest in how the hands were played. He thought it was another one of her acts; trying to please the grown-ups. As always, she had dressed to show her cleavage, the buttons of her blouse undone to reveal the top of her bra. The men looked, although they pretended not to, as she bent over to fill a glass or ask a question. He saw this and hated her for it; her flirtatiousness, the way she encouraged them with her girlish laughter and double entendres.

As the afternoon came to an end, he made coffee for those who wanted it, and took a cup out onto the terrace to sip while he smoked another cigarette. The sun had slipped away from the garden, and a dull light fell on the grass and the shrubs. The confusion he had felt in the cupboard earlier, a mixture of fear and anger, and yes, desire, was troubling. And was Amanda's cruelty towards him some sort of an expression of desire on her part? Nothing was clear to him, least of all why she was really here.

He ground out his cigarette and went back into the house; taxis were arriving to pick up the guests. As they left, Richard started to clear up the glasses, cups and plates from the tables and carry them out to the kitchen. He took the chairs, one at a time, back to the dining room, and stayed to look at the Verelst.

Coming through the hall he heard Amanda and his grandmother giggling. They sounded like two schoolgirls making jokes only they could understand. Was this Peter's 'something'? He stopped and watched the two women through the open door. He hadn't consciously walked quietly, but now he knew he was being furtive. His grandmother was still sitting at one of the card tables. Amanda was standing beside her and pushed two tablets out of a blister strip, the way she had done before, at the beginning of the afternoon. She passed them to the old woman, who swallowed them down with the remains of a gin and tonic, and with the same expert flick of her head.

When he walked into the room the green and white packet of Tramadol was lying on the table. It confirmed what he thought; his grandmother had had another dose of painkillers. Amanda, he realised, had seen what he was looking at. She must have sensed that he was about to say something, and before he could, she turned to their grandmother.

"Richard doesn't like you taking painkillers, Nana."

"What? He ought to try the bloody pain. He's a silly boy, isn't he?"

"Do you remember we used to call him Dickie?"

"Dickie?"

"You know. When he was little, we used to call him Dickie. Don't you remember?"

"Yes, Dickie," said his grandmother, her voice slurring. Dickie! Little Dickie!" She clapped her hands and started to shriek, a strange hysterical laugh.

"Yes, that's right, Nana. Little Dickie," said Amanda, looking at him with her arms crossed and that bloody smile on her face.

11

"So?" said Peter.

"Here comes our coffee," said Richard, meaning wait until the waitress has gone.

They'd met in Di Marco's, around the corner from the gallery. Richard was sitting on the banquette by the window, his favourite seat in the little Italian caffe. On another day the chatter of foreign students and the Europop on the sound system would have cheered him up.

But Peter was getting impatient. After the waitress had left their cappuccinos, he leaned across the table and asked again.

"So?"

"The painkillers," said Richard. "Is it something about the painkillers? Is that what's worrying you? I saw Amanda give her two doses, but to be honest, I don't know if the second was too soon after the first."

"And she's drinking with them. Amanda encourages that."

"She's always been a drinker. Isn't that why she fell down and broke her hip in the first place?"

Peter nodded. He bent forward and took a sip of coffee.

"Can I get a cake or something?" he said. "The doctor said I shouldn't drink coffee on an empty stomach."

The Gaggia machine hissed behind the counter and Richard looked over and caught the waitress's eye. He ordered a lemon and almond tart for Peter and tiramisu for himself.

"You're always fixing her g and t's, aren't you? How's it any different?"

"I mix them weak. Not much gin," said Peter.

"I think she's noticed."

"Amanda's starting to take charge of things. Indulging Jane. Trying to control her. Is it her money she wants?" said Peter, narrowing his eyes. "It can only be that, can't it?"

"Can't you take Nana away for a while? You were planning something, weren't you?"

"Jane would like that. I know she would."

"Stick to the original plan, Peter," he said after the waitress had brought their cakes. "The one you had before Amanda ever turned up."

"Don't you think we should ask someone to look into things? You know, to investigate?"

"You can't mean the police. Do you mean the police?" he said taking a forkful of Tiramisu. "What would you tell them?"

"We've got to do something."

When Peter left, he walked across the street with his head down. Richard watched him through the window, wondering if he should have said that his Aunt Emily had died of an overdose. But were Lisa McKee's suspicions of murder credible? Could Amanda have been capable of it? It could have been suicide after all, or just a terrible accident. Perhaps Peter was right, they should get someone to look into it. There must be some official channel they could resort to. But the police? That would make a lot of noise. His grandmother would hate him for it. And in the end, could anything be proved? There was no proof. None at all.

He ordered a double espresso, and asked the waitress to bring it to one of the tables outside because he wanted a cigarette. The two young men at the next table were talking in Arabic and smoking. Tobacco was meant to be some sort of consolation. It was meant to help you think things through, like Sherlock Holmes and his three-pipe problem. Richard smoked two cigarettes, lighting the second off the first.

If Amanda was up to something, he thought she would have waited until he'd gone before giving their grandmother the second dose of Tramadol. Unless she was trying to throw him off balance by letting him see what she was up to. There was always that; she'd always taken perverse delight in provoking him.

The barrier was raised, sticking up like a red and white barber's pole. Richard drove through into the car park and reversed into a space between two white vans. He got out of the car and looked around, but he couldn't see Robson's Porsche and that bothered him.

The site office was in a Portakabin that smelled of sawn wood and sweat. A man with a shaved head sat behind a desk covered in paperwork, stubbing his fingers onto the keyboard of his computer and swearing.

"Johnny's having his picture taken," he said as he looked for Richard's name on a printed list. "Up for some award, apparently. He loves all that stuff, doesn't he?"

Richard clipped a visitor's badge to his lapel and took the safety helmet and the Hi Vis vest the man handed him. The vest was grubby and someone had written *Dave the Rave* in black felt tip pen on the scuffed helmet. It was too tight at first, and even though he adjusted the headband until it fitted, it still felt ridiculous on his head.

The building was meant to be almost finished, but the windows and doors still had protective tape on the glass, and inside the lobby swathes of polythene sheeting protected the floor. The vague shape of a reception desk was visible under thick translucent plastic, an apparition in pale beech veneer. Richard heard frantic banging, the whirr of drills and the stutter of electric screwdrivers.

Robson was getting ready to have his photograph taken. He stood by the balcony rail on the mezzanine with his legs apart, holding a clean white hard hat in his hand. In the other hand he held a long roll of paper, which Richard thought might actually be an architect's plan. Today though, like the fluorescent Hi Vis vest and the expensive suit, it was just another part of an elaborate costume.

The photographer, the same young woman that Richard

had hired for James' opening, adjusted one of her lights and began to take pictures. She called out instructions to Robson. He unrolled the plan and pretended to look at it, looked into the distance, or up at the skylight, put his helmet on and took it off, turned this way and then that. Playing the role he had defined for himself. That of a confident man of his time, a builder of things; the kind of man who actually made things happen.

Robson had enjoyed posing for the portrait; he was flushed and a little breathless when it was over. Richard wondered how he would react if he were to discover he was a cuckold. Johnny's vanity, he imagined, would require some awful, full-blown revenge.

"I'm up for Northern Businessman of the Year," he said, shaking Richard's hand.

"I heard there was something in the air. Congratulations."

They looked over the balcony to the atrium below. The walls of original Victorian brick had been left exposed. The region's past, Richard supposed, was having its rough edges smoothed away and contained by contemporary architectural design and bourgeois taste. The old industrial space had been transformed into offices. Offices for legal firms, software companies and call centres. Whatever there was a demand for these days.

It was on those bare brick walls that Richard proposed to hang James Heath's canvases with their wild gestural sweeps of bright colour. He had brought images with him on his Macbook; Photoshop mock-ups of how the paintings would look in the space. He proposed to hang the big pictures on the opposite side of the atrium where they could be seen from both the ground floor and where they stood now.

"When will the building be finished?" said Richard.

"There's just some wiring for the lighting and comms to do. The main offices are finished. Ready for clients to move into."

Richard said he wanted to arrange for his technicians to install the work as soon as possible. "I need to give them notice," he said.

"You're in a hurry, aren't you?" said Robson.

"Storage is an issue at the gallery, that's all."

"And you want paying." Laughing, he clapped Richard on the back. "Don't be ashamed of that. The building will be finished by the end of next week. You can hang the paintings at the beginning of the week after. That suits me, the opening's on the Friday at the end of that week. I want them up for that. Get your guys to call the site office."

The two men walked out of the building to the car park. Robson waited while Richard returned the hard-hat and vest to the site office, and they walked over to the Saab.

"Is this what you drive?" said Robson, kicking one of the front tyres as if he were buying a used car.

"It's a classic," said Richard. "A 900 Turbo."

"If you say so."

"Where's your Porsche?" said Richard. "I didn't see it."

"Rhi's got it. I'm driving her car," said Robson. "Come and have a look at the state of it."

They walked across the car park and stopped in front of a black Range Rover. "Have you seen the state of this?"

Richard looked. The left front headlamp was smashed, the front bumper cracked and hanging loose. The wing was dented and all down the side, along the door and rear wing, was a deep wide scratch, the glossy paintwork down to bare metal in places. This was the car Rhiannon had been driving on the night she and James had come to his house looking for cocaine. Christ, he thought, she must have been really out of it.

"What happened?" he said.

"Ask Rhi," said Robson, shaking the front bumper. "Had a girl's night out last week when I was away. Looks like she had an argument with a house, doesn't it? It's a fucking mess. She doesn't want to be seen driving it, so Muggins here has to take it to the body shop. Women, eh?"

"Don't talk to me about women," said Richard.

"Stick with that assistant of yours. She doesn't look like she'll give you too much trouble. Rhi's a spitfire, alright." Robson laughed. "A real woman. You know what I mean?" He winked, put his hard hat on and walked back towards the building with his hands in his pocket, whistling.

Richard sat in his car. His stomach felt queasy. Robson's macho cockiness and the damage to the Range Rover unsettled him. As soon as the paintings were hanging in Robson's building, he could send the invoice; then he could chase it up. On the basis of the money they were due he might be able to persuade James to take a trip somewhere. And then perhaps Rhiannon would find someone else to amuse her, someone who had nothing to do with him or the gallery.

Catherine was at the desk out in the gallery.

"Wolfgang called. He wants a set of keys for the gallery so that he can start taking the show down on Sunday. I said that was okay."

"Yeah, sounds good. Let's get everything moving. We need to book him in to install the paintings, anyway," he said and went into the office.

Catherine went into the kitchenette to make coffee and leaned against the door-frame with her arms crossed as the filter machine burbled and hissed.

"Well?" she said. "You've got a date from Robson?"

Richard was groping about in the top drawer of his desk. He shut it and opened the next one down, moved things about and bent down to peer inside. Catherine was getting annoyed with him, he could tell. He told her about the Range Rover, what Rhiannon had done to it.

"She's trouble," he said, slamming the drawer shut. "This whole deal could go down the drain because of her."

"You've got a date to deliver the paintings, haven't you?" she said. "Anyway, you're panicking."

"Am I?

He bent down to open the bottom drawer. After a moment he slammed that shut too, and looked up.

"What are you looking for?"

"That spare set of keys," he said, pushing his chair away

from the desk. "I'm frightened of Robson, you know. I think he's dangerous. And I don't trust him."

"If he finds out, he finds out. It's nothing to do with you."

"He'll think we've made a fool out of him. Or that I have. He thinks he's an alpha male and that he can control Rhiannon, but he obviously can't. When he finds that out, well, we'll be in the line of fire. Where the fuck are those keys?"

"They'll be in the key box, silly."

"Silly? Don't you think that was the first place I looked?" he said, standing up and going over to the grey metal key box on the wall. He opened it and pointed inside. "See? No fucking keys. Silly."

Richard knew she was about to cry. It was obvious, in the way she stood, her body open to him, that she wanted him to cross the room and hold her. But he wasn't going to. Starting the affair had been a mistake. The problem was that he still needed her. Without her help the gallery wouldn't be able to function.

"I'm sorry," he said.

"It's her, isn't it? Amanda. Something's been off since you came back from Toronto. And it's been even worse since she came. You've been different. Has she followed you? Come to finish off something you started over there?"

"It's not what you think."

"And what do I think?"

"That Amanda and I are having a relationship. A sexual relationship."

"Aren't you? I've seen the way she looks at you. It's the way a cat looks at a mouse." She reached her arm out and made a claw with her hand and snarled. "Is it even legal?"

"It's not that," he said. "It's family stuff. It's too difficult to explain. Things will calm down, you'll see."

"I thought we were doing so well together, with the gallery. Well, with everything really. Have I even still got a job?"

"Of course you have. If you still want it. You must know that I need you here. The gallery needs you, for God's sake. Can't that be enough for now? Until I sort myself out?"

He went over to her. She fell against him and he put his arms around her, but he didn't look down at her face. Because he knew she would be looking up at him, her lips and eyes imploring him to kiss her. She would look pathetic and desperate. He knew that he could have, did have, a power over her. Even if he used her badly, she would come back for more. The thought made him feel ashamed. Amanda, he imagined, would think him a coward.

Peter's Mercedes was parked at the bottom of the steps. Richard pulled up behind it and let himself into the house. He called out, as he usually did, and went into the sitting room.

His grandmother was sitting at the table by the window looking at her iPad. Peter stood behind her, his hand on the back of her chair, leaning forward to look at the screen. They were watching a video. As Richard bent to kiss her, he saw footage of a blue sky and a large white building overlooking the sea. Amanda was in an armchair flicking through a copy of Vogue.

"They're getting excited about a holiday," she said, closing the magazine and tossing it onto the coffee table as if she was bored with it.

"Madeira, for a bit of winter sun," said Peter. "We're looking at Reid's Hotel."

"Winston Churchill used to stay there," said his grandmother, turning to look up at Peter and patting his hand. "It'll be like old times, won't it?"

"Who's for a drink?" said Amanda. "It's after six."

She asked Richard to come and help her. They went into the kitchen and she pushed him up against the peninsular unit. He could kiss her if he wanted to; he knew she would let him. His head swam at the thought of it, like the first time he'd inhaled a cigarette. It was the old confusion of wanting her, of being frightened of what she would do to him, where it would lead. Perhaps he should just submit to her, give up all resistance.

"Isn't this cosy?" she said. Her arms were around his waist, her lips close to his.

"What do you want, Amanda?" he said, pushing her away.

"We need to talk about Nana," she said. "This thing about going away. Peter's got her all worked up about it."

"It'll do her good, won't it?"

"I should take her. Not him."

"You'd like that. I can just see you pushing Nana around in a wheelchair."

"She's getting old. She's vulnerable, and creeps like Peter Morgan are going to try to take advantage of her. Getting her to pay for his luxury holiday at that hotel. She's a very wealthy woman, but you know that. You've been taking advantage yourself. I've seen her bank statements. You've put him up to it, haven't you? Turning up like this to add your weight to it. It's a conspiracy. That's what it is. It's a fucking betrayal."

"Peter's a very wealthy man," said Richard. "He doesn't need Nana's money."

"Are you sure? We're her family. We're the ones who should be looking out for her."

"What do you know about looking out for family?"

"You're pathetic. Do you know that?" she said, coming back towards him. Her eyes went hard. The way they did when they were children. The way they did just before she hit him. "All those years ago, looking for sympathy with that story about your noble father and that fucking deer. He still killed your mother though, didn't he?"

12

If only he knew the words, he wanted to spit out at her. But he couldn't speak and fled the kitchen in a dumb rage.

He went down the garden to the bench behind the shrubbery. He lit a cigarette and sat smoking with his elbows on his knees to try and stop his hands from shaking; Amanda had touched on the truth.

On the night of the accident both his parents had been drunk. They were arguing. His father had wanted to go to Toronto, but his mother was against it. They'd been at it for days, on and off. It erupted as they were coming back in the car.

Richard wasn't really paying attention, he'd tried to shut the whole thing out because it was his birthday, but he heard his mother say that she wasn't prepared to play happy families anymore, and then something about 'that bloody girl'. She started screaming and hitting his father around the head as he was driving. He told her to be quiet, that she should 'think about the boy', but she lashed out at him again. He tried to hit her with the back of his hand and lost control of the car.

The story Richard had always told about a deer appearing in the road simply wasn't true. There was no deer, he'd invented it, to make it seem as if their deaths were the result of a foolish, heroic act.

He stubbed out his cigarette and walked back up to the house. Amanda was waiting for him in the kitchen, leaning against one of the units with a large cut glass tumbler in her hand.

"I was going to bring one out to you," she said, raising the glass to her lips. "You need one to take the edge off."

"I can make my own bloody drink."

Richard went over to the worktop. Amanda had everything ready, she'd filled the ice bucket and sliced a lime on the small wooden board. He filled a tumbler with ice and poured in a good measure of gin.

"We had something special, didn't we?" she said, coming very close to him.

"Did we?"

"You wanted to. You always wanted to. I was your first so I'll always be special to you in that way. That's true, isn't it? Someone said that to me once. Can you guess who it was?" She started laughing, looking him in the eye, as if he was the butt of another one of her jokes. And she was standing too close to him.

"I'm glad to see that you two are getting on so well," said his grandmother. She was standing in the doorway, leaning on her walking stick. "But some of us are dying of thirst in here."

He mixed two more drinks and carried them into the sitting room on a tray. Peter and his grandmother were still looking at the iPad, watching the promotional video about Reid's Hotel. Richard looked over her shoulder to offer encouragement, but he was just going through the motions because he knew that Amanda was watching him. If he left the room, he knew she would come after him. This was the game they played as children; she would stalk him around the house without anyone else noticing.

Richard had to go into the kitchen to mix more drinks. Amanda followed, leaning against the worktop and watching him. He made a great effort, pretending to be calm, using tongs to put ice into the glasses and pouring the gin slowly, with a steady hand. It was important that he appeared quite normal, unperturbed. But he had the feeling that if he ran from the room, if he tried to get away from her, she would sprint after him.

"I'm going to buy a car," she said. "Did you know?"

"Nana mentioned it," he said, picking up the tray.

She followed him into the hallway.

"Will you help me choose one? I know nothing about cars."

"Of course I will." It surprised him that he meant it. Hadn't he always wanted to please her?

"What do you think I should get?"

Amanda had stopped in the hallway as if she was waiting for a reply, and Richard turned towards her. She moved her eyes towards the staircase, as if she was suggesting that they went upstairs. He didn't know how long they stood there; it couldn't have been any longer than a second or two. But it seemed as if something was wrong with time. His mouth went dry and there was a hammering in his chest.

Peter saved him by stepping into the hall.

"Ah, the drinks are coming, at last," he said. "Everything alright?"

"Yes," said Richard, going through to the sitting room. "Amanda wants to buy a car. Needs some advice."

"Oh, talk to me," said Peter, sitting next to Amanda on the settee. "I know people in the trade."

Richard knew that Amanda was only pretending to be interested, just as he was pretending to be interested in the guidebook to Madeira that he found on the coffee table. He sensed she was watching him. It was evening now, and Jane began complaining about the cold. She wanted her wrap, a Pashmina, from her bedroom.

"It's on the chair by my bed," she said.

Richard put down the guidebook, and went up to his grandmother's bedroom to get it. As he came back out onto the landing, he heard a door opening and closing downstairs. From the top of the staircase he saw Amanda standing in the hall. She was looking up at him with that awful smile on her face. As he stood there, she kicked off her shoes and began to take the stairs two at a time, laughing as she came up towards him.

When she was nearly at the top, he realised what she was up

to; he headed down the corridor towards the bathroom. But she was behind him pushing hard against the door as he tried to close it. He staggered back, surprised at her strength. Amanda was in the room now, locking the bolt with one hand behind her back. Then she came at him grinning, her arms wide to stop him getting away. He remembered that was an old trick of hers, just as she kicked his legs away, and he fell down onto the floor.

Amanda unzipped her skirt and stepped out of it as she walked towards him. She began to tug at his belt. Blood pounded in his head and he felt himself swoon. She undid his zip and he raised his hips so that she could pull his jeans and pants down. Then she mounted him.

"Do you like that?" she said.

"It feels like…like…" But he didn't really have a word for it, although he had tried to answer this question a very long time ago. He obeyed her body, echoing the rhythm of her movements until they both came at the same time.

"See what you've been missing." She got to her feet and stood with one leg up on the toilet bowl, wiping herself with tissue. Richard was still lying on the floor. "You'd better jump to it and clean yourself up," she said. "Nana's still waiting for that wrap."

Something had changed in the sitting room; there was a look of unease in Peter's face. And something simmering behind his grandmother's eyes. She demanded to know where Richard had been, and then started crying when Amanda followed him into the room.

She was carrying the wrap. "Dickie didn't know where it was," she said.

"Oh, my darling girl," said Jane, holding out her hand. "Come to me, come to your Nana. Why did I let Ray take you and Emily to Canada?"

"She's drunk or something," said Peter in Richard's ear.

"Come on, darling," said Amanda, kneeling down by Jane's chair. "I think an early bed is called for. This holiday thing's got you too worked up. I've always thought it was a silly idea. Didn't I say so, Nana?"

Amanda took their grandmother by the arm and led her out of the room. Richard stood by the sitting room door, holding it open just enough so that he could watch them going up the stairs. He pushed the door to and turned to Peter.

"What the fuck happened?"

"Is there something between you two? You were out of the room for a while. I heard noises. Jane heard them too. We thought, well I thought, that you were fighting."

"Don't,' said Richard.

He went upstairs to say goodnight to his grandmother. She was already in bed and asleep. Amanda was in the en-suite and came out when she heard him.

"Be quiet, Nana's just gone down," she said, beckoning him to the door.

"Is she on sleeping tablets?" he said when they were standing outside the room.

"She gets them on prescription. But she doesn't need them tonight. She's tired out. And this stupid holiday thing has just jangled her up."

"Perhaps we should hire a nurse. It must be a lot of work for you."

"I looked after my mom," she said. "I can look after my grandmother too. Someone has to."

"She's my grandmother too. I get a say in these things."

"Ask her tomorrow morning if she wants a nurse. Stay the night," she said, coming very close to him, and fingering the open collar of his shirt. "We had fun before, didn't we?"

"I've got to go," he said. "I don't want to stay."

Amanda pushed him away. "Fuck off then."

"Did you give her something earlier?" he said. "Painkillers or something?"

"Be careful, Dickie. You're speaking out of turn."

"We'll see," he said, turning and walking down the stairs.

Was his grandmother just drunk? Or did Amanda have something to do with his grandmother's change in mood? It might have had something to do with the Tramadol or some other drug. Perhaps Peter was right; they should get someone to look into it.

At the bottom of the staircase he stopped to look at the marble bust of Diana on the console table. It was another of his favourite pieces. Richard wanted to look at it longer, to reach out and touch it, to feel how smooth it was. He used to do that when he was a boy, but Amanda was watching him from the first-floor landing so he left, closing the front door behind him.

As he drove out onto the road, he had to stop the car, pulling over to the kerb because he suddenly felt nauseous. A feeling of disgust, a sense of self-loathing erupted from deep inside him, up into his throat and he had to open the door to vomit. A car came towards him from behind and he looked up. The headlights dazzled him and the driver blasted the horn. The blare seemed more of an admonition than a warning. Richard felt as if he had been caught in some unspeakably seedy act by an anonymous, unseen eye. He pulled the door to, but even though he'd shut the world out, he felt ashamed as the car drove by, and he turned his head away.

This had been how he'd felt in Toronto all those years ago when Amanda had started giving him her 'sex lessons'. It was always painful to acknowledge his feelings of desire when it came to her. There was always the feeling that he'd been ruined in some way. And that it had been against his will. 'I was your first,' she'd said, as if that made him her property, and meant she could do exactly what she wanted with him.

Catherine was waiting for him, sitting in her car outside his house. He recognised the distinctive shape of her old Citroen as he pulled up. Shit, he thought. He should have known that she would try something like this. She hadn't taken their 'separation' well; he knew that from the way she had been looking at him in the gallery.

She got out of her car as he reached the gate, waving at him the way a little girl waves, with a bottle of something wrapped in tissue in her other hand.

"I thought we could have a drink together," she said. "You know, catch up. I wanted to see you."

"We'll see each other in the morning," he said, unlocking the front door.

"I don't mean like that."

They went down the hall and into the kitchen. Even under the electric light he could see how soft and smooth her skin was. Seeing her so unexpectedly made him realise he had forgotten how attractive she was. He pulled the cork on a bottle of wine and began to fill a glass for her.

"Here," he said, still pouring it as he passed it to her so that it was almost too full.

Richard poured another glass for himself and drained it quickly.

"Yes," he said. "Let's have a drink and catch up."

He felt angry, and he hated that she had a pretty face and that she was kind.

"What's wrong?" she said.

"I'm just trying to give you what you want," he said.

Catherine looked surprised, shocked even, as he took her glass from her. He put it on the worktop and pulled her towards him. He used to like the smell of her, like fresh sheets dried in the open air, and now, right now, he thought that was the smell of a stupid naïve innocent. Didn't all girls smell like that? Clean and fresh. Amanda smelled of musk and sex, and he was angry about that too; that his thoughts pulled him back to *her*. And that he'd helped her in the bathroom, lifting his hips to help her pull down his jeans.

"This is what you've come for, isn't it?" he said, grabbing her buttocks and pushing his groin forward, backing her up against one of the units.

He kissed her hard, the way Amanda kissed him; there was no tenderness in it, only lust.

"Do you want to go upstairs?" he said. "Or shall we just fuck here?" At that he swept his arm across the kitchen table. Everything fell, mugs, cups, the teapot, keys; apples from the fruit bowl rolled around on the floor. The bottle of wine fell too, and smashed, and the dark liquid spread across the quarry tiles.

"What's wrong with you?" said Catherine, stepping back.

"Come on. You know this is what you came for," he said, grabbing her by the shoulders, trying to push her back onto the table.

Catherine slapped him across the face and he fell back in shock.

"You need to sort yourself out," she said. "I don't need to put up with this."

He didn't say anything; he just stood there with his head down, touching his face, unable to look her in the eye. It never occurred to him that she would resist him, not go along with what he wanted. He'd never resisted Amanda, never fought back. He heard Catherine walking out of the room, and muttered 'I'm sorry, I'm sorry,' under his breath as she went down the hall and slammed the front door behind her.

Opening another bottle of wine, he took it outside and smoked one cigarette after another. Behind him the house was empty and dark; he'd turned out all the lights. The bright thin crescent of the moon was cut into the dark sky. Whether it was waxing or waning, he had no idea.

He took out his phone and called Lisa McKee in Toronto. She must have been watching television, because he heard voices and loud music until she turned the sound off.

"I think she's up to her old tricks with pharmaceuticals," he said.

"You don't think she'd try the same thing again? Christ, I'd come over and tell the cops if your grandma dies of an overdose."

"You really think she killed her mother, don't you?"

"Oh yes. That's for sure. What's the matter? Don't you think she's capable of it?"

"She's up to something. I just don't know what it is."

"You need to do what I didn't do."

"What's that?"

"Confront her. Tell her you know what's she's up to. Stop her."

Richard didn't say anything. He was silent for so long that Lisa asked if he was still there.

"I thought the line had gone dead," she said.

"It's the signal here sometimes." Then he told her about the car crash; blurting it out. "I lied to you all those years ago," he said, his voice cracking.

"Have you been drinking?"

"Just a little."

"A bottle's not much company, is it?"

"I can talk to you."

"Oh wow, it's Richard who calls me up when he's drunk. You know how to reel a girl in, don't you?"

"What are you doing?"

"I'm watching a dumb cop show on TV."

He laughed to himself, thinking about Lisa and her murder mysteries, and remembered the bottle of wine lying broken on the kitchen floor. He thought of the dark liquid pooling on the tiles like blood; evidence of a crime he'd have to clean up in the morning.

13

The gallery was between shows and the walls were empty.

"Do you want me to work my notice?" said Catherine.

She stood just inside the office door. The shoulders of her raincoat were wet, the belt still tied tight, as if she wasn't staying, and was ready to rush back out into the rain. Richard sat at his desk, unable to look at her. He picked up the bright yellow fountain pen she'd given him for his birthday, and turned it over and over in his hands.

"You don't have to leave," he said. "I don't want you to."

"Why should I care? You were horrible last night. Maybe that's what you're really like and you're just good at hiding it. I think you're good at hiding things."

"What do you mean?" he said, putting the pen down.

"Whatever it is that's going on between you and Amanda."

"Not this again," he said. "You really think I'm having an affair with her, don't you?"

"I still think there's something going on between you. Something that's a little bit off. Is it sexual? You tell me."

"It's not that," he said, not looking up, not wanting to meet her eye. "It's not what you think it is."

"So tell me what it is," she said, dropping into the chair on the other side of his desk and folding her arms across her chest.

"I'll tell you," he said, and hesitated, and then he spoke very quickly. "I was terrified of her when we were kids. She was an awful bully. But that doesn't seem like the right word. It doesn't explain it properly. She was always at me for as long as I can remember, but she was clever with it. No one noticed. I thought that when her family moved to Canada, that was it. It was over. But here she is again. And even though I'm meant to have grown up…" He laughed, but there were tears in his eyes and he had to catch his breath. "It's as if nothing has changed. I can't face up to her. Really, I can't."

"She's certainly exploded into our lives, hasn't she?" said Catherine. "I hate her for it. Have you ever talked to anyone about this? You know, properly?"

"A shrink, you mean?" Richard said, taking the tissue she offered him across the desk and wiping his eyes.

"You shouldn't keep it all to yourself," she said.

He watched Catherine take her coat off and hang it up. She said she would make coffee. It was as if something had been settled between them, even if he wasn't quite sure what it was. She was tougher than he'd thought; the slap she'd given him last night should have told him that. Perhaps he should tell her more. Tell her about Lisa McKee's suspicions, or Amanda's predilection for pharmaceutical high jinks. But the sex thing, well that was something else.

A shadow fell across the street window. James Heath had parked his Land Rover up on the pavement. There was something comical about his outfit; a tweed jacket with shorts and paint splattered work boots. He charged towards the office, shoulders down, fists clenched. He was pale-faced and unshaven, and his eyes were bloodshot; he was hungover.

"When do I get my money?" he said. The stench of stale alcohol on his breath made Richard wince. "Robson's got the paintings, hasn't he? The big opening's tonight, isn't it? Canapés and fucking fizz. So everyone's happy. Except me. I want my fucking money. I need it."

"Are you panicking for the same reason I am, Jimmy? You know, if Robson finds out you've been diddling his wife then the whole bloody deal's off, and you'll have a bit more clutter in your studio. I'll tell you one thing, if that happens, if this goes tits up, then any understanding between us is over."

"What Richard means is that you can go and find another gallery to deal your work," said Catherine.

"We're going away. I need the money to go away."

"Are you serious?" she said. "Are you seriously suggesting that you and Rhiannon are going to run off together?"

"Are you mad?" said Richard.

"It's the real thing. This is the real thing."

"And won't Rhiannon miss the fancy motors and the designer clothes?" said Richard. "Did you see what she did to her car? Robson just laughed it off. It's small change to him."

"I just want what's due to me."

"Leave town, Jimmy," said Richard. "Stay away from the cookie jar for a while. You'll get your money when I get the money. That is, when the cheque's cleared and there's nothing Robson can do to queer the deal. He'll be as mad as hell if he finds out. When he finds out. And then we'll have to pretend we knew nothing about it, and hope that means we get to keep the money."

"You're being selfish, James," said Catherine. "This could ruin the gallery."

"It's love," said James. "What wouldn't you do for love?"

Richard wanted to laugh, not at the absurdity of it, but because he saw a traffic warden through the window, sizing up the Land Rover. He told James, who sprinted down the length of the gallery and out onto the pavement.

"It's the shorts," said Richard. "They don't look quite right on an angry man."

"He just looks like a schoolboy in a strop," said Catherine.

They stood in the gallery and watched James gesticulating and shouting at the warden. She was a large woman with dyed red hair, who calmly took a photograph of the Land Rover, wrote out a ticket, stuck it on the windscreen and walked away.

Richard and Catherine looked at each other with grins on their faces; something had come right between them. Even if it wasn't quite what Catherine wanted, he knew that she would stay at the gallery now and help him through this.

When James came back Richard made him sit on the sofa in the office and gave him a cup of green tea to try and calm him down.

"I've got a cottage up on the coast. Why don't I lend it to you for a couple of weeks? A few weeks, even. Until all this is sorted. That'll give you a bit of time to reflect on things. Sketch the sea and the sky. Get real."

But James wasn't listening. He barely touched the tea, and was obviously anxious to leave.

"I'm going to get myself ready for tonight," he said, getting to his feet.

"Don't tell me you're seriously coming to the opening," said Richard. "Please don't tell me that."

"My paintings are hanging in that building. I want to see them."

"Haven't you been listening? You've got to stay away from Rhiannon."

"Don't tell me what to do. Nobody tells me what to do."

After showing their invitations to the security men, pumped up nightclub doormen in dark suits, they were greeted by a line of young Japanese women hired by Robson from an agency. They wore black mini-dresses with white Peter Pan collars and held trays loaded with flutes of champagne, offering them with a smile as guests came into the lobby. Richard and Catherine took a glass each and hovered near the doors to watch for James. They'd made a plan of sorts for the opening; one or both of them would stick to him like glue in an attempt to keep him away from Rhiannon.

Catherine spotted him first. He'd trimmed his beard, and if he'd lost the wild-eyed look he'd had earlier that day, he was still on edge. He had no conversation and kept looking around, raising himself up on his toes to look over the heads of the crowd. Richard fetched another glass of champagne and pressed it into his hand. They distracted him by taking him up onto the mezzanine to look out from the balcony at his paintings on the far wall.

The height and spacing were perfect. Wolfgang and his team had done a terrific job and Robson had taken the trouble to have good lighting fitted. The paintings, with their expressive sweeps of colour glowed in the space. But James was anxiously scanning the crowd on the ground floor.

Richard nudged Catherine; Robson was holding court down below, standing in front of a temporary stage that had been set up with a microphone stand. His shaved head glistened in the light as he waved his arm towards the paintings, showing them off to the small group surrounding him. Rhiannon was on his arm, laughing. James had seen them too and, gripping the balcony rail with one hand, he drained his glass.

"I need more fizz," he said, and set off for the stairs.

Richard and Catherine followed. At the bottom of the staircase James took another flute of champagne from a table set with rows of glasses on a crisp white cloth. He started to push his way through the crowd towards Robson's gleaming head, towards Rhiannon.

Richard got held up; one of the men Robson had introduced him to at James' opening was interested in buying some artwork for his office. Could they arrange something? Perhaps he could bring his partners to the gallery? Could they do some business?

When Richard got to Robson, he was clapping James on the back.

"Here he is, the bloody talented bastard," he said.

Rhiannon kissed Catherine, Richard and then James on the cheek and laughed. She introduced them to an attractive woman with dark hair. Richard recognised her; she was a well-known actress, the star of a well-received TV series in the nineteen nineties. Rhiannon was flushed with excitement. If she had adultery in mind, she didn't show it. In fact, she seemed determined to ignore James, and made a show of clinging to her husband's arm.

"Isn't this brilliant?" she said.

At that moment Robson climbed on the stage and took the microphone from the stand. He called for everyone's attention and people began to move closer to the platform, creating a crush that made it difficult to move.

Richard took his eyes off James. He should have paid more attention to the expression on his face, the confused anger, and he should have stayed with him. Instead he'd turned to hear what the man of the future had to say.

"Thanks for coming. I won't keep you too long, there's drinking to be done," said Robson raising his glass, grinning as the audience laughed. Someone cheered. "Those of you who know me know that I love this city. I love this region and I love the people. If there's a problem, it's because we're all caught up in nostalgia. You know what I mean, this idea that the past was a golden age of shipbuilding and coalmining and heavy engineering. All cloth caps and whippets. We forget the slums and the poor sanitation. In our minds we're too ready to see ourselves defined by romantic images of pigeon lofts and an endless stream of men on bicycles coming out of the shipyards at knocking off time. But that's all gone. Anyone who tells you different is lying or mad.

"Once this building was an engineering workshop, and it was part of that past. But times have changed, and the world has changed. This building was left empty and derelict for years, and it's not a blink from the city centre. Now, it hasn't just been tarted up and prettified for no purpose. It is going to be a centre for economic and cultural renewal. The problem is that we've gotten used to thinking that the best is behind us. Well, I've got news for you. The best is ahead of us. This building is part of the past, that's for sure. But now it will be part of the future of this city."

The audience applauded. They whooped and cheered. As the hubbub died down Robson began to list the people he wanted to thank: the architect, and the CEO of the building firm. He asked them to come on to the stage. Then he pointed to the paintings up on the wall behind him.

"James Heath, the artist who created these fantastic paintings. Where are you, James?" Robson had to put his hand up to shield his eyes from the lights. "I've just seen you. Come up and take a bow. Either he's shy or he's gone for a Jimmy Riddle," he said, raising another laugh.

Richard stood on tiptoe and scanned the crowd. He couldn't see James. Nor, he realised, could he see Rhiannon, and he tapped Catherine on the shoulder as Robson called the actress up onto the stage. "A great ambassador for this city," he called her. She said how glad she was to be home. How she thought that the energy and spirit of the people of the city was a great cause for optimism. She asked the audience to raise their glasses.

As people cheered, Richard and Catherine began to push their way through the crowd. There were office suites behind the glass wall that ran around the back of the atrium. The lights were out, and the doors were locked. They took the stairs. Up on the mezzanine a crowd had gathered by the balcony rail. The speeches were finished and they were beginning to come towards the tables that had been set with drinks and food.

"This is hopeless," said Catherine. "What are we going to do when we find them? Throw a bucket of cold water over them?"

Richard put his finger to his lips. He knew she was right, but he turned, and began to walk slowly past the lift doors and along the corridor that led off into the heart of the building. The smell of new flooring and adhesive was overwhelming. Light from the streetlamps outside seeped into the offices, and showed as a pale-yellow glow on the blinds of the interior windows that lined the corridor. He could see down its length. For a moment he thought all the doors were shut, but halfway down on the right he noticed a thin shaft of light showing on the carpet tiles. One of them was open.

The hubbub of the opening party seemed far away. Richard felt uncertain as he walked towards the slightly open door. He stopped and listened; he was too late; they were having sex. There seemed to be no point in confronting them; it would change nothing. But Richard was curious, a curiosity he didn't know he possessed, and he pushed the door open just enough to see them.

Rhiannon was leaning forward over a meeting table, the skirt of her dress pulled up to her waist while James, his Levi's around his ankles and his jacket still on, was moving vigorously, the way a dog humps an ankle. Richard was transfixed. In a way he was excited, but then he had another thought. Was sex really so ridiculous? Had he and Amanda looked as comical? The thought made him shudder. He stepped back and pulled the door to, hard enough to make a sound. And the catch clicked.

As Richard walked away, he heard James' voice calling out, "Who's there? Who's there?" and he was glad to have spoilt it, their desperate little act. But he knew that was little compensation for what might come after it.

Catherine was still waiting for him by the lift and they went and mingled with the other guests, innocent and smiling, as if they were ignorant of what had happened upstairs. Rhiannon reappeared, hanging on Johnny's arm, brass-necked and fearless. James had disappeared, but the glasses of champagne continued to be served by the Japanese waitresses, and Richard thought that they might as well get drunk.

"For tomorrow," he said to Catherine, raising his glass to hers.

Of course, he should have known they would spend the night together. He woke with an aching head and the smell of Catherine in his bed at seven o'clock in the morning.

His phone woke him, ringing up through the house. It stopped ringing and then it rang again. And again. He had to remember where he'd left his jacket, and he pulled on a shirt and staggered downstairs, the depth of his hangover revealing itself with every jolting step. There were five missed calls on his phone. Two from Peter and three from Amanda. He called Peter first.

"What's the matter?" he said.

"Jane's in a state," said Peter. "I can't get any sense out of her. I'm going over there now."

Then he called Amanda.

"Where the fuck have you been?" she said.

"Asleep," he said.

"There's been a burglary. During the night. While we were in our beds. Nana's beside herself, Dickie," she said. "And they took that painting you're so fond of."

"Which one?"

"The one you said was worth money."

"The Verelst?"

"Yes, that's right," said Amanda, and Richard could hear the smile in her voice. "That's the one. The one you liked so very much."

14

The police were already at the house; a van and an unmarked Ford saloon parked by the steps that led up to the front door. Amanda must have been listening for Richard's car; she was waiting for him when he stepped into the hall.

"Come and have a look at the scene of the crime, Dickie."

She grabbed his hand, and led him into the dining room. There was a chill in the air and the curtains billowed in the breeze. A uniformed policeman was examining the lock on the French windows. One of the panes had been smashed out and jagged glass stuck out around the edges of the frame. More broken glass was scattered over the parquet floor. It crunched under Richard's foot as he stepped forward for a better look. The officer swirled black powder over the paintwork with a brush, leaving a trail of oily marks across the surface.

"Fingerprints," the policeman said, looking up at Richard. "They jemmied the gate to the back lane. And then smashed the glass. Small pane, single glazed. Easypeasy."

"We must have left the key in the lock," said Amanda. "Whoever it was just reached in and used it to open the door."

"The insurance people are going to love that," said Richard, staring at the fingerprints. "Is that lot any use?"

"Can't tell," said the policeman. "I'll have to take yours. For elimination purposes, obviously."

"Obviously," said Richard, going over to stare at the dark patch of wallpaper where the Verelst had hung.

"I'm not used to putting the alarm on before I go to bed," said Amanda. "It's upsetting, isn't it?"

"It was a wonderful painting, you know," he said, turning to face her, but he couldn't read her expression. "I just hope we see it again."

They went into the sitting room. A young woman in a navy trouser suit, her red hair tied up in a ponytail, was sitting on the sofa with a notebook in her hand. Richard supposed she was a detective interviewing his grandmother. Jane sat on the edge of her chair looking down at a tissue in her hands, and pulling at it obsessively.

"Nana," said Richard.

"Oh, darling," she said, taking his hand. "This is such a terrible thing. We were asleep in our beds. Anything could have happened to us."

He squeezed her hand and kissed her on the cheek. The detective was looking at him expectantly.

"I'm DS Walsh," she said. "We're just trying to find out what's been taken."

"Nana, have you checked to see what they took?"

"Is that all you care about?" said Jane. "Don't you care what might have happened to us?"

"Our handbags have gone," said Amanda. "And with them all our credit cards and the keys to the house."

Walsh told them that the handbags had been found in the back lane.

"Empty, of course," she said.

"I don't understand," said Amanda. "The TV, the computer, things like that, they're still here. Isn't that what they'd normally take?"

"They might come back," said Jane. "They have the keys now. They can just let themselves in whenever they want to."

"Do you know what else has been taken, Nana?" said Richard.

"No, I haven't looked. Anyway, I don't know about things like the painting. They were your grandfather's things."

"These things," said Walsh to Richard. "What are they? Antiques?"

"My grandfather was a collector. There's definitely a painting missing. I can check around the house to see if anything else is gone."

"The house doesn't feel safe anymore," said Jane, still tugging away at the tissue, pulling it to shreds.

She began to cry. Richard was shocked; he'd thought his grandmother was tougher than this. Today she was an old woman, a frail old woman.

"I think you need to rest, Nana," said Amanda, helping her to her feet.

While Amanda took their grandmother upstairs, Richard made coffee for them all, and after leaving the tray with a cafetière and cups in the kitchen, he went around the house, upstairs and downstairs, to see if anything else had been taken. But nothing else had. He was surprised; there were a set of Hogarth prints, Marriage a la Mode, in the corridor by the bathroom that would have been particularly easy to sell.

The painting had been a particular favourite of his. He found it difficult to imagine that a random burglar had a grudge against him. The break-in had been personal, an act of spite. If indeed it had been genuine. He wanted to dismiss the thought as mere paranoia, but the idea that it was one of Amanda's tricks unnerved him. She must have known that he would suspect her; it was just another one of her taunts. Like a poke or a pinch or a punch.

As he passed Amanda's room, he stopped outside the door. If he found the Verelst, stuffed under the bed or in the back of the wardrobe, then he would be able to unmask her. And everyone would see she was playing dirty tricks on them all. He had his hand on the door handle, but he heard her voice, and thinking she might come looking for him, he went downstairs.

Amanda was drinking coffee with DS Walsh when he got back to the sitting room.

"Nana's in her room. I put her to bed. She's still in a lot of pain. I gave her something for that, but she's probably asleep now."

"It's a terrible shock," said Walsh. "It can hit people hard. Especially the elderly."

"Nothing else from my grandfather's collection appears to have been taken," said Richard, sitting in one of the armchairs. "Just the painting. Just…" He shrugged, and looked at Amanda. Was that smile finally emerging, curling up at the corners of her mouth?

"And this painting?" said Walsh. "I presume it's valuable? What kind of value would you put on it?"

"Richard said it was worth about fifty thousand pounds," said Amanda. "Didn't you? When you were showing your friend around?"

"Ms Johnson tells me you're an art dealer."

"I have a gallery, but we deal in contemporary art. It's not the same sort of thing at all."

"Do you know how someone would get rid of this sort of thing?"

"It's not easy to sell, you know. It's a seventeenth century Dutch painting. It's unique. My grandfather bought it at auction in the nineteen sixties. It's not the sort of thing that someone would try and sell you in a pub. As to the trade, I don't know. We'll have paperwork showing its provenance, somewhere. And you'd need that to sell it. Legitimately, at least."

"And how would you go about selling it illegitimately?"

"Isn't there an art or antiques squad that deals with this sort of thing?"

"You've just got me for the moment, Mr Waverley. Who's this friend Ms Johnson mentioned? The one you were showing the painting to?"

"You're barking up the wrong tree there."

"You'd be surprised."

"It was my gallery manager."

"Isn't she your girlfriend?" said Amanda. "Although I never know if you two are on or off from one day to the next."

Walsh closed her notebook. She said they needed to have their fingerprints scanned.

"We'll need them to progress the investigation."

"I know," said Richard. "For elimination purposes."

"Is there anyone else we need to fingerprint?" said Walsh. "Anyone who comes to the house a lot?"

"There's Peter Morgan. He's a friend of my grandmother's. And everyone in her bridge club. The cleaner. Lots of people, I suppose."

"It doesn't seem to be a very sophisticated break in. But they must have known what they were after. They must have known that the painting was in the house. Why that one in particular, do you think? Do you know anyone who liked it particularly? A member of the bridge club? This Peter Morgan? Your... girlfriend?"

"Not her,' said Richard. "She was with me. I'm her alibi."

"And she's yours," said Walsh, smiling. "We'll have to see if it turns up somewhere. Sometimes drug gangs use these things as collateral for big deals. But this is Tyneside. Our villains prefer hard cash."

"So, what will you do?"

"We'll need photographs. Something we can send out to antique dealers especially those that deal in paintings. The Met have an Art and Antiques Squad. They might turn something up in London. And we might get lucky with the fingerprints, but I doubt it. I'll check if there's anyone local who might be worth a visit. There's not much else we can do, to be honest. Best you get in touch with your insurers. Get the money, if that's what you want."

"Those things are irreplaceable," said Richard.

"And difficult to sell. You said so yourself. So the motive... well, that's the key, isn't it?"

Walsh closed her notebook. She began to tap her pen against it, looking at them both, her face impassive.

Richard and Catherine had barricaded themselves in the office against the noise of electric screwdrivers and drills whirring and shrieking. Wolfgang and his assistants were installing the next show, the work of a German artist, large paintings of clubbers in Berlin that had been copied from colour photographs.

Peter called unannounced and paced about the office, pretending to look at the framed pictures on the wall. He picked up one of the catalogues that was lying on the desk, and tossed it down immediately. DS Walsh had been to see him that afternoon.

"They came to my house," he said. "And took my fingerprints."

"I'm a suspect too, apparently." said Catherine. "It's quite funny, really, isn't it?"

"It's ridiculous," said Peter, rolling his eyes at Richard. "Absolutely bloody ridiculous."

Richard realised that Peter wanted to talk to him alone. They headed out to the Bacchus.

"Catherine's very young, isn't she?" said Peter as they walked down the cobbled street to the pub, the nearest thing Richard had to a local. "I hope you're not taking advantage of her. It's so easily done."

The pub was busy; the early evening crowd were in, men and women in suits fresh from the office. They managed to get a table in a corner and Richard fetched two large glasses of Shiraz from the bar.

Peter took a long pull on his glass and sat back in his chair as if exhausted. The idea of outsiders poking around in his affairs had unnerved him, and Richard wondered if any of his business affairs had been shady. Besides that, he lived alone, and had no one to vouch for him. But the visit from the police wasn't the only thing that had unsettled him. Amanda had refused to let him see Jane when he'd called at the house earlier.

"Said Jane was resting and couldn't be disturbed. Virtually pushed me out of the front door."

The thought crossed Richard's mind that if Detective Sergeant Walsh could see the two of them now, she would think they were meeting up to get their story straight. Were they suspects? If so, he wondered if Amanda was on Walsh's list as well.

Richard had more or less convinced himself that she was behind the break in, and that she didn't care if he knew. She used to pinch and punch him when he was a child and then, like now, she knew that there was nothing he could do about any of it.

Peter went to the bar to get another round. Left alone, Richard looked around at the early evening drinkers. A group of young women were shrieking with laughter. He caught the eye of one of them and she smiled back. He looked away; to be caught looking embarrassed him. In that moment, he envied them their camaraderie, and realised that he felt dreadfully alone.

He wanted to confide in Peter, but he wasn't sure how much to tell him. Lisa's suspicions that Amanda had killed her own mother might, after all, be fuelled by bitterness. It might just have been a tragic accident. But then again, she'd drugged him with Rohypnol in Toronto, hadn't she?

He wanted to share this with Peter. They were both concerned about Amanda's influence over his grandmother. Her history of using drugs on other people was pertinent. But if he laid it all out, then he would have to touch on what Amanda had done to him. Any mention of her sexual assaults would make him seem deranged. And it would make him look weak. He was a grown man, after all.

When Peter came back from the bar Richard told him that he thought Amanda had something to do with the burglary.

"She's certainly up to something," said Peter. "There's the thing with painkillers, and she was trying to put the kibosh on Jane going on any kind of holiday. Not one of life's angels, although Jane can't see it."

"We'll both go round tomorrow, Peter," he said. "She can't keep us out."

His phone rang and he looked at the screen. It was Catherine and he ignored it.

He had decided, he said to Peter, to search his grandmother's house. If Amanda had staged the burglary, the painting would be hidden somewhere, probably in one of the outbuildings. If he could find it, then perhaps he could challenge her, and find a way to force her out.

They made a plan. Peter would try and persuade Jane to go out for lunch to help her get over the shock of the burglary, and ask Amanda to join them. Beg her to come. Richard would say he was going to look through his grandfather's papers, because he had to find some photographs of the painting to give to Walsh. It would take some time, easily giving him the opportunity to search for the Verelst.

"What are you so happy about, Waverley?"

Richard looked up. James Heath was standing over the table. He'd gone feral; his hair was a tangle, his t-shirt and shorts covered with spatters of paint. He must have called at the gallery, which was why Catherine had called, to warn him.

"Have you got the money from Robson yet?"

"No," said Richard. "But we're having a meeting. Come to the gallery tomorrow and we'll talk about it."

"Well, I've heard he doesn't like to pay his bills," said James, putting his hands on the table and leaning forward. "Likes to keep people waiting."

"Where'd you get this?" said Richard, but he knew. Rhiannon.

"I did try to warn you," said Catherine when he got back to the gallery.

Richard sat at his desk and said he hadn't heard his phone. It had been too loud in the Bacchus. It had been someone's birthday and they were a rowdy bunch. He couldn't very well say he hadn't wanted to answer her call or that he went on and off her according to his needs.

But if what James had said was true, and Robson didn't like to pay his bills on time, then he needed her. Peter had been right; Catherine was an innocent. It was her naivety that allowed Richard to exploit her. He needed her more than he cared to admit. That she saw some worth in him was an antidote to the self-loathing that Amanda provoked in him, and he knew he should be more grateful for it.

Catherine came and sat on his lap, put her arms around his neck and kissed him.

"What you need to do is to go and see Mr Robson and use your not inconsiderable charm to persuade him to write you a cheque."

She was right. It was the only chance they had. Otherwise Robson would let the whole thing drift. But if he wanted to be seen as a patron of the arts, and Richard knew he wanted the kudos, then it was beholden on him to settle the bill. How close James and Rhiannon's affair was to being discovered, well that was out of his hands.

15

Richard rang the bell and banged on the door until Amanda opened it. The security chain was on and her eyes, the lashes sharp with mascara, glared at him through the gap.

"What's all the noise?"

"It wouldn't work," he said, holding up his key.

"That's because we've had the locks changed, Dickie. That's what you do after you've been burgled."

She closed the door to take the chain off and opened it again.

"I'll need a new set of keys," he said.

"You should have let us know you were coming," said Amanda, closing the door behind him. "We're still having breakfast. I suppose you'll want a cup of coffee."

He said the thing about the keys again, but she ignored him and he followed her into the kitchen. So the burglary had given her an excuse to change the locks. She was trying to make life more difficult for him. Like those little punches when they were children; they weren't just meant to hurt him, they were meant to keep him off balance.

His grandmother was sitting at the table in the kitchen eating a slice of toast with delicate disinterest. Richard thought she looked half asleep. He kissed her on the cheek and sat down. She grabbed his hand and squeezed it.

"Was it you making all that noise, Richard?" she said.

"My key wouldn't work in the lock, Nana."

He noticed she wasn't wearing any make up, which was unusual; she always put on what she called 'my face' before coming down in the morning. She'd done it for as long as he could remember. Now she looked her age and that shocked him; he'd always thought of her as invincible.

"Your key? What's wrong with your key?" she said.

"We've had the locks changed, Nana," said Amanda, passing Richard a cup of coffee.

"You'll need to give me a new set of keys," he said.

"So you said."

"Well?"

"I will."

"When?"

"When I feel like it."

"What is it?" said Jane. "What are you two bickering about?"

"She won't give me the new keys, Nana." He heard the whine in his own voice.

"Why can't he have them, Amanda?"

Amanda said something about Richard not having a sense of humour. She got up and went and opened one of the kitchen drawers. She came back and put a bunch of keys down hard on the table.

"You'd better check they work, Dickie," she said, crossing her arms.

"I need to find the insurance policies for the artworks," he said, picking up the keys and looking at them. "There should be photographs of the Verelst. We need them for the police. Do you know where they are, Nana?"

"Look in the study. They'll be in there somewhere."

"Have you kept up the premiums? Otherwise we can't make a claim. I'll need to see your bank statements if you're not sure."

"He's always thinking about money, isn't he, Nana?" said Amanda.

"I'd like to help the police catch the bastards who broke in. Then we might get the Verelst back," he said, looking at Amanda, ever more convinced that the whole business was some game on her part.

"Do you really think there's a chance you'll see your precious painting again?" she said. "There's more of a chance they'll come back and steal the rest. Don't you think we need to make the house more secure?"

The doorbell rang. "That must be Peter," said Richard, glancing at his watch.

"Have you arranged this?" said Amanda. "You should have given us some warning. You can see how things are here."

"He wants to help Nana, that's all."

Peter had brought a large bunch of yellow roses and a bottle of champagne. Joking and making a fuss of Jane, he managed to raise a smile from her, and she seemed to brighten. He wanted to take her out in the Mercedes. She needed to get out of the house. "Let's go for lunch," he said. There was a country pub he had taken her to before. Jane couldn't walk far, but there was a bench nearby that offered a terrific view over the Tyne Valley. Amanda declined his invitation. She said she was going shopping because she had nothing to wear.

"I must put my face on," said Jane, picking up her stick and struggling to her feet.

"Do you need any help?" said Richard.

"I can help," said Amanda, standing up.

"I can still manage the stairs, darlings," said Jane.

Richard followed her out into the hallway and watched her take the stairs slowly. When he came back into the kitchen Amanda was leaning against the worktop, watching him as she sipped her coffee. She forced a smile at him; on and off, the way she'd done when they were kids.

"When are you going to help me buy that car, Peter?" she said. "You promised, remember?"

Amanda had decided she wanted a Range Rover and Peter asked her how much she wanted to spend. She said she didn't want to scrimp; she had plenty of money. Richard thought that was a dig at him because she knew he was broke. He finished his coffee and went across the hallway to the study.

His grandfather had fantasised about being a gentleman scholar from the nineteenth century. The large Victorian desk and the mahogany swivel chair attested to that, but the beige metal filing cabinet looked out of place. It was there, in one of the drawers, that Richard found a hanging file marked Art and Antiques. There were receipts, out of date insurance policies, and certificates of provenance. And in a bound folder with clear plastic pages were a set of colour photographs of all the paintings and artworks in the house. He undid the binding and spread the pictures over the leather-topped desk, leaning on his hands to look over them, to marvel at the sheer quality of the collection. He heard a car engine and looked out of the window. Peter's Mercedes was heading down the drive.

Amanda came into the room and he glanced up at her. She was wearing a navy blazer with gold braid on the cuffs and jeans with white sneakers. She had a way with clothes, of making herself look as if she had walked out of the pages of one of the celebrity magazines she read.

"I'm taking Nana's old car," she said. "You won't get scared, will you, all alone in the house?"

He turned back to the photographs, ignoring her, or at least pretending to, because he could sense she was looking at him.

"I bet Peter's going to bring up the idea of that trip to Madeira again."

"Well, it would do Nana good to get away," he said without looking up.

"Well, it would do Nana good to get away," said Amanda, her voice high-pitched like a cartoon character.

He turned and looked at her, trying to appear relaxed, trying to face her down. This had been one of the things she had done when they were children, repeating everything he said, and making it sound stupid.

Amanda walked slowly towards him. He thought that she wanted to have sex because she parted her lips and touched her teeth with the tip of her tongue. He wanted to kiss her and he wanted to say no. But he knew the word would stick in his throat, the way it had when she'd attacked him in the bathroom.

She was very close to him, so close he could smell her perfume, and almost taste her moist lips. At that moment she

126

brought her knee up into his thigh. His leg gave way, and as he crumpled against the desk, holding on to it, to stop himself from falling, she smacked him around the head with her open hand two, three, four times and he fell to the floor, covering his head with his hands to protect himself.

"What was that for?" he said, looking up.

"What was that for?' she said. The cartoon voice again. "Don't forget to lock up when you leave, Dickie. You've got a nice new set of keys to play with."

As he heard the old BMW drive away, it dawned on him that he wouldn't find the Verelst. Amanda had made it all too easy for him, leaving him with the run of the house. The thing with keys had been a blind, a fake victory, just something else to keep him off balance.

He decided to search the house anyway and to start with Amanda's room. As he closed the door behind him, he felt a tingle of excitement rather than a fear of being caught.

Getting down on his hands and knees he looked under the bed. If she had taken the painting, she might simply have hidden it there. But there was nothing. He opened the wardrobe and pushed his hands amongst her clothes, parting them so that he could see right to the back. There was no sign of the painting, but his fingers slid over a white silk blouse. The slippery smoothness of it excited him. He held it to his nose, and inhaled Amanda's smell.

For some reason he went over to the chest of drawers, and opened them. There was no possibility that the painting could be hidden there, but suddenly he was standing with a tight chest and a dry mouth feeling through a drawer of Amanda's underwear. He saw a pair of red satin panties, and held them to his face. He had done this once before, in Amanda's room in Toronto when he was a teenager. That was over twenty years ago, but it might have been only yesterday; the compulsion was still so strong. Was this the real reason he'd wanted to search her room the other day, the reason for the thrill he'd felt just now when he closed the door behind him?

It was finding the drugs that brought him back to himself, the packets of Xanax, the white plastic bottles of Oxycontin, the boxes of other drugs whose names he couldn't take in. Painkillers, he thought. There were two foil strips of Rohypnol. He slipped one into his jacket pocket, closed the drawer and left the room.

He was shaking, and needed to mask his odd behaviour by making a methodical search of the house and the grounds. And so he looked in all the wardrobes and cupboards, under all the beds, up in the attic, the garage, even the outhouses in the garden, so long unused that the doors that had to be forced open. As he had expected, he found nothing. But when he felt the foil strip in his pocket, he knew that he hadn't wasted his time. The Rohypnol meant something.

He was in the kitchen making a cup of coffee when Peter and his grandmother came back. She looked quite flushed; the outing seemed to have done her good, and she was excited.

"We're going to Madeira," she said. "Isn't that wonderful?"

"It's bloody brilliant," said Richard.

Robson kept him waiting in reception. The receptionist, a blonde woman wearing a white blouse and a black pencil skirt, brought him a cup of coffee. Richard sat in a low chair, black leather, chromed steel and uncomfortable, drinking the awful coffee and looking through one of the daily papers that had been laid out for visitors.

None of the articles held his attention. His mind kept returning to the same thing; what was Amanda up to? Earlier, he'd driven round the back of the gallery to park the Saab. His grandmother's BMW had been there, parked at an awkward angle next to Wolfgang's van. He wondered what the hell was going on.

"She asked if she could leave the car," said Catherine. "I couldn't very well say no. Could I?"

A voice called his name and snapped him out of his reverie. Another young blonde woman took him up in the lift to Robson's office. She showed him in and Robson came out from behind his desk, red braces, shirtsleeves rolled, his arm outstretched. He apologised for keeping Richard waiting. A phone call from Hong Kong, he said, that had gone on and on.

"Coffee for two, Jasmine. And not that muck we serve in reception." Robson laughed. "I was surprised you'd called," he said, dropping down onto a black leather sofa, and gesturing for Richard to sit in one of the armchairs opposite him. "You know, there was actually something I wanted to talk to you about. But it's personal. More the sort of thing we should talk about over a drink, like mates. But what was it you wanted to see me about?"

"I just wondered what sort of reaction the paintings were getting. The gallery's mission is to get people to invest in the arts. If they can see that as worthwhile, if they want to develop that, well there are other benefits too."

"What other benefits?"

"Social benefits. People are already talking about you as a patron of the arts, Johnny. There's a lot of kudos in that. Look at Saatchi."

Robson smiled. "If you've come for your money you should just ask for it, straight out," he said.

Jasmine brought in a cafetière and cups on a tray. Like the woman Richard had seen in reception, she was wearing a black pencil skirt and a tight white blouse. Robson watched her walk out of the room.

"I have to remind myself I'm a married man," he said, shaking his head. "Look but don't touch, that's my motto." He reached over to push the plunger on the cafetière down. "Marriage isn't the same as it used to be, is it? There's a different morality these days. You know why? No God. No Hell. No Damnation. Does that make straying easier?"

"I'm sorry, Johnny. I don't follow."

"You're divorced. That's what you told me, isn't it?"

"Yes, that's right."

"So what brought that about? Were you shagging on the side?"

"That's personal, Johnny."

"I'm after perspective, Richard," he said, sipping his coffee. "That's a good cup of coffee, isn't it?"

Richard drank a little from his cup. "Yeah, it is good," he said.

"So why did you do it? Commit adultery, I mean. Were you bored?" Robson shifted in his seat. "Were you out of love?"

"Out of love's a good way to put it. And yes, I was bored. Because I wasn't really happy, I suppose."

"I think I give too much time to the business. Perhaps if we'd had kids."

"What's all this about, Johnny?"

Robson leaned forward, his elbows on his knees, his head down. "I think Rhiannon is having an affair. And it's driving me crazy."

"Are you sure?" said Richard. He wanted to ask, who with? He wanted to look surprised if Robson knew.

"She's been going out a lot on her own. And staying out late. Said she was with friends. Which friends, I ask. She tells me. One friend in particular, just got divorced, likes a night out, making up for lost time. That sort of thing. You follow me?" Richard nodded. "Then this friend phones the house looking for Rhiannon when they're meant to be out together. Hasn't seen her in weeks. What do you make of that?"

"Have you asked her about it?"

"It's not an easy thing to ask, is it?" said Robson.

"No. Nor an easy question to answer, I remember that. I got so used to lying I couldn't tell the truth when I was asked a straight question about anything. It was like confessing to a crime, you don't want to 'fess up unless you have to. And divorce? Well that's a messy business, Johnny. There's blame, and blame has financial implications. Somebody has to be found guilty, and that person has to pay for it. In hard cash. I was lucky to hang on to my house."

"Money?" Robson went over to his desk and sat down. "She does like to spend money, I know that."

Richard stood up and looked out of the window towards the cathedral. Rain was hitting against the glass. Another shower. If the conversation hadn't taken this peculiar turn, he would have said something about the weather or what a great view it was. He knew Robson was writing him a cheque at that moment, and he held his breath. Best not to speak, he thought.

"Thanks for listening," said Robson, holding up the cheque.

Richard took it. "What will you do?" he said.

"If she's just staying for the money, I'll crucify her. I didn't know what to do until now. All this stuff's just been going round in my head. Talking about it out loud, well that's helped me see the way things are. I'll tell you what I'm going to do. I'm going to hire a private detective and find out what the fuck's going on. That seems a bloody good idea, don't you think?" Robson stood up and clapped Richard on the shoulder. "Once again, thanks for listening."

"Don't mention it."

"You won't tell anyone, will you?"

"No, of course not."

"If you do, I'll crucify you too," said Robson, and laughed.

Richard folded up the cheque and put it in the inside pocket of his jacket. He laughed too, to show he understood the ways of the world.

Catherine said that Amanda had come back for her car with about half a dozen bags, all with designer labels, and that she'd insisted on showing off all the things she'd bought.

"She had them all out of the bags, in the office, holding them up. Asking me if I liked them. It was funny. Funny odd. You know, you'd think I was her new best friend. Anyway, I couldn't help wondering. Where does she actually go to wear all that stuff?"

Richard shrugged; Amanda was too difficult to read. Thinking about it didn't do any good, and he was glad to have avoided her. The meeting with Robson was still on his mind. On his way back to the gallery he'd waited for the rain to ease off in a disused shop doorway that stank of stale urine. Seized with paranoia, he'd taken the cheque out of his pocket and looked at it, checking the details two or three times in case Robson had played some awful trick on him.

He handed the cheque to Catherine. She looked at it and whistled. Normally, this amount of money would be an excuse to celebrate. They would have opened a bottle of fizz and gone out for dinner. It was as real as any cheque could be, but it didn't mean anything until it had cleared. And how long would that take? Five working days, she said. It was too late for the bank now, and with the weekend coming up that would mean a week. And then there was the fact, Richard told her, that Robson suspected Rhiannon of being unfaithful, and what he was planning to do about it.

"But how long will it take him to get a detective on the job?" said Catherine.

"And how long after that before he finds out about James?" he said.

Richard was distracted by the sound of an electric screwdriver. He stood up and looked through the floor to ceiling window that separated the office from the gallery. Wolfgang was on a stepladder fixing a painting to the wall. It was the last canvas to go up. He and his assistant, John, had finally finished installing the show. They packed away their tools, and took the boxes out through the storeroom to their van.

"They've finished," said Richard. "We should pop a cork on a bottle of something to celebrate that at least."

"I'll check what's in the fridge," said Catherine.

She took a chilled bottle of prosecco and four glasses out into the gallery. Richard called out to Wolfgang and John, and asked them to come back through. He popped the cork and handed around the glasses.

"Before I forget,' said Wolfgang, taking something out of his pocket. "I found these on the floor in the storeroom, just now when we were loading the van. Just kicked them as I walked through." He held up a bunch of keys.

"The spare keys," said Catherine.

"Funny thing," said John. "The back door was unlocked."

"Oh, that's just me," said Catherine. "I must have forgotten to lock it when I let Amanda out."

But Richard wasn't listening; he'd had enough of Amanda for one day. He was looking at the paintings, how they filled the walls, how his idea for sequencing the work allowed it to unfold for the viewer. The installation was immaculate and he knew, just knew the show would be a success. He'd done this; he'd made it happen. He turned to the others and raised his glass.

16

Richard kept talking. James pretended not to listen. He kept painting, attacking the canvas with a large brush. It was clear he was struggling; free expression was giving way to a mess of paint.

Richard heard himself. His voice had become a drone; he was nagging.

"Stop telling me what to do," said James, and dropped the brush into a can of turps. He wiped his hands on a rag and began to roll a cigarette.

"I'm waiting for the penny to drop, Jimmy. That's all."

The studio reeked of turps and oil paint. Richard wondered if the fumes had some effect on the sanity of painters, and made them pig-headed. He opened the metal-framed window to let in some air, lit one of his own cigarettes, and looked at the industrial units and the new blocks of flats being built on the other side of the valley. A train rattled over the Metro Bridge, punctuating the silence between them.

The new exhibition at the gallery was opening in a couple of days. He'd left all the arrangements to Catherine, aware that he was becoming too dependent on her again. It would mean that she would cling to him even more, become more cloying, fishing for her reward with declarations of love.

But he had too many other things on his mind. He couldn't tell James about the private detective; it would get back to Rhiannon. She would have it out with Robson and then it would become clear that Richard knew about the affair. And Johnny wouldn't like being made a fool of twice.

James had to stay out of the way, at least until the cheque cleared.

"It's just a week, Jimmy," he said. "Just disappear for a fucking week."

But James just stood, smoking and looking at the painting. Still not listening.

"What do you think?" he said, waving his hand towards the canvas.

"You're just going through the motions."

"I'm working the way I've always worked," said James, placing his hand on his chest.

Richard wanted to laugh out loud at the theatricality of the gesture. It was so at odds with James' feral look. A wild man's hair and beard, and his clothes; t-shirt, cargo shorts, tan work boots, all spattered with paint. Even his cigarette, made with brown liquorice paper, looked like a small twig stuck between his lips.

"I don't doubt your sincerity, Jimmy. But I'm your dealer and I've got your artistic interests at heart. You know that. Just like you know that painting's a pile of shite."

"I know," said James.

He dropped his cigarette to the floor. From amongst the paint tubes lying on the table next to his easel he picked up a Stanley knife. He slid out the blade and slashed the painting in a criss-cross motion. The canvas gaped under the weight of all the paint he'd used and made an ugly hole.

Richard sighed. "Look at the state you're in. For one thing, you need to stop seeing her. And for another, Robson's dangerous."

"That bastard owns four of my best paintings."

"And you're fucking his wife," said Richard.

"It's not the same thing."

"You'll need to be careful when he finds out."

"I can handle Johnny Robson," said James, and started rolling another cigarette.

"Go up to the cottage, will you?" said Richard, dangling a

set of keys. "Take your sketchbooks, whatever you need. Go out and look at the sea and the sky for fuck's sake. Draw and paint. Reconnect with something other than your cock. It's obvious you don't paint from down there."

James snatched the keys and looked at them. "A week?" he said.

"The longer the better."

Richard tore a page out of one of James' sketchpads and wrote down directions to the cottage. Rhiannon was a bored trophy wife; she would tire of James eventually. Perhaps this forced separation would speed things up.

Amanda had joined a gym. She told Richard it was very exclusive, and it was becoming too embarrassing for her to turn up in their grandmother's old BMW. She was making friends at the gym. That's why she needed a new car. "These things matter," she told him. "That's just the way things are." And she was looking for a place of her own, and was pestering him to come and see a flat in the Art Deco block overlooking the Town Moor. If Richard had ever clung to the hope that this was just a passing visit, he was beginning to realise how wrong he was; Amanda was staying.

She summoned him to come and see the Range Rover. And like a fool he turned up. He saw the thing as he came up the drive, a glossy hulk of black paint and dark tinted glass parked in front of the house, and set at an angle as if it was about to be photographed. Amanda must have been watching for him, because she came skipping down the steps onto the gravel as he drew up. She made him climb into the passenger seat so that he could admire the cream leather upholstery.

"Just smell it," she said, getting into the driving seat. "It smells like money in here."

Amanda sat with her hands on the wheel. He half expected her to make noises like an engine revving. She'd done that when they were children, when she'd made him sit in one or other of the family cars. Then she would pretend to drive him somewhere. 'We're off to a deep dark wood,' she used to say. A place he couldn't find his way back from.

"We could go for a little ride in the country and try it out in the back, if you like." She looked straight ahead but he saw the smile on her face. "You look as if you could do with a little bit of fun, Dickie. I bet, what's her name? Catherine? I bet she doesn't know what you really like."

She squeezed his thigh and began moving her hand up towards his groin.

"Is that all you think about?" said Richard.

He was getting an erection, and got out of the car before Amanda discovered it; that would only make her think he welcomed her attentions, that he enjoyed them. And that wasn't quite true. It never had been. Had it? He started walking towards the house.

"I know you think about it," she said.

"Just shut up, Mandy."

She repeated what he'd said in the high-pitched cartoon voice as she caught up with him, and then she slipped her arm through his. "It's been a long time since you called me Mandy."

Richard didn't say anything, or pull free of her, and they walked up the steps to the front door.

Peter was sitting in the kitchen with his grandmother. His laptop was on the table in front of them. They were finalising the details of their trip to Madeira. According to her consultant, Jane's hip had healed, and she could start to reduce her reliance on painkillers. But she was reluctant, encouraged by Amanda's mantra of "Take them when you need to, Nana." Today she had the hazy look in her eyes that Richard had seen all too often in recent weeks.

On Sunday, as an experiment to gauge the effects of the drug, he'd taken one of her Tramadol tablets. After twenty minutes his body became heavy. Overwhelmed by lethargy, he spent the afternoon lying on the sofa watching television, hypnotised by the vivid colours of a quiz show.

It was Peter's plan to reduce the dose while they were in

Madeira, and to bring Jane 'back to herself' as he called it. They were leaving in two weeks. Now it was time to make the final payment online. But Richard's grandmother became confused as she searched for her credit card; it wasn't in her handbag.

Amanda was sitting at the end of the table, flicking through a copy of Hello magazine as if she had no interest at all in what was happening. Richard knew it was just a pretence; she was watching them all very closely.

"Don't you remember, Nana?" she said, looking over the top of the magazine. "We had to change our cards after the burglary."

Amanda got up and went to fetch the new card. She came back and tried to hand it to her grandmother, but she didn't want it.

"You do it, darling. Really, it's best if you do it. I haven't got my glasses."

The thing with the credit card bothered Richard. He caught Peter's eye and nodded towards the door. Amanda didn't notice; she was busy tapping the card number onto the laptop's keypad.

Peter followed him out to his car when he left, and they stood as if they were admiring the Range Rover. We're like conspirators, thought Richard. Amanda was probably watching them from the house, watching him at least. The truth was they were watching each other; the sense there was a game or a secret war between them was as palpable as it was unspoken.

"What did you make of that?" said Richard. "Amanda using Nana's card as if it's the normal thing to do."

"I think it's going to get worse. She's going to try to get power of attorney. Just something Jane said the other day, about how managing money was getting too much for her. How helpful Amanda was with things like that."

Richard told Peter about his experiment with Tramadol. "She's using the painkillers to control Nana. Things will change while you're away, though. Won't they?"

"I don't know, Richard. I don't know what I can hope to

achieve. Amanda is actively encouraging us to go on this trip. If she gets the legal paperwork done before we go, she'll have complete control of Jane's finances."

On Saturday night Richard and Catherine had a row. A friend of hers was having a party and she wanted him to go. But her friends were too young for him and he couldn't be bothered. At least that was the beginning of it, but it turned out that they were really arguing about commitment.

She wanted him to say something definitive about their relationship, and although he pretended he didn't know what she wanted him to say, he knew she wanted to get married and have children. She threatened to move out and go back to her flat, and although he didn't have the courage to say so, that was what he wanted. In the end she lost patience with him and phoned for a taxi to take her to the party.

He started drinking and thinking about Amanda and the way she'd always tormented him. The sexual stuff didn't come until Toronto, and that happened just after he'd met Lisa McKee. Lisa had been kind to him then, when he was reeling from the death of his parents. The first time they had sipped ice cold Coke on the porch of her mother's house there had been an attraction. The feeling was new to him, not just sexually, because there was something else. A tenderness: something that might have saved him from what came next.

But Amanda had ruined it for him. And he knew she had corrupted him too. Those 'sex lessons' of hers had followed him all his life, tainted him and ruined every relationship. Sex was power, and he picked on women like Catherine because he knew he could dominate them. He resented them for that, the very thing he'd chosen them for, just as he resented them for not being Amanda.

He took one of the Rohypnol capsules he'd stolen from Amanda's room. He had looked the drug up on the Internet; it had once been popular on the club scene as a way of losing yourself in the moment. When taken with alcohol, its effect was stronger, more unpredictable. He'd done that with antidepressants when he was younger; he was an expert in self-medication in that it hadn't killed him. Now he was falling into another fug, dredging up the past, regretting what might have been. He wanted to get out of his head.

Staggering outside with a packet of cigarettes and a bottle of wine, he sat at the wrought iron table in the dark looking out across the garden. He felt very drunk and wondered if the Rohypnol was having any effect at all. A bird or a bat must have tripped the sensor of the security light. It clicked on and lit up the patio and the lawn beyond it. Out on the grass he saw a deer looking at him. It was very still and he wasn't sure if it moved at all. He'd seen it before; it was the deer that he'd memorised from a photograph in a wildlife book, the deer, he'd told everyone, his father had swerved to avoid on the night of the accident. And suddenly he wasn't on the bench on the patio, but in the back of the BMW, watching his parents punching each other in the front seats of the car. The security light timed out and he saw a bright afterimage as if he'd been dazzled by a flashgun.

He fumbled for his phone and called Lisa McKee.

"Have you been drinking?" she said. "I think you only call me when you're drunk."

"I wanted to say that you're the place I'd start from if I could start again," he said. "But it's too late."

"I don't understand, darling."

Richard told her things that he had never been able to tell anyone else. There was no one else he could tell.

He woke up, still slumped on the patio bench at five o'clock in the morning. The thin, grey light and the dawn chorus made everything unreal. He knew he'd been crying. His phone, still in his hand, was dead; the battery had run down. He remembered talking to Lisa McKee, but if the drug had enabled him to let it all come out there was no release, no catharsis; he remembered too little of the night before.

Catherine had stayed the night at her friend's house. She came home at about eight o'clock and found him in the kitchen.

She made him sit down and spooned coffee into the cafetière while the kettle boiled.

"You look awful," she said.

"It was just a bad bottle of wine," he said, sitting at the table with his head in his hands.

"Don't lie to me. You've taken something. You've done something stupid."

"It's my business. Not yours."

"I don't know you," she said, putting a cup of coffee down in front of him.

"You should go to your place for a while," he said. "There's too much shit going on in my head right now."

17

Catherine said she would pack a bag and leave him to it. Richard heard her moving about upstairs as he lay on the sofa in the sitting room with the curtains drawn. Sweat crawled over his skin and his chest ached from too many cigarettes.

But he was used to hangovers; he'd started drinking as a teenager after he'd come back from Toronto twenty years ago. At first, he'd drunk alone, stealing whisky or gin or brandy from his grandfather's drinks cabinet; merely wanting, as he had last night, to get out of himself. At teenage parties it made him feel braver, less inhibited, and more inclined to get into trouble.

His first year at university was worse; he became ever more unpredictable when he was drunk. Sometimes the hangovers weren't enough punishment and his self-loathing drove him into carrying a rucksack weighted with stones for days at a time. He would spread them out over his bed and sleep on them, making his nights even more restless and covering his body in patches of red skin and small bruises.

The thought that he was not fit to be a member of the human race was at the core of every hangover. Trawling through his memory of the night before, as he did now, was automatic, a prelude to raking over the past. Memories came to him unbidden and he was unable to find any sense of redemption; he was ashamed of everything he had ever done. Of course, it was always this way after any sort of bender. But the familiarity of the self-contempt didn't alleviate the crushing depression it induced.

Catherine came into the sitting room; she was wearing her coat and carrying an overnight bag. She had come to say goodbye, and Richard looked at her for a clue as to what she thought of him. Her mouth was straight, and her face showed no emotion. There was something in her eyes though, something less stern. She looked like a nurse about to impart bad news to a patient. Perhaps that's what he needed, a twenty-four hours a day psychiatric nurse. Twenty-four fucking seven.

"You still look awful," she said. "Tell me honestly, did you take something last night?"

"Just too much wine," he said. "I got into a fug and thought I could drink my way out of it."

How could he tell her more? To mention the Rohypnol would bring more questions. Questions he couldn't answer because they would lead to Amanda. And that would only prove his weakness and his shame.

"Do you really want me to go?" she said.

He shook his head, mouthing a 'no'; he needed someone to pull him out of this pit. Catherine loved him, he was certain of that, and she knew how important the gallery was to him. It was obvious that she thought he was worried about money, and that explained his behaviour. She told him everything would be fine, the opening on Thursday would be a success, and Johnny Robson wasn't the only man in town who wanted to buy art.

She brought him a glass of water and some painkillers.

"Don't worry," she said. "Everything will be alright. I promise."

Catherine was happy, he could hear it in her voice. She had what she wanted, their little spat cleared up, and she went to make coffee.

Richard tried to remember his phone call to Lisa McKee. What had he said to her? Until Aunt Emily's funeral he hadn't seen her for over twenty years, and he wondered if they still had a claim on each other. Their teenage affair had been all too brief; too innocent. But there had been something between them after Emily's funeral. He was sure of it.

Catherine came up behind him while he was sitting at his desk and put her arms around him.

"I bring good news. Isn't that worth a kiss?"

"I'll hear the news first, and then we'll see if you deserve it," he said, swivelling his chair around to face her.

"The cheque has cleared. I think that's worth a kiss, don't you?"

"I think it might be," he said.

"You're such a tease," she said, and sat on his lap and kissed him. "You must think I'm being soppy, but I do love you."

"I love you, too," he said. He'd always been good at lying about these things.

The money was important. Not only did the sale of the paintings make the gallery viable, it enhanced its reputation. Richard knew that Robson was a catch because he had a chip on his shoulder; a self-made man sneered at by those born into the middle classes. They were jealous of his money and thought they had taste because it was their birthright. A rich man like him could be persuaded that he needed the kudos that art could bring. But even if such a notion was irresistible to someone like Johnny Robson, Richard still needed his goodwill.

If Robson discovered the identity of Rhiannon's lover, it would taint everything, and the relationship between gallerist and patron could come to an ugly end. Richard had decided to keep a straight face and feign ignorance when the truth about the affair was uncovered. Then he might ride out the storm that would follow by offering a sympathetic shoulder. More than that, he was willing to be Johnny's friend.

Robson and Rhiannon came to the opening of the new exhibition. Richard was glad to see them together, her arm through his. He hoped it meant that the affair with James had run its course. He went through the crowd to say hello, shaking Robson's hand and kissing Rhiannon once on each cheek. Robson was certainly in a good mood.

"Are you going to try and sell me any of these?" he said.

"Only if you like any of them, Johnny."

"Are they any good, though?"

That Robson was unsure of himself when it came to art gave Richard some satisfaction. But he wasn't sure he wanted to sell any more paintings to the man. At least not until he was sure that the affair was well and truly over. And tonight Rhiannon seemed distracted, looking around the room as the two men chatted. Normally he would have suggested that they walked around and looked at the pictures together, but he was tired of the whole thing and happy to allow all the usual distractions of the opening to get in the way; too many people he wanted to see, or who wanted to see him.

Catherine came to his rescue, bringing over the artist, Kirsten Dressler. Robson was obviously beguiled by the young woman in black leather trousers and a crisp white shirt speaking perfect, German-accented English. Rhiannon appeared bored with the whole thing and said she was going to get another glass of wine. Robson didn't notice her walking away and Richard knew then that the affair with James had merely been suspended.

He was about to make his excuses and walk away himself when Amanda appeared. She had said she might come, and Richard hoped it had been meant as an idle threat. And she had made an effort, her hair in a chignon; a low-cut sheath dress and high heels that made her tall.

Now he was forced to introduce her, 'my cousin, Amanda' to Robson and Kirsten. In the social fog of smiles and polite handshakes, the fake kisses for Catherine, and her proffered cheek demanding a kiss from him, he felt as if the gallery was becoming a new zone of her infection.

"Are you an American cousin?" said Robson.

"No, I'm a Geordie, but I've been in Canada for over twenty years. We went out there for my stepfather's work and Mom died out there. Richard came to the funeral and that made me think. I knew it was time to come back." Amanda put her arm through Richard's and pulled him closer to her so that he felt her body against his. "Family is what counts, don't you think?"

"Welcome home," said Robson and raised his glass.

"Why thank you, Johnny," said Amanda. "That's the first time anyone's actually said that to me, you know?"

"Richard's invited us to the restaurant after this. Are you coming?"

"Am I?" said Amanda.

"I wasn't sure if you were. You hadn't decided, remember?" said Richard, pulling himself free of her.

He excused himself. There were other people he needed to see, he said. But he went into the office and closed the door behind him. He could still hear the babble from the gallery as he slumped down on the sofa. There was a soft knock on the door. He heard it open, the noise of the crowd suddenly louder, and looked up, expecting to see Catherine, come to offer him consolation or Amanda come to taunt him. But it was Rhiannon. She stood in the open doorway, glancing behind her before coming into the room.

She closed the door slowly behind her as if she was frightened of making too much noise. Richard felt trapped and his thoughts ran into one another. If Robson had seen her come in, if he saw her leave, if he suspected they had been alone together, then he would think that Richard was her lover.

"You can't be in here," he said. "What would Johnny think?"

"It's alright. He's gone outside for a cigarette with some woman."

"What is it? What do you want?"

"He's having me followed, you know. He thinks he's being clever or that I'm stupid. Or both. But I've noticed the same car behind me too many times, the same man who's there every time I meet a friend for lunch or go shopping."

"I don't want him to think that there's anything between us."

"I just want to know where Jimmy is."

"I don't know. He's gone up into the country to paint. He needed to get away."

Rhiannon began to cry. She had drunk too much.

"You should leave him," said Richard, getting up quickly.

Opening the door a little, he slipped out through the gap,

and pulled it to behind him. Catherine was with Kirsten talking to one of the Fine Art lecturers from the University. Richard stood by her shoulder and began to speak into her ear.

"Go into the office now. Rhiannon's there. She's in a bit of a state. Wants to know where James is, but don't tell her. Just try and calm her down, will you?"

Catherine didn't hesitate and Richard watched her make her way through the crowd and go into the office. When she had closed the door behind her, he went to get himself a glass of wine, making small talk with the young women behind the drinks table. He was getting himself back in the mood he needed to be in when he saw Robson coming towards him.

"There you are," Robson said, his large hand bouncing up and down on Richard's shoulder. "I like these paintings, you know. We should have a meeting, a proper chat, you know. About this gallery business."

"What about it?"

"Does it wash its face?"

"That's a trade secret," said Richard. He was laughing, but he wanted the joke to put an end to Robson's probing. The man was drunk, clearly drunk and putting on his alpha-male act.

"You need money," said Robson. "I'll give you money."

"Why?"

"I like all this," he said, putting an arm around Richard's shoulder. He raised the hand that held his glass and gestured across the room with it. "I want to be part of this. I want be a patron of the arts."

"We should have a meeting if you want to talk about it. That is, if you're still serious about it in the morning," said Richard, stepping back slightly so that he moved out of Robson's embrace.

"You think I'm too drunk to know my own mind."

Amanda joined them and wanted to know what they were talking about.

"Money," said Robson, smiling at her.

"Is there anything else to talk about?" said Amanda, touching Robson's arm.

"Rhiannon's had too much to drink," Richard said. "Catherine took her into the office to try and calm her down. You should take her home, Johnny."

"She'll be alright, man," said Robson. But it was as if he hadn't heard him; his full attention was on Amanda. "We're all going to the restaurant. You're coming, aren't you?"

"I'm not sure," she said, looking at Richard.

Like a vampire, he thought, she needs to be invited in. No, she would come without his permission, he knew that, but she wanted him to ask her out loud, in front of Robson. And what of Johnny? Is this how he would take things over if Richard took his money? They were both looking at him, waiting for him to speak.

"Of course. You must come, Amanda."

"Oh, thank you darling," she said, and kissed him on the cheek, which for some inexplicable reason filled him with relief.

At the restaurant, an Italian place near the gallery, the six of them were seated at a long table. Amanda made a point of sitting next to Robson. Rhiannon sat on the other side of him. She barely touched her food, reaching across the table for the nearest bottle of wine whenever she'd drained her glass.

Robson didn't notice; he was anxious to play up to the idea of being a patron of the arts, leaning across the table to tell Kirsten how much he liked her paintings.

"I'm going to buy one," he said. "Maybe two."

Richard explained his hopes of taking the work to an art fair next year, and Robson nodded as if he understood what that meant.

"Richard knows all about art, you know," said Amanda, demanding Robson's attention by squeezing his arm. "Sometimes I think it's all he knows about. He can't get his priorities right, Johnny. We were burgled, you know. I mean our grandmother's house was burgled. All they took was an old painting. And do you know, he was more upset about that painting than he was about Nana's feelings. She was terrified. Family should trump everything, don't you think?"

Richard looked at her across the table and she winked at him. He was angry. Not just because she was trying to humiliate him, but because of the way she was hanging on to Robson. He was seething with jealousy.

The next morning Richard went to the bank and transferred money into James' account. Then he drove up to the cottage with the BACS receipt. He wanted to persuade James to go away. The affair would die without contact, he was sure of it.

Richard pulled up behind the Land Rover. James had left the five-bar gate open and parked on the short grassy drive that led up to the cottage. There were no other vehicles outside any of the other cottages; not many people came up at this time of year. Those who could afford it went away to Madeira or Tenerife where, he'd heard, the sun always shone. Today the light at the coast was dull and heavy. It was difficult to tell where the sea ended and the sky began; there was no horizon, just a wall of grey.

Richard beeped his horn and got out of the car. James opened the front door and they went into the kitchen together, and stood there while he made coffee in a stovetop expresso maker. He wasn't bothered about the bank receipt. He wanted to know about Rhiannon.

"How is she?" he said. "Have you seen her?"

"She's fine."

"We want to be together, you know."

"So why doesn't she just leave him?" said Richard.

James just shook his head and looked at the bank receipt again.

He said he'd been using the conservatory at the back of the cottage as a studio because it looked out over the sea and Richard went to see what he'd been doing. There was a painting on the easel; a great swirl of black paint hovering in white space.

"It's grim and grey up here at the moment, isn't it?" said Richard when James brought the coffee through. "You should use some of the money to go to the South of France. Pretend you're Van Gogh or something."

"I'm fine here," said James. "The weather changes all the time. More than you'd think. There was a storm out at sea last week." There was a light in his eyes, and he pointed at the painting. "I actually made sketches for this out in the rain."

Richard thought about Turner lashed to the mast of a ship to paint a storm. Or Ulysses, desperate to hear the sirens' song. He wondered if James was going mad. But he didn't say anything.

Nor did he say anything about the mess, the paint drips on the quarry tiles that would clean off and the old bamboo table, covered in tubes of paint and cans of turps, which was ruined. Painting was a messy business. Better James was here than in the city. And at least he was working. He wanted more blank canvasses from his studio, and Richard promised to get Wolfgang to deliver them next week.

On the way back to the city his mobile rang as he approached the A1. He pulled over into a lay-by. It was Lisa McKee.

"You were really out of it the other night. Do you remember what you said to me?'

"Bits and pieces," he said.

"What do you want from me, Richard. What do you actually expect?"

"I'm not sure," he said, reaching for the ignition key and turning off the engine. "But I want to see you again."

"I can't cure you of Amanda, if that's what you think. I'm worried that you'll keep picking away at it, and that she'll always be there."

"We could get to know each other again, couldn't we?" He remembered what he had said to her that night. "Then we'd know if it was too late, wouldn't we?"

"You'd come here?" said Lisa. "You'd come back to Toronto?"

"Third time lucky," he said.

18

A supermarket delivery van came down the drive and Richard pulled over to let it pass. Amanda had started ordering groceries online. Peter didn't like it; shopping had been one of the things he did for Jane, one of the ways he demonstrated his affection for her. He was standing by his car holding a bunch of flowers, waiting for Richard to park up.

"I want to have a moan," he said.

"If it's about Amanda, moan away."

"I used to take your grandmother to Waitrose in the wheelchair," he said. "It wasn't much, but it got her out of the house. There's no reason to go now. Amanda's ruined it."

"Perhaps she wants to make you redundant," said Richard, lighting a cigarette. "Make sure Nana notices the flowers. Put them in a vase yourself, and make a show of it. Or Amanda will do it and try and take all the credit."

"You do know that she's taking Jane to the solicitor's after lunch?" said Peter.

"About this power of attorney thing? It's really happening?"

"Jane's all for it. Says it's a weight off her mind. Thinks things are getting on top of her."

"That's just the painkillers, isn't it?" said Richard.

"And Amanda's pushing for it. And what Amanda wants…"

"What could she do?"

"Well, she could access all Jane's accounts. Empty them of cash. It depends on what she's after, doesn't it? Jane's property portfolio is where the real wealth is, and that would take time to access. Amanda would have to stick around for that. She might be playing a long game."

"So she's unstoppable, is she?"

"You tell me. She's your cousin," said Peter.

Richard didn't say anything. He looked up. The sky was heavy with dark clouds. "It's going to rain," he said. "We should go in."

Amanda had invited them both for lunch, just a little family thing. Nothing fancy, she'd said, which was why they were eating in the kitchen. All the same she had put on a rather smart floral dress, with heels and an apron, which made her look domesticated. She reminded Richard of his Aunt Emily when he'd first gone to Toronto all those years ago. He knew she was just playacting, acting out whatever she thought was expected of a hostess, like the way she made a big fuss of Peter's flowers and admired the way he arranged them in the vase so that, despite his efforts, all the attention was on her.

"Beautiful flowers for a beautiful lady," said Amanda.

Richard looked at his grandmother. She was wearing make-up, and he thought she was wearing too much of it; her lipstick was too red and too bright, like the blusher on her cheeks and the bright turquoise eye shadow. Amanda had done it.

"We had a girly session, didn't we, Nana?"

Jane giggled. Today she seemed brighter. Perhaps she was becoming habituated to the painkillers, or perhaps Amanda had stopped being so cavalier in administering them. She asked Peter to open a bottle of Champagne, which he rushed to do. Richard realised he was more than happy to be useful again.

When the glasses had been filled, Amanda proposed a toast.

"To a wonderful Nana," she said.

"You are an angel, Amanda," said Jane. "You don't know what it's meant to have you here. After all the awful things that have happened to this family."

"And here's to you, Peter," said Amanda, raising her glass again. "For all you've done for Nana." She came around the table and kissed him on the forehead. Peter blushed, grinning like a schoolboy.

Richard was annoyed. Since his parents' death he'd never felt much affection for his grandmother. Her idea of family was like this version of Amanda's; it had always been for show. He remembered how Christmas was in this house when they were children. Everything appeared to be as it should be; the crackers, the paper hats, and the pudding that had to be eaten until the pound coin hidden in it had been found. During the compulsory games afterwards some of the adults got drunk and made mistakes or gave up. They didn't take it seriously enough, and in the end, there was no joy to it. Christmas always fell short of the perfection his grandmother demanded. "Thank God that's over for another year," his mother used to say when they got home, which used to annoy his father and they'd have a row.

The rain had held off and Richard said he was going for a cigarette. He stood on the terrace, just outside the French doors that led out from the kitchen. Amanda was working her magic; he heard his grandmother and Peter laughing. He turned to look into the room, watching them through the glass. He wasn't part of the fantasy being played out around the kitchen table.

Amanda looked up and saw him standing there. She got up from the table and came towards him. At first, he thought she was coming out to have a cigarette, and he stood back from the door as she pulled it open. But she just looked at him.

"You're being creepy," she said. "Standing there watching us like a weirdo."

She'd said it loud enough so that his grandmother heard.

"I don't know what's wrong with him," she said. "He was like this when he was a boy. Leave him to it, Amanda. He'll only spoil it for the rest of us."

The rain had been falling for over an hour, painting the city grey and thickening on the windscreen of the Saab. Now and again Richard flicked the wipers to clear it, and wound the window halfway down so that he could smoke. He sat listening to the traffic hissing in the wet, his eyes fixed on a Victorian doorway between a pizzeria and a sandwich bar on the other side of the street.

After about an hour he saw Amanda and his grandmother come out onto the pavement. Huddled together, arm in arm under a bright red golf umbrella, they walked to the Range Rover. When it pulled away Richard got out of his car and sprinted across the road, the rain running down his face.

The offices were up on the first floor and he grabbed the banister rail and pulled himself up, two steps at a time. It was not as grand as it had seemed when he'd come here after his parents' death; the stair carpet was shabby now and the paintwork chipped. Everything smelled musty as if the air had never changed, but Stephen York had been the family solicitor for a long time, and his grandmother kept coming back. The connection made him feel he could be pushy with the receptionist; he needed to see Stephen very quickly, it wouldn't take a minute, surely he could have a minute?

York was embarrassed to see him. Richard saw it in his face as they shook hands. He realised how desperate he must look; his woollen coat and scarf were soaked; his hair was plastered to his face and he felt clammy.

"Do you want a towel? A cup of tea?" said York.

"I'm fine. I just got wet," said Richard, using his fingers like a comb to push the hair off his face.

"I'm originally from the south coast," said York, walking over to the window and looking out. "I've never come to terms with the rain up here. It's always so bloody grey. I should go and live in the South of France, like Dirk Bogarde."

"Sounds like a good idea."

"There's no money in the law anymore." He sat down behind his desk, leaned back and let out a groan. "Algorithms, whatever they are, seem to be able to do all the things I can. Look at all this," he said, gesturing at the stacks of legal folders piled along the wall, stacked on the table behind him and underneath it. "The legal detritus of human life. Not wanted on voyage. Cyberspace looks tidier, I suppose, but it can't be, can it? I can never find anything on my computer."

"You should retire, Stephen."

"I should. I would. But I made some bad investments. The old clients, like your grandmother, keep me going. The analogue generation. Perhaps I'll go when they're all gone."

"My grandmother was just here, wasn't she?"

"What can I do for you, Richard?" said York, sitting up, suddenly attentive and alert.

"Why was she here?"

"I'm sure you appreciate the concept of client confidentiality, Richard. Put simply, I can't tell you."

"Something's going on, between my cousin and my Nana. Something that's not right."

"What do you mean? Not right?" said York.

"My aunt died of a drug overdose. I think Amanda had something to do with it. She wanted her mother's money and her house."

"Was there an investigation?" said York, drumming his fingers on his desk. "Was your cousin suspected of wrongdoing? Were the police involved?"

Richard put his elbows on his knees and shook his head.

"There was just some talk about it, that's all."

"Just gossip, then?"

"I suppose so," said Richard.

Saying it out loud, that Amanda had killed her mother when he had no proof. And admitting that it was just tittle-tattle. Well, that made it sound all too ridiculous, like a family feud in which slights are imagined and blown out of all proportion.

"Can't I stop her?" he said, looking up.

"Who?" said York, picking at some papers on his desk.

"Amanda. Can I stop her getting power of attorney?"

"You seem to have got yourself into a bit of a state, Richard. I wish I could help but I can't answer your question. You'll need to see another solicitor."

"So there is something going on."

"Richard, I can't tell you what we discussed. I can't talk about things like power of attorney or changes to wills, even to another member of the family. I really can't. If I were you, I would try and make things up with your grandmother. If something's happened between you, perhaps it's time to build bridges. Now, that's all I have to say. I think you'd better go." York pretended to look at the papers in his hand. "Really, I'm very busy."

Richard got up and went out of the office. The young woman behind the reception desk looked up from the magazine she was reading and smiled at him. It was a melancholy smile; there was no one else waiting to see Stephen York.

On his way down the stairs Richard stopped and gripped the banister rail, flushing because he thought he'd made a fool of himself. But he realised that York had either made a slip, or warned him on purpose. The will. His grandmother was going to make, or had made, changes to her will.

"What happened to you?" said Catherine when he got back to the gallery. He threw his coat and scarf over the back of his chair and slumped down on the sofa.

"Rain and dirty tricks."

"What tricks?"

"Amanda, who else?" He told her about the power of attorney and York's hints about the will.

"It's a shame you can't just get rid of her."

"Don't think I haven't thought about it."

And he had. Stuck in a line at traffic lights the other day he'd fantasised about following Amanda through the streets at night, ready to seize on any opportunity to attack her. He imagined the look of fear in her face and wondered if there would be any satisfaction in seeing it.

Catherine threw a towel at him and put his coat on a hanger.

"Don't do anything stupid," she said. "Promise me you won't do anything stupid."

Richard took off his shirt and rubbed the towel through his hair.

"Only if I could get away with it," he said, opening the tall cupboard where he kept a couple of the white shirts he wore at openings. He took one off a hanger and slipped his arms through the sleeves.

"They must all think they can get away with it," said Catherine, coming up to him and buttoning the shirt. "Sometimes people just snap, I suppose, with someone like her in their lives. Fucking everything up." She kissed him. "You're cold. I'll make you some coffee to warm you up."

"I was only joking," he said, calling through to the kitchen.

"I know," she called back.

Did she know? Was she sure of it? For a moment Richard wondered if Catherine would help him if it came to it. But it hadn't come to that yet, had it? Yet? Was there a point at which he might commit murder? If Amanda persuaded his grandmother to leave him nothing, well that might drive him to it before a new will was made. It was bad enough that she would cut off any money for the gallery and force him even more into bed with Robson, but his inheritance?

His grandmother was eighty-four, she could live to ninety, even a hundred. Amanda wouldn't be able to wait even a few years, never mind sixteen. What if Lisa McKee was right and Aunt Emily had been murdered?

When Catherine brought him the coffee, he nearly told her about Lisa's suspicions, but he remembered York's reaction. Perhaps Lisa watched too many murder mysteries on television and their dislike of Amanda, the spell she cast over them, made them imagine the worst.

He knew he needed to concentrate on the matter in hand and attend to gallery business. They had sold another of James' pictures, one of his smaller works, to a private collector. Catherine reminded him that Wolfgang was calling to pick it up later and he went into the storeroom to get it ready for collection.

After unrolling a length of bubble wrap on the table, he went over to the storage rack to fetch the painting. Then he saw something he didn't quite understand. A fleece blanket, like the one his grandmother used to cover her knees when she felt the cold, had been wrapped around something, obviously a picture, and pushed into a slot at the far end of the rack. Taking hold of it, he felt the bulk of an ornate frame, and caught a glimpse of gold leaf.

Richard knew what it was even before he laid it down on the table and pulled the blanket away. But the painting still surprised him. As always, he was seduced by the exquisite brushwork. The flowers bloomed in front of him; caught in light that was straining through the window of a room in another world in another time. His eyes rested on the butterfly, and he held his breath in case it took fright and fluttered away.

A banging on the back door startled him out of his reverie.

"I'm coming, Wolfgang," he said.

Wrapping the blanket around the painting he pushed it back into the rack.

19

His first thought was to get the Verelst out of the gallery; Catherine might find it and think him guilty. He took it outside, still wrapped in the blanket, and put it in the back of the Saab.

As he slammed the tailgate shut, he struggled to catch his breath. He'd had this feeling before, years ago when Amanda used to come into his room at night and he could hear her creeping towards him in the dark. This business with the burglary was like that. She was trying to catch him out. Trying to get him into trouble. For a moment he had to lean against the car to steady himself.

The alley seemed greyer than usual. It was getting dark and he felt rain on his face. Drops of it showed in the light of the streetlamp above the parking bay. He lit a cigarette, his hand trembling as he worked the lighter. He stood and smoked, holding onto the car, struggling to get his thoughts into some kind of order.

Richard didn't know what to do with the Verelst, other than hide it amongst all the junk in his garage, but for how long? The burglary was too singular a crime; besides the credit cards, the painting was the only thing of significance that had been stolen. Sooner or later the police might take a look closer to home. They might come at him with a search warrant, and Amanda might cook something up to point them in his direction.

He flicked the remains of his cigarette into the alley, and went back into the storeroom. Catherine came through just as he was locking the back door.

"You're all wet," she said, pushing his damp hair from his forehead. "What's wrong?"

"I needed a cigarette, that's all," he said.

She'd come to tell him that Robson had called and wanted to set up a meeting.

"Do you really think that's a good idea?"

"Are you still worried about James and Rhiannon?" she said.

"That's a fucking time bomb," he said. "And Robson's unpredictable."

"You could always say no, I don't want your money."

"Really?" he said, and went into the office and picked up the phone.

Peter phoned Richard the next day. His grandmother wanted him to call at the house for morning coffee. No reason was given, but it was a summons. As he walked into the sitting room Amanda was flicking through one of her magazines and looked up.

"Oh look, it's Dickie, Nana," she said. "I wonder what he wants."

"A cup of coffee?" he said.

Amanda snorted. "You can give me a hand." She got up and he followed her into the kitchen. "If you want money from Nana, you'll have to ask me for it from now on," she said as she set up the coffee machine.

"What does that mean?"

"It means that I'm taking care of that sort of thing now."

"What sort of thing?"

"Managing Nana's affairs. It's become too much for her."

"But it's still up to her, isn't it? Whether she wants me to have any money or not."

"You're a very manipulative person, Richard. You were like that when you were a boy. You used to take advantage of Nana even then."

"Why did you come back home, Mandy?"

"Nana asked me to. She needs me to look after her."

"You looked after Aunt Emily. That didn't end too well, did it?"

"You little shit," she said, coming around the table to face him. Richard turned his body away from her. But it was too late; Amanda's punch caught him in the stomach and he doubled over. He looked up at her. There was anger in her face. But there was a fear too. "What do you know about it?"

"I don't actually need Nana's money," he said after he caught his breath. "But this power of attorney thing. I don't understand. Why are you doing that?"

"I told you. I'm looking after Nana. Looking after her interests."

Peter came into the kitchen.

"Have you two been arguing about something?" he said. "We can hear you, you know. Jane sent me to find out what's happened to the coffee."

"So she sent you to break it up?" said Amanda.

"What was all the noise?" said their grandmother when they took the coffee things into the sitting room.

"Richard was arguing about money, Nana."

"That isn't true. I've got a backer," said Richard, grinning. "Johnny Robson wants to come in with me." He turned to Amanda. "You must remember him. You were all over him the other night."

"He's having his wife followed, you know."

"Is he?"

"Christ! It's not you she's having an affair with, is it?"

"Is she having an affair?"

"Ha, ha," she said. "I think Richard's planning to run off with another man's wife."

"That's Amanda's idea of a joke," he said, taking a cup of coffee from the tray. "She's always joking, Nana. It's her way of showing affection."

"You were like this when you were children," said Jane. "It was boring then and it's boring now."

Amanda went back to flicking through her magazine and

Richard sat and drank his coffee and their grandmother told them she was having a little party on Friday and she expected them both to be there.

"What are we celebrating?" said Amanda.

"You'll just have to wait and see,' said Jane.

"What?" said Catherine, when Richard told her about the party. "I'm not invited?"

"I didn't think you'd want to come. Amanda will only try and bait you. And I could do without watching that."

"It's you I'm worried about."

"It's just family stuff," he said. "I'll cope."

Richard knew he'd rattled Amanda when he'd mentioned her mother's death, and he thought there was a chance he could make her angry enough to talk. If he could get her alone after she'd had too much to drink, she might incriminate herself.

That afternoon he spent an hour on the Internet and bought a sound recorder disguised as a pen. It could actually write as well. He thought he could use it to make notes in the notebook he always carried, and to be seen doing it. And it wouldn't take much, he thought, to touch the pen and run his thumb over the switch without Amanda thinking anything of it.

The next day he met Robson for lunch at a restaurant behind the County Court. Johnny was standing at the bar with a glass of red wine in front of him when Richard arrived.

"I'm in the chair. What'll you have?"

Richard said he would have a glass of Muscadet. Robson ordered himself another large Shiraz. A group of lawyers were being loud at a table by the window. "Listen to that lot, probably getting oiled up before an afternoon in court. Some poor sod could get a raw deal if one of those bastards is too pissed to defend them properly."

"Do you think the law's an ass?"

"In my experience you have to make your own justice."

"Maybe you're right," Richard said, thinking about Amanda.

Robson told him how much he'd enjoyed the opening.

"Your cousin's a very attractive woman," he said after the barman brought their drinks.

"She's more complicated than she looks," said Richard.

"She looks sexy. What's so complicated about that?"

"You told her you were having Rhiannon followed. That's too much information to give someone like her. Someone you don't even know."

"You think she'll blab about it?"

"She likes to pretend she knows more than she does. And she's just joined a gym, so a bit of gossip might prove useful. Give the newbie some traction with the other gym bunnies."

"It doesn't really matter. Rhi knows about the detective, anyway."

"How come?"

"Because I hired a bloody amateur, an absolute fuckwit," said Robson, leaning towards Richard and keeping his voice down. "She spotted him. Gave me hell about it."

"Because you don't trust her?"

"Because she's got something to hide."

They finished their drinks at the bar and were shown to a table upstairs. Richard ordered the roast lamb; Robson wanted a steak cooked rare and chose a bottle of Australian Shiraz from the wine list.

Richard explained his strategy for the gallery. How he'd chosen the artists he represented very carefully. They were all painters; he didn't go near video or photography, or even sculpture. And it was a small group. Some, like James, were local. Others, like Kirsten, were from Europe where they already had a reputation.

"How will anyone get to know if the paintings are any good?"

"We need to get them maximum exposure. Publish catalogues with essays by respected academics for each exhibition. But it's the art fairs that are really important. London, New York, Berlin. The work gets seen by serious collectors and the gallery gets a reputation."

"It's a bit of a gamble, isn't it?"

Richard shrugged. "It's what I do."

"I've always had to work for a living. Does this thing even wash its face?"

"It could do."

"All this guff about me being a patron of the arts. Have you been trying to reel me in all along, Richard? You're more of an operator than you look."

"Straight up, Johnny? I tried hard to sell you those paintings. That's true. And I thought you might get the bug and buy more. But I thought that was it. You told me you wanted to get involved, remember?"

"I did, didn't I? I just want to know what it's going to cost me. My accountant wants me to get rid of a wodge of cash. And quick. So I can write it off against tax. And anyway, I think it might be a blast to come in with you."

The waiter brought their meals and Robson cut into his steak; the meat was red with blood beneath the chargrilled surface. He grinned at Richard as he reached for the bottle of Shiraz and topped up both their glasses.

"You don't like your cousin, do you?"

"And I don't want to talk about her, either."

"Just enough to warn me off, eh? I can take care of myself," said Robson. He laughed and refilled their glasses.

On Friday evening Richard took a taxi to his grandmother's house. He'd brought a couple of bottles of wine, a Costieres de Nimes that he liked, and took them into the kitchen. Amanda was fussing over the buffet. She was wearing a satin dress that showed her figure, and high heels that made a hard sound as she paced about the tiled floor.

"I've bought you a present," said Richard. "To say sorry for the other day. That crack of mine about Aunt Emily. It was unforgivable." He took a package from the side pocket of his jacket and held it up for her to see. It was wrapped in gold paper with a bright red ribbon tied in a bow.

164

"Yes," she said, taking the package from his hand. "It was shitty of you."

He stood and watched Amanda as she pulled at the ribbon, tore the gold paper apart and let it fall to the floor. She took the silver bracelet from its final wrapping of tissue paper. Richard had bought it from a jeweller who had a workshop out at the coast. It was handmade, one of a kind, and he had taken a great deal of care in choosing it. It felt odd; how much he wanted her to like it.

Amanda slipped the bracelet onto her wrist. "It is lovely," she said, holding her arm out to look at it. Then she came and kissed him on the mouth.

They went into the sitting room. The party was really just like a meeting of the bridge club with no cards and more booze. Amanda flirted with the old men in their bright sweaters and made them laugh. Richard watched her, realising that he was as beguiled as they were by her performance. That she was beautiful was undeniable, and as Robson had said, she was sexy. But the fact that he was attracted to her disturbed him. It was a sign of his own weakness, just as he'd been desperate for her to like the bracelet.

An insistent chinking sound broke into his reverie; Peter was knocking a spoon against the side of his glass. Gradually the chatter in the room died away as he called softly for everyone's attention.

"I've got an important announcement to make," he said, pausing and looking around the room to make sure everyone was listening. "I've asked Jane to marry me. And she's said yes."

Everyone started to clap, and as Jane used her stick to get to her feet, Richard turned to see Amanda's reaction. For a moment her eyes narrowed in anger, but she quickly smiled and came forward to kiss her grandmother, and then Peter. Richard followed her lead, shaking Peter's hand and kissing his grandmother on the cheek.

"Richard. Amanda," said Peter. "You'll find a few bottles of champagne in the fridge. Could you do the honours?"

In the kitchen Amanda started getting the flutes out of one of the wall cupboards. She set them up on two trays, and Richard began opening the bottles. He was good at it; he had a gentle touch when it came to sliding the corks out. But one of them surprised him; with a loud pop it flew out of his hand and ricocheted off the fridge. He laughed.

"What's so funny?" said Amanda.

"Oh, it's bloody marvellous," he said as he carefully poured out the champagne, "And at their age, too. Don't you think so?"

"Oh, it's a big surprise, alright," she said. "Ho, ho."

They took the trays into the sitting room and after they'd handed round the glasses, Amanda started to make a speech. It was addressed to Peter. She was so pleased about the wedding and all he'd done for her grandmother.

"It shows that you're never too old for love. And I know Richard will join me in welcoming you into our family," she said, kissing Peter on the cheek.

Everyone started talking about the wedding. Jane and Peter held court, sitting next to each other on the settee. The trip to Madeira was to be their honeymoon. They looked at each other, smiled and held hands as their friends took photographs with their smart phones and drank champagne.

Amanda switched to red wine, draining her glass quickly and refilling it. "It's time to celebrate," she said, and went over to the CD player and put on a Smokey Robinson album. She swayed to the music and tried to get one or two of the men to dance with her. But they were old and they were tired, and by eleven thirty the pre-ordered taxis came to take them and their wives home. Peter was staying in one of the spare rooms that night, and he and Jane went upstairs.

Amanda took a packet of Marlboro from her handbag. She put on a wrap and they both went out on to the terrace to smoke. It had rained and the chairs and the bench were wet so they had to stand. Richard clenched his cigarette between his teeth. As he raised his jacket collar against the cold, he slipped his hand inside to touch the pen and activate the microphone.

"It was a mistake to come back," said Amanda, taking a draw on her cigarette. "I'm not really needed. I can see that now. Anyway, I'm bored with handing out snacks at the bridge club."

"So what will you do?"

"Perhaps a cruise. You get to dress up for dinner and everything's done for you. You get treated properly. That sounds nice, doesn't it?" she said, stubbing her cigarette out in the ashtray.

When she looked at him, he bent to kiss her. She pulled her head back.

"Hey, where's this come from? You were an absolute shit the other day and now you want to play," she said, reaching down to cup his groin. "But then you always were keener than you pretended."

"Let's go in," he said, slipping his arm around her. "It's cold out here."

"Yes. Let's have another drink," she said. "And see where that gets us."

Richard took another bottle of wine and two glasses from the kitchen, and they went into the sitting room. He'd brought the Rohypnol tablets he'd stolen from Amanda's room. Earlier that evening, on a visit to the toilet, he had popped one of the tablets out of the foil strip and put it into his shirt pocket. Now, as Amanda knelt down to turn on the gas fire, he dropped it into one of the glasses on the coffee table and poured wine over it.

Sitting on the settee he picked up his own glass. Amanda sat beside him.

"To us," he said.

"Do you really think there's an 'us'?" she said. "You've had a funny way of showing it."

"Can't people change their minds?" he said, watching her drink from her glass, and trying to remember how long the drug would take to have an effect.

"Sometimes it's too late."

"Before I forget," he said. "I meant to tell you that I found the Verelst."

"Oh, you mean that painting. Where did it turn up?"

"Where you put it. In the gallery storeroom."

"Well, I know you liked it so much. I thought you ought to have it," she said, smiling at him over her glass.

20

Her smile irritated him. It said there are things you don't know; that he was the butt of another one of her jokes. His usual defence was to feign indifference, to show no fear, and he picked up one of her gossip magazines from the coffee table. He turned the pages quickly; glanced at the photographs of celebrities he didn't recognise, and tossed it aside.

"You don't seem very pleased," said Amanda, pushing her empty glass across the table towards him. "After all, I went through a lot of trouble to get it for you."

"I can see that. Breaking into the house. Lying to the police. Smuggling the painting into the gallery. It does seem like an awful lot of trouble," he said, and refilled their glasses.

"You always were ungrateful," she said, moving closer to him.

"I bought you a present, didn't I?"

Amanda held out her arm and looked at the bracelet again. "It is pretty," she said. "You're good at getting people to like you, aren't you? It's one of your tricks. He was like that. A real charmer."

"Who?"

"Your father." She took a long pull from her glass, and then another until she'd emptied it. "I thought we were having a drink together. You're falling behind."

But Richard didn't want to talk about his father. He filled her glass and topped up his own. "What happens when the police come looking for the painting? You want me to get the blame for the break in. Is that it?"

"Everybody gets what's coming to them. What goes around comes around. Isn't that what they say?"

"What do you mean by that?"

"You really look like him, you know?"

"Do I?"

"It's not just the face. It's in the way you stand, hold your hands, things like that. And now this is funny. You really look like him when you come." Amanda half closed her eyes, opened her mouth and groaned in mock ecstasy. She started laughing. "Oh, poor Dickie. Are you shocked?"

"What are you saying?" he said, sitting up. "What the fuck are you talking about?"

"He used to make me feel special. He could see I was unhappy, you see. 'You're my little princess.' That's what he used to say. It was nothing much at first. Just a tiny little bit at a time," she said, walking her fingers up Richard's thigh. "I can see that now, but I was smitten back then. I was thirteen when he fucked me properly."

Amanda paused as if to let what she'd said sink in.

"You're fucking sick," he said, feeling the blood rush to his head.

"I know it wasn't right, the things he did to me," she said, going on as if she was ignoring him. "But there's a bit of you that likes it. But you know that, don't you?"

Richard's gut lurched. A memory came to him unbidden, the image of an Easter lunch long ago, a family gathering at the house. His father coming into this very room with a funny look on his face, and Amanda coming in a little after. But he didn't want to believe her. She was unreliable and he didn't want her to go on. He wanted her to shut up.

"You're lying. Nana would never let anything like that happen."

"Oh, Nana knew. Your mum knew. Even my own mother knew. Oh, they all fucking knew. When Mom met Ray and we went to Canada, you'd have thought I'd have been glad to get away, wouldn't you? I actually pined for him. Do you know that? But whatever I felt, I knew it wasn't right."

"And what about what you did to me?" said Richard. "Was that right?"

"Do you mean the sex lessons?" said Amanda, leaning back and smiling at him. That fucking smile! He saw how her dress flowed over her body, the red gloss of the satin revealing the shape of her thighs as she parted them. She was very close to him, her arm was touching his, and she grabbed his hand and pushed it into her groin. He felt the wiry texture of her pubic hair through the material.

"You always liked it though, didn't you?" she whispered, flicking her tongue into his ear.

Richard pulled his hand away. She was smiling. Mocking him. Suddenly he was on top of her, pushing a cushion down onto her face. He gritted his teeth as she struggled beneath him, arms waving and legs kicking out. One of her feet caught against the edge of the coffee table and knocked it hard. He heard the bottle and glasses falling onto the rug and the sound of glass breaking.

Richard was aware of taking his time to sit astride Amanda in order to trap her legs. And he was aware of the prosaic details of the moment; her chignon falling apart as her head hit against the arm of the settee, the tassels on the cushion shaking as she struggled.

He casually wondered how long it would take for her to die. She made strange noises, the pathetic whimpering of an injured animal. The realisation of what he was doing, and what his intention was, came to him all at once. That he had an erection shocked him most of all, and he lifted the cushion away from her face and dropped it to the floor.

Amanda's mouth was open as she wheezed and panted for breath. Perhaps the drug had taken her strength away; she looked like a frightened child now. Tears, streaked with mascara, ran down her face. Trembling, Richard went over to the drinks table and poured them both a brandy. He pushed a glass into her shaking hand, and drank his own down in one.

Still trembling, heart pumping with adrenaline, sweat oozing from his pores; he wanted air. Opening the French window onto the terrace, he stood on the threshold and lit a cigarette. A gust of wind whipped cold air onto his face. In the light from the house he saw yellow leaves drifting from the trees. It reminded him of Corot's Coup de Vent, a painting he'd seen a long time ago, when he was a student. He had an urge to see it now, to escape to Paris, and lose himself amongst the tourist swarm in the Louvre.

What Amanda had said about his father had made him angry, but that wasn't the only reason he'd attacked her; it was her assumption that she had the right to do whatever she wanted to him. And he hadn't wanted to believe her, but he did. There was his own lie about the deer, the deer he'd so much wanted to believe was real. He'd always wanted to imagine that the accident was the result of bad luck, a foolish sense of nobility on his father's part, rather than anything more sordid. Amanda must have been 'that girl'. The one his mother had been shouting about as she and his father fought like crazed drunks in the front seat of the car.

As he smoked, he turned and looked back into the room. Amanda was sprawling on the settee, trying to sit up. Her movements were lazy, and her eyes glassy as if she were in a trance. The Rohypnol was having its full effect. He threw his cigarette out into the garden and closed the door.

Wine had spilled onto the rug in front of the fireplace and he set about tidying up, picking up the bottle and pieces of broken glass, and fetching a damp cloth and cooking salt from the kitchen. He rubbed at the red stains with the cloth, and poured a mound of salt onto each one of them. In the morning he would tell his grandmother that they'd just drunk too much. Red wine and Persian rugs were, after all, a dangerous combination.

"You tried to kill me," said Amanda, waving her finger at

him. "You're not as sweet as everyone thinks. Are you? When they find that painting Nana will know."

"I don't understand," said Richard, sitting on the edge of one of the armchairs. "Tell me what you mean."

"Draw you a picture? You like pictures, don't you, Dickie?"

"Yes, draw me a picture, Mandy."

"She didn't want to leave Little Dickie out of her will." Her eyelids were fluttering, her voice was slow and slurring as if she was talking in her sleep. "But the police will find that painting wherever you've hidden it, and it'll all be alright." She sat up, pointed her finger at him like a pistol. "Bang," she said, and slumped back on the settee.

Amanda was having difficulty concentrating. She picked up the magazine that Richard had been looking at.

"Isn't she beautiful?" she said, holding it up so that Richard could see the double page spread: a photograph of a glamorous woman in an evening gown standing on a grand staircase. "She said she's the happiest she's ever been now. It's a lovely house. And she is so beautiful."

Catherine had once asked him what Amanda did all day. He'd said he didn't really know. She filled her time with going to the gym, or went for lunch with some of the women she'd met there. But mostly, she sat around the house flicking through her magazines or went out shopping for clothes.

He remembered how she'd looked at her mother's funeral, as if she'd seen a feature on mourning chic in Vogue. She always had the right outfit for the occasion, but she had a penchant for being overdressed. She wore dresses and heels for the bridge club, when jeans and sneakers would have done, and was compelled to flirt, to make the old men find her attractive even though she didn't really like them.

"Give me another drink," she said, sitting up with her elbows on her knees.

Richard sighed, went into the kitchen and fetched another bottle of wine and two glasses. Amanda was semi-conscious on the settee and he kicked her with his foot. She looked up at him.

"I used to love coming to this house when I was little. I remember when you were born. Funny thing is how well I can remember it. Everybody coming to see the new baby. I managed to get a look at you, all burbling and happy in your little Moses basket. I hated you then. When no one was looking I pinched you, just to see what would happen."

Amanda seemed lost, an actress on the stage of an empty theatre, hoping to play a princess in front of a painted backdrop. Her fantasy to be on a cruise ship, with an outfit for every timetabled moment, was a pathetic dream, thought Richard. He looked at her now, the dishevelled hair and the crumpled satin of her dress; all her glamour had evaporated.

As if she was conscious of being studied, she sat up. "It's so boring, isn't it, Dickie?" she said. "Handing out snacks at the fucking bridge club. What a life. I can't wait around here for her to die."

"So what are you going to do?" he said, handing her a glass of wine. "If you can't wait around here forever, what are you going to do?"

"Burglar. Nana in the library with the lead pipe," she said, moving her arm up and down if she was beating something, a grimace on her face. "Blunt force trauma." She laughed. "And now there's this fucking wedding business. What am I going to do about that?"

"Did you kill your mother, Mandy? Did you kill Aunt Emily?"

"I only held out the little pills in the palm of my hand. She picked them up one by one and put them in her mouth. Did it all by herself. She was addicted to them, you see."

"Why did you do that?"

"Come on. The money. And she had it coming. Just took them from my hand," she said, holding her own hand out towards him.

With the thumb and forefinger of her other hand she dipped into the palm and mimed the act of taking a pill and putting it into her mouth. She did it over and over, and started giggling.

174

Richard got to his feet. For a moment he wanted to hit Amanda, to slap her hard around the face. But he'd had enough of her and walked out of the room.

Putting on his coat in the hall he heard a soft 'psst' coming from above. Peter was at the top of the stairs, standing in bare feet, his shirt tails out over his trousers. "What's all the noise?" he said, holding onto the banister rail and leaning forward. "You'll wake Jane."

"It's nothing, Peter. Go back to bed."

"Is Amanda alright?"

"She's pissed," said Richard, opening the front door. "She's just pissed."

Amanda's giggling changed to something else, a lonely sobbing. He hesitated, thinking he should go back and comfort her. But he didn't; he stepped out into the cold night air and closed the door behind him.

The wind rushed through the trees and whipped shoals of leaves across the drive. Turning up the collar of his coat, he walked home, following The Great North Road past the open spaces of the Town Moor. The weather seemed to have kept everyone indoors and the only other person he saw was a lone cyclist struggling against the wind on the other side of the road.

The house was dark; Catherine wasn't there. She had either stayed at her own place or at a friend's. For all he knew she was in bed in some dingy flat with one of the young men who mooned over her at gallery openings, and he didn't care.

His first thought was to call Lisa McKee, but he wasn't sure what the time was in Toronto. But it wasn't just that; there was nothing to crow about. None of what had happened felt like any kind of victory.

21

He was lying in bed with his eyes closed, but he wasn't sleeping and he wasn't dreaming. Images came in and out of his head: the deer that never was, Lisa McKee when she was fourteen, bright and blonde in the sun, and smiling at him. And Amanda's face.

It was a ringtone from the other side of the room that got him out of bed. It was a conditioned response, the curse of the modern world, the need to answer the bloody phone. He staggered around the bedroom until he tracked the sound to his suit jacket, lying on the floor with one of its sleeves inside out. He caught a glimpse of grey daylight through the gap in the curtains as he fumbled in the pockets for the phone. Pulling it out, he looked at the screen. It was Peter.

"She's dead," he said.

"Nana?" said Richard.

"Amanda. Jane found her this morning when she went downstairs. She's in a terrible state now. I can't console her. You'd better come."

Richard's first thought was that he ought to be dressed. Holding the phone in one hand he tried to sit on the bed to pull on his trousers with the other, but he slipped down on to the floor. He was trying to catch his breath.

"How?" he said, clapping his hand to his head.

"The paramedic said she must have passed out and choked on her own vomit."

"She was alright when I left," said Richard.

He had a sudden, terrible fear; that everyone would think it was his fault.

"The police are here," said Peter. "Can you come quickly?"

The drive was crowded with vehicles: an ambulance, marked police cars, a van and a saloon car. Richard parked and pulled down the sun visor to check his face in the mirror. The hangover still showed in his eyes and in the pallor of his skin. He took a deep breath, opened the car door and went up into the house.

The hall was full of people in uniforms of one kind or another. As Richard walked towards the sitting room a flash of light lit it up. He tried to go through the doorway, but a uniformed officer in a Day-Glo jacket stopped him. As he felt the policeman's hand touch his elbow, gently forcing him to turn back, he caught a glimpse of Amanda's legs, the bright hem of her satin dress, lying on the floor between the settee and the coffee table. The mounds of salt he'd poured onto the Persian rug were tinged with pink. They looked odd and out of place, a hint that something had got out of hand. A figure in white overalls, a forensic suit, was holding a camera over the body and the flash went off again.

Richard looked in the dining room and then wandered into the kitchen. His grandmother was sitting at the table, twisting a handkerchief in her hands, her face rigid, her eyes cold. She gave him a look he didn't like, and turned her cheek to receive his kiss. It was a mechanical movement, a rebuff. Peter, fussing over at the worktop, asked him if he wanted a coffee.

"Not too much milk for me," he said, sitting at the table, hoping that the atmosphere might dissipate if they behaved normally as far as things like coffee were concerned. He reached for his grandmother's hand and felt the soft skin over the thin bones of her fingers.

"Was it drugs?' she said, snatching her hand away.

"We were just drinking, Nana. That's all."

How easily the words slipped out of his mouth. This was the basis of the story he'd been rehearsing in his head since Peter's phone call. It was the story he would tell the police, his voice calm as if he had nothing to hide. It had just been a dreadful accident as far as he was concerned. He wondered if an autopsy would find the Rohypnol in Amanda's blood. Well, he would have to bluff that one out.

As Richard sipped his coffee a voice called his name and he turned. A woman in a navy-blue trouser suit and a white shirt stood in the doorway. Her dark red hair was pulled back in a ponytail and she had a notebook in one hand, knocking her pen, a cheap Biro, against it as she looked at him. It was DS Walsh, the detective who was meant to be hunting for the Verelst.

"I believe you were the last person to see Ms Johnson alive, Richard."

He didn't like Walsh using his Christian name like that. There was no deference, just that patronising familiarity the police used to put everyone on edge, whether they were guilty or not.

"I'm going to need a statement," she said, still looking at him and still banging her pen against her copper's notebook.

Richard thought she's sizing me up and said he was more than happy to come down to the station later. He wanted more time to think things through, but Walsh was insistent. She wanted him to follow her into the dining room.

"It's just a preliminary thing, to try and get the basic facts," she said. "Best we get this over with, and then we can get out of your hair. You don't need a house full of plods at a time like this."

Richard thought it odd, as they sat at the polished mahogany table, that the dining room was being used for a police interview. Walsh's black notebook and her cheap Biro, even Walsh herself, looked out of place amongst the antiques and the paintings on the walls.

Then there was the space where the Verelst had hung, the rectangle where the wallpaper was less faded. Its absence haunted him. And if it were discovered in his possession, then he would be implicated in the burglary, just as Amanda had intended. At the very least it would complicate things for him now she was dead.

Walsh saw him looking at the place on the wall. "No sign of it, I'm afraid. We need to look elsewhere, but we're understaffed and there's always something else, isn't there?" she said, looking straight at him. Her eyes were bright, her skin glowing. DS Walsh had him at a disadvantage; she didn't have a hangover.

"What happened to my cousin?"

"I was hoping you could tell me that. You were the last person, etcetera, etcetera. So you tell me."

"We were drinking. Quite a lot, I suppose. We knocked a bottle of wine over. Broke a glass. Made a mess of the carpet," he said, watching Walsh write in her notebook, her ponytail flicking about as she scribbled away.

"You must have been very drunk," said Walsh.

"Not really," said Richard. "I walked home."

"Did she take anything else?"

"What do you mean?"

"The paramedics think she choked on her own vomit," said Walsh. "A bit of a rock star's death, isn't it? You know, sex and drugs and rock and roll. Was she like that?"

"She had some drugs. She showed them to me. Not last night. Another time, when she first came here. She was showing them off."

"What sort of drugs?"

"Oh, prescription drugs, I think you'd call them. They were in her underwear drawer. Some were in packets, some in foil strips. She tried to push some on to me, wanted me to have them, but I gave them back to her. She said we could take them for fun. They were good with booze. That's what she said. Painkillers, and something called Xanax. I remember that because of the name. There was Rohypnol too."

"Rohypnol?"

"That's the date rape drug, isn't it? She said that people took it in clubs."

"Where did she get this stuff, Richard?"

179

"Do you think that's what happened? That she took some of these drugs?"

"Do you know where she got the drugs from?"

"She brought them from Canada."

"Did she suggest you took any last night?"

"No."

"How did you get on?"

"I was very fond of her. She was very kind to me after my parents died. There was an accident."

Of course, Walsh wanted to know about the accident. Richard thought she would. He told her the version with the deer: his father swerving to avoid it, the car coming off the road. And him in the back of the car, knowing his parents were both dead. He told it well, and at the end there was that reliable, yet genuine, tremor of emotion that he hoped would stand him in good stead. It made it easier for him to cry, to let out the emotion, the guilt, the fear of being caught. Amanda's death had hit him harder than he thought. He wanted his grief to show.

"I went to Canada afterwards to stay with them. Mandy and I bonded then. We had a very special relationship. She was a couple of years older than me. She showed me a lot of affection."

"So you didn't have a fight last night?"

"No, but we started talking about our parents. That upset us both and we got a bit loud. Peter Morgan must have heard all that because he came and asked us to keep it down."

Walsh closed her notebook and put the elasticated band over the cover.

"Is that it?" said Richard, and stood up. He went over to the window and looked out so that Walsh couldn't see his face. There were a few policemen in the garden, their Day-Glo jackets bright against the dull autumn light as they poked about in the shrubbery.

"Are you having the grounds searched?" he said.

"Just covering the bases. We'll have to wait for the autopsy. See what that tells us."

"Do you want me to show you where those drugs are?"

"Oh, there's no need. I found them amongst her frillies."

When the police left, they didn't take the atmosphere with them. That hovered around the house, lodging in the kitchen where Richard's grandmother glowered at him. Peter tried to keep the peace, making a lunch of soup, with bread and cheese. Richard was glad of it, but his grandmother didn't eat a thing, or say much. But she was happy to drink half a bottle of Pinot Grigio. When she was drunk enough, she got her mood into words.

"You never wanted Amanda here, did you, Richard? This family has had more than its fair share of tragedy. But you couldn't welcome her home, could you? We could have had happiness as a family at last. I could have some peace in my final days. But now this. Did you fight with her last night? Were you just so full of anger the last time you saw her alive? Is that going to be your lasting memory of her? You were spoilt as a boy, and you resented her because other people loved her more than they loved you. That's it, isn't it?"

"Did you know about my father and Amanda?" said Richard, leaning across the table, his voice breaking. Peter came and held him by the shoulders and he sank back in his chair.

"What are you talking about?"

"She told me, Nana. She told me."

"She had a crush on your father, that's all. It was a misunderstanding. She was always flirting with him. And then she thought he loved her and wouldn't leave him alone."

"A misunderstanding? Is this the famous misunderstanding? Is that why Aunt Emily took her to Canada?"

"You really don't know what you're talking about."

"She told me last night. She told me everything."

"You're an unlucky person. You pass your bad luck on to others. How does anyone die from having a few drinks? Tell me that."

Richard had no other response but to storm out of the room, out of the house. Peter followed him out and caught up with him by his car.

"Jane's upset. But there's a question to be asked, isn't there?"

"What? Whether I had anything to do with it?"

"Well, Amanda's death solves a lot of problems for you, doesn't it?

"Are you going to ask me the question, Peter?" said Richard, opening the door of the Saab.

"Did you have anything to do with it?"

"Fuck off," said Richard.

"That's not an answer to the question, is it?"

Richard slammed the door and started the car. Peter stood with his hands in his jacket pockets and watched him drive away. He shook his head and went back into the house.

There was just about enough light left in the day for what he had to do. Raking leaves into a pile, he started a fire using some of the small branches that had come down during the summer storms. Using the garden fork, he tossed leaves onto the bonfire and as smoke rose up in dense plumes he went into the garage.

He took the Verelst from where he'd hidden it and put it down on the workbench. Using a club hammer he knocked the canvas out of the frame. The frame itself, gilded plaster and wood, he smashed up, working quickly so as not to lose his nerve.

If he was guilty of causing Amanda's death, well that was one thing. But this? This was a crime of a different nature. He thought he would vomit as he picked up a Stanley knife from his toolbox. Sliding out the blade, he took great care in cutting a rectangle from the painting. Now he had an image of the butterfly hovering above two of the flowers, which he thought was the essence of the work. Then he slashed at the remains of the canvas, again and again.

He took everything outside and threw it onto the fire. The smouldering leaves were too damp to burn so he fetched the can of petrol he kept for the lawnmower. Dowsing the fragments of canvas and plaster and wood he struck a match, tossed it on, and then another. There was a loud whump, and the flames jumped out at him, and he staggered back. The smell of singed hair made him beat at his head and his clothes like a demented drunk.

There was more work to do. Under the fluorescent tubes he began to search the dank garage for anything else that might burn. He found discarded lengths of two by one and two by two, an old Lloyd Loom chair that had been here when he bought the house. He broke everything up with an old blunt axe and fed the flames. It was a good hot blaze, and he took the strip of Rohypnol tablets out of his pocket and threw it into the fire. If asked, he would say he'd decided to tidy the garden of leaves to take his mind off Amanda's death. Grief had made him do it; sent him haywire, he'd say.

The brightness of the flames had fooled him; as they died down, he realised how dark it had become. Now, he wouldn't be able to see how well the fire had done its work. Knowing he would have to come back in the morning and rake amongst the ashes, for anything left of the frame and the canvas and the foil strip of tablets, he went back into the house and poured himself a large glass of Shiraz.

He stood in the dining room with the lights off, and looked out over the garden, watching the fire burn out. He had given up not smoking in the house (it was *his* house, after all) and lit a cigarette. It was the middle of the afternoon in Toronto. Time, he thought, to call Lisa McKee and tell her the news. He wondered if she would think it was good news or not.

"Do they think she died from drinking?" said Lisa. "I suppose that can happen."

"Well, I don't know but I'm having a drink right now," he said. "Will you have one with me? I don't like drinking alone."

He waited, listening to her moving about as she poured herself a glass of something. "What are we celebrating?" she said. "An accidental death?"

"The police think she might have taken something. They won't know until after the autopsy."

"Taken what? What are they hoping to find?"

"Rohypnol," he said, and poured himself another glass of wine.

"Is that possible?"

"Amanda had a load of prescription drugs she'd brought from Canada."

"The bitch, excuse my French, was a regular little pharmacist, wasn't she?"

"And she killed Emily. Fed her the painkillers like sweets. She told me that."

He looked out of the French windows. The fire had finally died out.

"You know there's something I want to ask you," said Lisa.

"Ask me some other time," he said. He had a terrible thought; that someone might be listening.

"Well, here's to an accidental death," she said.

"She told me other things as well, Lisa. Things that made me feel sorry for her."

"Hold your nerve, darling. They have to prove it, you know."

"I'll come to Toronto when this is all over. If you'll have me."

"You don't have to ask that, Richard. You just have to mean it."

22

Early on Monday morning a grey mist came off the river and crept up into the city. Richard sat at his desk with the lights off. When Catherine came in at ten o'clock, he told her Amanda was dead.

It gave her an excuse to try and comfort him. As she embraced him, he thought it was a mistake; coming back across a bridge he thought he'd burnt. She kissed him on the lips. But it didn't feel right; she didn't taste like Amanda. That he'd made the comparison shocked him. Nor could he hide his reticence; his body stiffened, and she pushed him away.

She went into the kitchen to make coffee. When she came back with the tray, she pushed it across the surface of the desk, and a pile of catalogues fell onto the floor. Richard bent down to pick them up.

"You were having a private party, were you?" she said. "Just the two of you?"

"That's not how it was," he said.

"Well, you didn't want me to go."

"I told you why," he said.

"I think you just wanted me out of the way," said Catherine, turning to look out into the gallery rather than face him. "There was something going on between you two. Something not quite right."

"What do you mean?"

"I don't know what I mean. It always felt odd," she said, and turned to face him. "Did you do anything stupid?"

"Now you're talking nonsense."

"Well, what do the police think?"

"I don't know," he said. "I suppose they think it was an accident."

"You suppose?" she said, shaking her head.

He'd come into the gallery early to plug the spy pen into his computer and listen to the recording. After he'd heard it, he realised that it would do him no good at all. What Amanda had said about his father wasn't something he wanted the world to know. Her confession couldn't help him either; he knew that. The sounds of their struggle implicated him; the microphone had picked up her muffled whimpering from under the cushion as he'd tried to suffocate her. He didn't know if the police thought her death was an accident; he just hoped they did.

"A rock star's death," said Robson.

Although Walsh had said the same thing, it sounded even more crass out of Johnny's mouth. He'd come into the gallery to talk business and, when Richard told him about Amanda, he insisted on taking him to the Bacchus to pour Shiraz down his neck.

"Remember when it seemed like a good idea to die young?" said Richard after his third glass.

"I think that might have been a poor little rich kid thing," said Robson.

They were sitting at the bar. There was a big crowd in and Richard wondered if any of them would get any work done that afternoon. He wasn't sure he would get anything done himself as Robson drained his glass and waved it at the barman.

Johnny had a swagger even when he was sitting down. He had one foot on the rung of his barstool, and the other on the floor. His jacket was undone, showing off his red braces. Splaying his legs wide, he turned and looked around the room. He was grinning because he was pleased with himself, and he wanted the world to know it.

"See her. The blonde in the white shirt?" said Robson. "Your four o'clock."

Richard turned and looked. A young woman was sitting at a table near the door with two men in business suits. She glanced up as if she sensed his interest, and smiled. He returned her smile and turned back to Robson.

"So, what about her?" he said.

"She's bored. Those two idiots are probably talking about football. I could just walk over there," said Robson. "And we'd be in a hotel room in fifteen minutes. Just like that." He clicked his fingers.

"And how would you make that happen?" said Richard, hunching over his glass on the bar. He'd had enough of The Johnny Robson Show.

"By acting like a man," said Robson, swinging himself around to face Richard. "This feminist stuff is just complete rubbish. All women want a real man. Someone who knows what he wants. Most people don't know what they want. But they're attracted to those who do."

"So do you think most people want to be told what they want?"

"Your trouble is that you spend too much time worrying about what other people think of you. Trying to get them to like you instead of telling them what it is you want. More importantly, what you want from them. Maybe you've had it too easy. That's why you don't know how to go out and grab it. Do you know what a real man is? A real man does just what he wants. Nobody tells me what to do. So, yes, I know what I want, and I make sure I get it. Do you know what you want, Richard? Do you?"

"I want the gallery to be successful. I know that much."

"Let's talk about that, then," said Robson. "But here's your problem. Your window of opportunity is shrinking fast. My accountant says I need to get rid of a bundle of cash. I need to do it ASAP. I've told you that I'd like to put it into your gallery. But do you want my money? Because if you do, we need to sort it now. Lawyers, contracts, that sort of thing. Or do I need to find some other way to hide it from the fucking taxman?"

"So you're a man who doesn't like to pay tax?"

"Tax is socialist bollocks. Why should I pay for some fucker not to work? They don't lift a finger to help themselves. I know people who have been on benefits for four generations. And they've always got their hands out when I'm around."

"This isn't a good time for me," said Richard. "There's probably going to be an autopsy. Then an inquest. And then the funeral. I've got a lot on my mind."

"You're not hungry enough."

When he couldn't stand his nicotine craving or Johnny's bluster anymore, Richard went outside for a cigarette. The blonde woman came out soon after, and asked him for a light. They had to huddle together in the doorway to shelter his lighter from the wind whipping up the lane. She wasn't wearing a coat, just a skirt and a thin white cotton shirt, and close up he saw how young she was; in her twenties.

"That's Johnny Robson you're with, isn't it?" she said, folding her arms around herself, shivering as she smoked. "That man's a fucking legend," she said. "If anything's going to happen in this town, he's the one who's going to make it happen. I'd like to grab onto those coat-tails, I can tell you."

"Do you want me to introduce you?"

"No need. I can pitch myself."

"He likes people who know what they want."

"I want to get on," she said. "Do you work for him?"

He told her about the gallery but she wasn't impressed.

"Is there any money in that?" she said.

"Money's not everything."

"You're kidding, right?"

"Of course I am," he said, dropping his cigarette to the ground and twisting his foot over it. "Go and tell Johnny I had to go. And tell him to call Catherine about the deal. Could you do that for me?"

"Why not?" she said. "It's a good intro. Your friend asked me to give you a message…"

"I envy you," he said. "You're one of those rare people who actually know what they want."

"Are you sure about this?" said Catherine.

Richard was sure; he'd made his mind up. He had that clarity which sometimes comes after a few drinks, when the drunken mind perceives what the sober one couldn't: the simple solution to a complex problem. That he wanted Robson to make the deal with Catherine made more and more sense to him as he walked down Grey Street towards the gallery. He wanted her in the business, but he didn't want her in his bed. With a wave of his hand it was done. This was the way to buy her off: to give her a stake in the gallery.

"I think you deserve it," he said, drinking from the bottle of mineral water he'd taken from the fridge. He was trying to sober up.

"And what about us?"

"We work well together, don't we?"

"You mean there is no us."

"You'll be a full partner in the gallery. I might go away for a while, so you'll be in charge."

"What about what I want?"

"I thought you wanted to be in the art business. Us is not working out. And now there's too much other stuff to deal with."

"I used to think that if Amanda went, then things would settle down between us again. But there are things I don't know anything about, aren't there? Things you're not saying."

"There's nothing for you to know," he said.

The door buzzer sounded; someone had come into the gallery from the street. But neither of them looked around.

"I hate to speak ill of the dead," she said. "But I can't help myself. She was a psychopath or something. An absolute witch. And she had something on you. Some kind of magic power."

As he was about to make some sort of denial, DS Walsh

rapped on the open office door. She stood straight-faced, wearing the same navy trouser suit she'd worn the last time he'd seen her, with that notebook in her hand. And she wasn't alone. A younger man in a tan leather jacket and jeans stood behind her with a folder under his arm. Richard wondered if they'd heard what Catherine had said. And why were there two of them?

"Am I interrupting something?" said Walsh.

She stood very close to him, and must have smelled the alcohol on his breath because she winced. Richard flushed. The other detective, DC Thomas, began to wander about the office, casually looking at the paintings and prints on the walls, as if he was there just to kill time. Catherine offered to make coffee and went into the kitchen.

"You should have called first," said Richard, sitting behind his computer and pretending to look at the screen. "I'm afraid there's rather a lot to do here."

"Have you been drinking, Richard?" said Walsh, standing on the other side of the desk, so close that her thighs were pushing against the edge of it. She was looking down at him and asking him the question as if she was a therapist.

"Boozy lunch with a client, a potential investor. It's an occupational hazard."

"I suppose you need to be careful, don't you?" She started knocking her pen against the cover of her notebook, tap-tap-tapping like a bird pecking at a windowpane.

"In what way?"

"Sometimes people do stupid things when they're drunk," she said. "Things they wouldn't normally do."

Catherine brought the coffee things in on a tray and Richard used the opportunity to deflect the situation, asking if they wanted milk or sugar or a biscuit. Thomas sat down on the sofa with his cup, and Walsh took the chair on the other side of the desk.

"We need to talk to Mr Waverley alone," she said.

Catherine took her coffee out into the gallery. Walsh watched her walk to the desk out there and closed the door. There had been a preliminary analysis of Amanda's blood, she said. They wanted to know if he could throw any light on what had come of it.

"What do you mean?"

"Did Amanda take anything, any drugs, in front of you on the evening of her death?"

"Such as?"

Thomas stood up and opened the folder. He took out an A4 print of a digital photograph and handed it to Richard. It was a close up of the coffee table in his grandmother's house. A small white plastic bottle, its cap discarded, was lying on its side.

"Did you see this that night? Or did Amanda show it to you at any point in the evening?"

Richard shook his head. "No," he said, relieved to be able to tell the truth. "What is it?"

"OxyContin. It's an opioid painkiller. Popular in the States for all the wrong reasons."

"I don't understand," said Richard.

"Your cousin took some of these," said DC Thomas. "Either while you were there, or after you left. We don't know exactly how many tablets she took, but the bottle's empty. The drug was probably a contributing factor in her death. It might have been *the* contributing factor."

"Did she have any reason to take her own life?" said Walsh.

"She was upset about her mother's death," said Richard. "That was from an overdose of painkillers, you know. An accident or suicide, no one knew."

"Did this come up in your conversation on the night she died?"

"We talked about our parents. All our parents are dead. Amanda has, had, a stepfather, but they didn't get on. She said we were both orphans now."

He remembered that she'd said something like that to him in Toronto, the night before Emily's funeral. There were things he could say that were true, or nearly true, and that made him feel safer. And if she had overdosed on the OxyContin, then perhaps the Rohypnol had nothing to do with her death, and perhaps he wasn't guilty of anything.

"Peter Morgan told us that he heard Amanda start to cry as you left. You didn't think to stay with her if she was upset?"

"We were both upset. We'd drunk too much. It was time to call it a night."

"The wine stains on the carpet. How did they come about?"

"We were drunk and clumsy. Amanda knocked the table when she got up to go out for a cigarette."

"You weren't arguing?"

"We were emotional. Since Amanda came home, we've been raking over the past. That can be upsetting. You must know that."

They were trying to rattle him; stirring things up to see what floated to the surface. Well, he wouldn't rise to it. They would have to come at him with something definite. But why was Walsh pushing at him like this? Did she think he'd talked Amanda into taking an overdose of the bloody things? Or that he'd poured them down her throat and wiped his fingerprints off the bottle? There was no evidence for anything like that or they would have taken him down to the police station and interrogated him properly, with tape recorders and video cameras.

"So, what do you think happened?" he said.

"That's up to the coroner to decide," said Walsh, standing up. "You'll be called as a witness. So, don't leave the country."

Neither of the detectives had touched their coffee. After they left Richard went into the kitchen to make a fresh cafetière; he needed to sober up. If Walsh had overheard what Catherine had been saying to him about Amanda, about her power over him, then she might have reason to be suspicious. In the scheme of things, simple hate was probably reason enough. But it wasn't as simple as that. And there was the business about the power of attorney, and the fact that his grandmother had been thinking about drawing up a new will. Money was a good, reliable motive for murder in anybody's book.

That evening he was alone in his house. He'd decided to have only one glass of wine with his supper, a grilled steak and salad; he needed to practise sobriety. Later he would telephone Lisa McKee; he always thought of her by her full name, as if she were a famous person. And then he tried to remember what kissing her was like.

Amanda had taught him how to kiss. Her kissing lessons had come before her sex lessons. When Catherine had kissed him this morning, his memory had triggered a comparison. If he had thought that Amanda's death freed him from her, now he began to worry that she'd ruined him. He was aware that he had been numbed by the news, but now the sense that she was no longer in the world overwhelmed him and he began to weep.

The doorbell rang and then there was a frantic knocking so he went through the house to open the front door. Rhiannon stood on the step wearing jeans, a leather jacket, and no make-up. Richard stood aside to let her pass, and she dragged a large wheeled suitcase into the hallway. Looking down the front garden to the street, Richard saw a taxi drive away.

"I've left him," she said. "I've come here for sanctuary until you can get Jimmy here."

"Why here?" he said.

"Because it's the last place that bastard will think of looking."

"You'd better have a drink," he said. "You look like you need one."

Richard led Rhiannon down to the kitchen. His pledge, to drink just one glass of wine tonight, was about to be broken.

193

23

Rhiannon sat at the kitchen table fussing over her nails. Richard took a bottle of white wine from the fridge and poured them both a glass.

"Look," she said, fluttering her fingers in front of his face. "Don't you think they're pretty?"

"Are they real?" he said.

"Of course not. I use the best nail bar in town. You drink champagne while they give you a manicure. Don't you think that's lush?"

She emptied her glass and Richard filled it again. She'd been drinking already. He knew that. Not just because her speech was slurred: the description of the argument she'd had with Robson made no sense at all. She had a drunk's conviction that he knew things he didn't; intimate details of her marriage and the justness of her cause.

"He thinks I don't do anything to improve myself. What the fuck's that supposed to mean?" she said, grabbing Richard's arm across the table. "I do my bit. Like when a dress feels tighter than it did last time I wore it, well I sort it out. Even if it means extra spin classes every week. And whatever diet everyone else is on." She cupped her breasts in her hands. "And if these start to go south. Well, he'd expect me to get work done. Go under the knife. He's only bothered about what I look like. If I look good, he looks good. If he puts weight on, I've got to keep my mouth shut. I'm married to a fat bloke with money."

She grabbed Richard's arm again.

"You should have gone to a hotel to cool off," he said, pulling his arm free. "You're another headache I don't need."

"You're not being very sympathetic."

"Johnny hired a detective once. He could hire another one. I bet you use the same cab company all the time. You've probably got an account," said Richard, and he saw from her face it was true. "Well, it wouldn't take much to find the driver. Or where he dropped you off."

Rhiannon glared at him and drained her glass. Richard pushed the bottle across the table towards her.

"Picpoul," she said, picking it up and looking at the label. "We all used to drink Pinot Grigio, and then it was Sauvignon Blanc. Or it might have been the other way round. Now we all drink Picpoul. I wore Jimmy Choo when it was the right time to wear Jimmy Choo. And I knew when to stop drinking the Sav Blank and start drinking the Picpoul de Pinet."

She mispronounced the name in a singsong voice and Richard corrected her because she was annoying him.

"You speak French? Of course you do. That's why Johnny likes you. That's why he hates you too. You'd think he didn't care, the way he acts, wouldn't you? All that take me as you find me, self-made man shite. But he wants respect. That's his weakness. He's a fucking gangster who wants to be a prince. He wants people like you to respect him."

"People like me?"

"People who speak French and pretend not to be impressed with his new Porsche. You can see that; your type always does. You sold him that culture thing. You're just taking him for his money. Perhaps he'll find himself somebody younger. Someone who speaks French and doesn't have a Geordie accent. Someone to have on his arm when he's a patron of the arts. Jimmy is still in touch with where he came from. Johnny wants to leave it all behind."

"Why did you come here?" he said.

"Because you know where Jimmy is. And I want to see him."

"Go back to your husband," said Richard. "He doesn't want to lose you."

"He doesn't want to get shown up, you mean. He doesn't like to lose face. Another man shagging his wife. Not a good look for a man like Johnny Robson."

Richard got to his feet. He rushed out through the front door and down the path to the street. When he got to the pavement, he lit a cigarette and stood and smoked, looking along the line of cars huddled up under the streetlamps. What did he expect to see? Johnny Robson's private eye sitting in a car with a cup of coffee steaming up the windscreen? He felt ridiculous and went back into the house.

But he knew that Johnny's ego, all that bluster about being a real man, would demand some sort of revenge for the affair, and he cursed Rhiannon for bringing it to his door. She was smoking a cigarette when he got back to the kitchen, her eyes glassy and unfocused. Richard took a heavy glass ashtray from the cupboard under the sink and let it drop on to the table. The thump startled her and he sat down.

"Go to a hotel," he said. "I don't want you here. I don't want you dragging me into this."

"You're already in it up to your neck. You didn't say a thing about Jimmy and me, did you? Johnny wouldn't have wanted to buy the paintings then, would he? You just wanted his money. And now you want more. So you're well and truly in it."

"James did alright out of it. He's got as much to lose as I have. Do you want to cause trouble for him?"

"Help me," she said. "Or I'll make a fuss. I can make a lot of noise."

"What will you do if I take you to him?"

"I don't know. We could go away, couldn't we? Disappear somewhere."

"Go to a hotel tonight. I'll take you to see James tomorrow. You can sort it out between you."

Rhiannon took a last draw of her cigarette, crushed it out in the ashtray and nodded. She took out her phone and called a taxi to take her to the Malmaison on the Quayside. Of course she'd called her usual cab company. She didn't believe him, or didn't care if it helped to trace her. When she'd left and the front door closed behind her, he sat at the kitchen table with a glass of wine and a cigarette.

He'd been in control when he pursued Robson. He'd known what he was doing. Culture was a proven antidote to the vulgarity of new money. But now the gallery was in danger; this bloody stupid affair could ruin everything. He would have to try and make things up with his grandmother and persuade her to open her chequebook again. At least Amanda couldn't stop that happening now.

But then he remembered the brief glimpse he'd had of her legs sticking out from behind the settee. And Walsh's questions were unnerving him. She thought he'd played a part in Amanda's death, that he was guilty. Rhiannon had mentioned disappearing. Sailing off into the sunset. Of course it was a fantasy, but suddenly it seemed like a very good idea.

Richard poured himself another drink; he wanted to stop the thoughts jostling around his head. He wanted numbness and sleep. His phone rang. It was Peter, anxious and agitated, with something on his mind.

"Meet me in the morning," said Richard. "But don't come to the gallery. Meet me at Di Marco's."

"The wedding's off," said Peter, pausing as the waitress set their cups down on the table. "Jane says it's just until this business is settled. But I think she's lost her appetite for it."

"I'll go and see her," said Richard.

"I'm not sure that's a good idea. She thinks you're to blame."

"For what?" he paused. He knew what. "Amanda took an overdose. How's that my fault?"

"Jane thinks that you pushed her too far. Got at her in some way by raking up the past. Some nonsense about Amanda and your father."

"What does she have to say about that?"

"She doesn't really. Sometimes she doesn't make any sense. But she knows that you went to see the solicitor. Thinks you're obsessed with money."

"And what do you think, Peter?"

"Amanda was trouble, I know that much. But there was something between you," said Peter, shaking his hand in the air. "Something a bit off."

"Does Nana know that Amanda was messing about with her painkillers?"

"You try bringing it up, Richard. See where it gets you. Amanda is the golden child now she's dead. And you're the naughty boy."

"Do you think I had anything to do with it?"

Richard waited for Peter's answer. He was worried now about how other people might see it. How it looked. He'd deliberately put the foil strip of Rohypnol in his jacket pocket on Saturday night. Dropping the tablet into Amanda's drink had been a premeditated act. What if that had been the deciding factor in her death?

Peter shrugged. "I don't think you forced the pills down her throat. But you were there just before she took them. So I don't know what to think, Richard. I really don't."

Rhiannon was waiting for Richard at the hotel, sitting on one of the low sofas in front of the reception desk and flicking through a magazine. She looked up when he came through the glass doors; he noticed her hair and make-up were immaculate but there were still faint lines under her eyes; the final trace of last night's booze. In that moment he saw something of the young woman she had been, her vulnerability and the need to be looked at. Robson would appreciate that; he enjoyed the way men looked at his wife, and Richard had to admit she was beautiful.

He wondered what James thought about it, whether or not it was important to him in the same way. Did he, for instance, appreciate her fashion sense, her long glossy fingernails and her talent for always being 'on trend'? Would he like her skinny jeans and the large Versace sunglasses nesting in her hair? It was upmarket, mainstream fashion, not the quirky aesthetic of the art crowd.

But Richard didn't want to feel sorry for her. Rhiannon must have sensed his lack of sympathy. She tossed the magazine down, pulled the sunglasses out of her hair and put them on, looking at him from behind their dark, impenetrable lenses.

"You're late," she said, and stood up.

"Come on then," he said, grabbing the handle of her wheeled suitcase.

He pulled it out to his car and put it in the boot.

She stood and looked at the Saab. "Is this why you need Johnny's money?"

"Just get in," he said.

As he opened the driver's door, he looked around the forecourt of the hotel. A blue BMW was parked across the road with two men in it. He wished that he'd thought to hire a car, an anonymous Ford saloon with a big engine. The Saab was an oddity, and that would make it easy to follow.

The BMW followed them up to the roundabout that led onto the central motorway. Richard kept checking the rear-view mirror as he drove across the city. The other car was always behind them, always two or three vehicles back. When he joined the A1 going north it was still there. He drove slowly to see if it was just a coincidence, but the BMW didn't overtake him.

"Is there something wrong with this car?" said Rhiannon.

"I think we're being followed."

Rhiannon turned in her seat.

"The blue BMW," he said. "It's been behind us since we left the hotel."

"They're not very good at it, are they?"

"It doesn't matter. Johnny knows. This is just a game now."

"You're up to your neck in it. What are you going to do?"

Richard checked his door mirror. He pulled out and accelerated. The turbo roared and he kept his foot down until he lost sight of the BMW on the long curving bend before the A1 changed from a dual carriageway to single lanes.

Slowing down, passing a junction where a black Mercedes van with tinted glass was waiting to come out, he took the next right turn to access the network of narrow winding roads that would take them to the coast. He'd checked the rear-view mirror as he made the turn. There was no sign of the BMW, only the Mercedes van, which had made the turn behind them. It was being driven too slowly to bother him, and soon they left it far behind.

"You just wanted Johnny's money, didn't you?" said Rhiannon. "People like you always sneer at people like him. You hate him because he's got money. Money you think you should have. Jimmy's different. He doesn't care about money. He's not a hypocrite."

"He cares about painting. I'm not sure you really know what that means. And he needs money to be able to do it. That's what all this was about. Money for James and money for the gallery."

"So you brought it on yourself."

"What do you think Johnny will do?"

"He'll do what he always does. Make a fuss and do some damage."

"The gallery. I suppose he'll take it out on the gallery."

"If he thinks you played him, he'll take it out on you."

"And you, Rhiannon. What will he do to you?"

They took the turn into the village. The cottage was detached, and sat on a rise above the beach. A glazed porch at the front faced the road, and at the back the conservatory looked out to sea. Richard pulled up behind James' Land Rover and beeped the horn.

He'd bought the place as a weekend retreat, but since his marriage had failed, he'd planned to do it up as a holiday let. But when he pushed open the front door and went into the sitting room, he didn't see the fantasy that the idea of a seaside cottage provokes in the English middle-class imagination.

Furniture that shouldn't have been in the room, it had come

from the conservatory, was stacked along the left-hand wall. A duvet and a sheet were twisted up on the sofa, and there was a pillow on the floor. The coffee table was covered in empty wine glasses and bottles, and dirty plates with liquorice paper roll-ups stubbed out amongst the remains of congealed food. The whole place stank of turps, oil paint and tobacco smoke. And sweat.

James came through wiping his hands on a rag, one of his brown cigarettes hanging from his lips. Richard saw the look in his eyes, the unkempt hair and beard. His clothes, Levi's and a thick sweater, were covered in paint.

"What is it?" he said. "Why have you come?"

"I've had enough of him, Jimmy," said Rhiannon. "I've come to be with you."

"Oh that," James said, turning to go back the way he had come. "Go away with that. I'm busy."

Rhiannon sighed and they followed him into the conservatory. Canvasses were stacked against the walls, more than there had been on Richard's last visit. There was a new painting on the easel, illuminated by the daylight falling through the glass roof, an image of a vast swirling sky. The kitchen table had been pulled through; it was covered in tubes of paint and cans of brushes. Paint had dripped onto the tiled floor. The table, thought Richard, was ruined.

James ignored them both. He picked up a brush and stood in front of the easel, waiting for them to go.

"I thought we had something," said Rhiannon, grabbing his sleeve.

"You've got the wrong end of the stick," said James, pulling out of her grasp.

"You fucking bastard," she said, and slapped him.

Richard not only felt excluded, he felt exhausted. He thought he ought to drive away and leave them to it. As he went back through to the sitting room, he heard car engines. And then he opened the front door and looked towards the road.

The blue BMW was blocking the Land Rover and the Saab in.

Behind it, on the road, was the black Mercedes van. Its side door faced the cottage. It slid open. Sitting inside, looking directly at him was Johnny Robson.

"Well, well. Look who it is," he said, stepping out of the van. "I recognised your stupid little car."

Robson walked towards him with an easy swagger, hands in his trouser pockets, his suit jacket buttoned with his overcoat undone. He thought of what Rhiannon had said about Johnny being a gangster. With his shaven head and his thick black spectacles, he looked like one.

Richard kept his eyes on him, a steady impassive gaze to hide his fear. He heard car doors open and close, and was aware of three men with close-cropped hair, two with neat beards coming towards him. And a woman with dyed blonde hair in a ponytail, wearing trousers and a black zippered jacket. She pushed past him and went into the cottage. The woman was for Rhiannon.

Richard felt Robson's minty breath on his face.

"What have you been up to? Rescuing the beautiful princess from the evil ogre?" said Robson, patting Richard's cheek. And then he slapped it. Hard. "So what does that make you? Fucking Prince Charming?"

"I'm not Rhi's lover, Johnny, if that's what you mean," said Richard, slumping against the doorframe. He rubbed his cheek and looked up.

"Funny that. I was just thinking that you're not her type. And then I got to thinking about all our little chats about art and culture. You've been playing me all along. You might not be shagging her, but you know who is."

From inside the cottage they heard women's voices, James swearing and then a loud crash as something fell over.

"So who's here?" said Robson. "Let's find out."

Richard followed Robson through to the conservatory. The blonde had a firm grip on Rhiannon's arm. James was sitting on the floor, looking sheepish. The easel had been knocked over and the canvas lay at an awkward angle against a chair.

"He got a bit uppity," said the blonde. "So I had to give him a smack."

Robson looked at James. "I won't say it's nice to see you again," he said, looking at the paintings stacked against the wall. He turned his head sideways to look at the canvas that had been on the easel. "You've been busy, Jimmy. It's very good work, isn't it, Richard? But I know what I'd like to do with them."

"Just leave them alone, Johnny," said Richard. "Or I'll sue you for criminal damage."

Robson shrugged and went back into the sitting room and the blonde woman told them to follow. The room was full of people. One of the men leaned against the front door. Another stood by the door that led off the sitting room to the bedrooms and bathroom, and the other one blocked the door to the conservatory.

James sat on a wooden chair and tried to roll a cigarette, but his hands were shaking. Richard gave him one of his Marlboros, lit another for himself and looked out of the side window with a partial view of the sea. Rhiannon perched on the windowsill beside him. Nobody spoke. Robson just paced the floor.

"This place is a fucking pigsty," he said, suddenly pulling the duvet and sheet off the sofa. He sat down. "Is that what you want, Rhi? To live like this?"

"What do you care, Johnny?" she said, and sat beside him.

"You think I don't care? Is that what all this is about? I'm in fucking pieces here."

"What are you going to do?"

"I don't know what I'm going to do. Take you back? Throw you out? But I'm going to have to do something, aren't I? And Jimmy's got to get what's coming to him. I can't let that go, can I? And it's got to cost him something," he said, jabbing a finger at Richard.

Robson had them held under guard while he drove off in the Mercedes van. One of his men, the clean-shaven one who was called Dave, sat on a kitchen chair blocking the front door to stop any of them leaving. The other two, the ones with beards were outside. Richard thought they had gone down onto the beach but he couldn't see them from the window, and the blonde woman stopped him from going into the conservatory.

He found a roll of bin bags in the kitchen, and started to tidy up the sitting room to work off his anxiety. Rhiannon helped him wash up and Danielle, the blonde, made black tea because there was no milk.

It was dark when they heard vehicles; two or three diesel engines outside the cottage. Richard went to the front window and looked out but all he could see were headlights. He tried to open the front door, but Dave dropped him to the floor in the same way that Amanda used to, by kicking his legs out from under him.

Robson came in and ordered them all outside. Richard wanted to know what was going on, but Johnny laughed. "You'll see," he said, and pushed him through the door. James and Rhiannon followed. They walked in single file, along the path that led down to the gate at the bottom of the dunes, and out onto the beach.

A bonfire blazed less than thirty yards from the gate. A gust of wind brought a whiff of petrol with it. The driftwood, collected by Robson's men that afternoon, crackled in the flames. Richard felt the heat on his face, and was drawn towards the fire, even as he feared its meaning.

A diesel engine was revving hard along the beach. Richard zipped up his jacket against the wind and looked to where a rough track led down from the road. He saw a white Peugeot van lurching over the rocks, and then turn towards them, headlamps on full beam. It stopped near the bonfire, the engine still running as the driver's door opened and someone got out. It was Wolfgang.

"What's going on?" said Richard. "Why are you here?"

"It's not my business to say," said Wolfgang.

He went to the back of the van and began opening the doors.

Richard followed him, wanting to see what was inside. But he knew. James' paintings, the ones that he'd sold to Robson, were stacked up against the side, tied to the inner frame with Wolfgang's usual efficiency so they wouldn't get damaged in transit.

"Ask Catherine," said Wolfgang, climbing up into the van and undoing the knots on the canvas tapes.

"She's here?" said Richard turning to look up at the cottage. He saw her in her raincoat up at the gate, just standing and watching.

There was shouting. They were getting ready for something. Two of Robson's men closed in on James and held him by the arms. Danielle stood next to Rhiannon.

"You can't do this, Johnny," said Richard.

"These paintings are bought and paid for," said Robson. "So I can do what the fuck I like with them." He stepped towards the bonfire. "Okay, let's do this."

Wolfgang and Dave took the first painting out of the van. They held it in the headlights as if they were showing it off at an auction, long enough for anyone who knew about these things to see how wonderful it was. Then, as James was forced to watch, Robson gave the order.

"Burn the fucker."

James wailed and struggled.

Rhiannon said something and grabbed Robson's arm. But she was fascinated, as they all were, by the flames flicking around the painting, blistering the surface paint, devouring the canvas and then the stretcher. The other paintings were brought out, one at a time, shown off in the light and thrown onto the fire. Richard watched. He'd burnt the Verelst to save himself, hadn't he? So how could he condemn Johnny Robson for this?

When it was over and James was weeping on his knees in the sand, Richard walked towards the cottage to find Catherine. She was still at the gate, leaning on it and smoking a cigarette as if she was waiting for him.

"You should have been down on the beach," he said as he came up the path. "You would have had a better view of it."

"I saw it well enough from up here."

"You helped him, didn't you?" he said, stopping and looking up at her.

"Of course I did," she said. "Johnny's going to buy me my very own gallery."

"You're as rotten as the rest of them," he said, not because it was true, but because he wanted to hurt her.

"I want something for myself," she said. "Something of my own that someone like you can't ruin."

Catherine tied her raincoat belt tight because of the breeze coming off the sea, and put her hands in the pockets. She looked down at Richard. He saw the bright glow of the bonfire reflected in her eyes and knew that he had no power over her anymore.

24

There was no getting out of it; he had to give evidence at Amanda's inquest. After all, he was the last person to see her alive. His guts twisted at the thought. On top of that, his grandmother and Peter Morgan would be there to hear what he had to say.

The coroner's court was at the Civic Centre and they'd arranged to meet in the foyer. Richard noticed how they greeted him: his grandmother's cursorily proffered cheek, Peter's limp handshake. And in the lift, he felt their silence squeeze the air out of him.

In the courtroom they sat at a long table covered in blue baize cloth and faced the coroner. Walsh was there. She'd chosen to sit directly behind Richard. He thought she was trying to intimidate him by sitting so close. And at the back of the room he'd seen a young man with a reporter's notebook, so he knew there would be something in the papers about it.

Walsh gave the police version of events, how officers had been called to the house that particular morning, how the paramedics had declared Amanda medically dead as she lay on the sitting room floor. Richard heard his grandmother gasp, and reached out to squeeze her hand, but she pulled it away.

The coroner, a middle-aged woman with dark hair, read out the results of the post-mortem. There was nothing to suggest there had been any violence, she said. But the toxicology report showed that there were other things in Amanda's blood besides alcohol. Prescription drugs; Oxycodone Hydrochloride, which was OxyContin, Alprazolam, which was better known as Xanax, and Flunitrazepam, which was Rohypnol.

When Richard was called to give evidence he went up to the lectern where Walsh had stood. He had to take the Bible from the court officer and hold it up in his right hand. The oath was printed on a slip of paper and he read it out, determined not to stumble over the words and give himself away.

"I swear by almighty God that the evidence I shall give shall be the truth, the whole truth, and nothing but the truth," he said. As he confirmed his name, he felt Walsh's eyes on him and his stomach spasmed.

"Did Ms Johnson take anything, any medication at all, in your presence that night?" said the coroner.

"No. We were just drinking," said Richard, looking at her, not daring to face his grandmother, or Peter, or catch Walsh's eye. "I think we drank a lot."

"Did you ever see her take anything at any other time?"

"No. But I knew she had the drugs because she showed them to me."

"In his statement to the police Mr Morgan said he was staying in the house, and that he got out of bed to ask you to make less noise. He said Ms Johnson was crying. So I presume she was upset about something."

"We were quite drunk and started talking about our parents. Her mother, my Aunt Emily, died from an overdose of painkillers. She had osteoarthritis and was in a lot of pain. Amanda was always worried that she'd killed herself."

"And was she upset about it that night?"

"Yes, she was."

"And you didn't think to stay and comfort her?"

"We'd been talking about our parents." The coroner nodded, wanting him to go on. "Then she said something that upset me. Something about my father."

"So you had an argument?"

"Not really," said Richard. "She upset me. And then she upset herself."

"How did she upset you?"

"She said that my father had killed my mother."

"Really?"

"My parents died in a road accident twenty years ago. Amanda said dad was drunk. I know that wasn't true. I was in the back of the car, you see. So I know that wasn't true."

Richard found himself slipping into telling the story about the deer in the headlamps, and how his father had swerved to avoid it. Everything always seemed to come down to this. He always used the story to provoke sympathy, even as he was trying to cover up the awful truth of his parents' marriage. And after Amanda's confession or accusation or whatever it was, there was more to cover up. More lies to tell.

The room went quiet as if he were being allowed to collect himself. He looked at his grandmother. She didn't look at him, but Peter did, something in his face that Richard couldn't understand. It was as if he was shaking his head and saying, 'oh, dear, oh, dear, not that again.' And there was DS Walsh, watching him with dispassionate curiosity.

He took a breath and went on. "Amanda was drunk. I think she was trying to upset me because she was upset about her mother. She blamed herself for her death, you see. But what she said was very hurtful. That's why I left. She started laughing about it and then she started crying. I just thought she was drunk. People say funny things when they're drunk. Things they don't mean. I thought we'd make it up in the morning."

Afterwards, when it was over, Richard saw Walsh waiting for him outside the Civic Centre. From the way she looked at him, he knew he had to go over and speak to her. She went and sat on one of the benches overlooking the pool with the sculpture of swans taking flight. The bronze looked dull in the grey light, and a bitter wind pulled at the surface of the water, making waves that glinted like broken glass.

She took the cigarette he offered her, and he cupped his hands around his lighter so that they could both get a light.

"Death by misadventure," she said, pulling her padded jacket around her. "No signs that anyone else was involved, no real proof that there was an intention of suicide. That's a good result for you."

"Is it?" he said, buttoning his own coat against the wind.

"It gets you off the hook."

"You think I'm guilty of something?"

"Your cousin had a lot of drugs in her, that's all. Quite a cocktail, in fact. You could have slipped her one of them."

"What are you getting at?"

"The Rohypnol. It struck me as the odd one out."

"I heard people take it when they go clubbing. Roofies, they call them. Have you heard of that?"

"Oh, I've heard of it. But you weren't in a club, were you? Seems an odd choice, given the circumstances. Did you want to have sex with her?"

"Don't be vile," he said. "Is this an official interview?"

"No. Off the record. Call it professional curiosity," she said. "I'm a student of human behaviour. Odd things pique my interest."

"We were drinking. People do odd things when they're drinking."

"They provoke each other sometimes. Isn't that what you mean?"

"I mean that people upset each other all the time. It's not illegal, is it? Anyway, as I told the coroner, Amanda was upset about her mother's death. And that was an overdose, too."

"And she blamed herself for that?"

"I think she thought other people did. She was looking after her mother, you see."

"Did you hear any gossip about that?"

"No, I didn't. But you can feel these things, can't you? Other people's suspicions. And you always feel guilt after your parents die. You always find something to blame yourself for."

Getting to his feet, he put his hands into his coat pockets, turned towards the entrance of the Civic Centre and started to walk away from Walsh. He saw Peter guiding his grandmother down the steps. She was walking without a stick now, but slowly as if she wasn't certain of the ground beneath her feet any longer. She glanced over at Richard, and he knew that she'd seen him, but she turned her head away. Peter led her through the pillars. He would probably leave her under the rotunda where the limos and taxis turned during civic events. Then he would go and bring the Merc round and drive her home.

Richard wanted to follow them, to make some attempt at reconciliation, but he was aware that Walsh had stood up too, and was walking beside him. She wasn't finished with her 'off the record' interview.

"There's something else," she said, grabbing his sleeve. "If you've got a minute."

"What?" he said, unable to conceal the irritation in his voice.

"We searched the grounds of your grandmother's house. Well, a bright-eyed bobby saw that something had been buried in one of the beds. Turned out to be a Jiffy bag with some credit cards in it. You know, the ones that were stolen in the burglary."

"Really?" Richard was pleased that he was able to show genuine surprise; his conversations with Walsh were so fraught with half-truths and feints that they were wearing him out.

"The forensic report's only just come in. Your cousin's fingerprints were all over them."

"What do you think that means?"

"What does it mean? Well, if I were to go with a hunch, I'd say your cousin took them from the house and buried them. Which would lead me to conclude she took the painting as well. In that case she must have staged the break in."

"What about the Verelst? The painting?"

"There's no sign of your painting. I wouldn't mind having another go at finding it. It must be somewhere. But the real question is why. Why did she do it?"

"Perhaps she was just playing a trick on the rest of us."

"A trick? Is that the sort of person she was?"

"What do you want from me? She's dead. The mystery of what she did, and why she did it, died with her. Didn't it?"

"The burglary's still unsolved. I'd like to have one last look for the painting. I'd like to search your gallery, your garden shed, and your garage, even your attic. We've already searched your grandmother's house."

"You think I was involved?"

"No, no. It's just weird. Like I said, it's just professional curiosity. She must have done something with it."

Richard told Walsh she could search where she liked.

"I'd be really pleased if you found it. I really would. Can I go now?"

Peter's Mercedes was driving off when he got to the rotunda, the brake lights bright as the car took the bend. He would have to go up to the house now to try and make things up with his grandmother. Perhaps it was just as well; Walsh's questions had upset him. She suspected him of playing some part in Amanda's death; she just wasn't sure what it was.

As to the burglary, she obviously thought that it was part of a psychotic game between them. Walsh's suspicions weren't that far off the mark; there was an element of truth to them. For instance, she thought that Richard might have given Amanda Rohypnol so that he could have sex with her. That touched on two things. One that he'd slipped the drug into her wine. And two, that there was a sexual element to their relationship. Of course, none of it made any sense to an outsider, so in a way he was safe. On top of that, there was no hard evidence against him. The coroner hadn't seen any, had she? The official verdict was 'death by misadventure.' He was off the hook.

Catherine had agreed to stay at the gallery to see out Kirsten Dressler's exhibition. After that Richard was going to shut up shop.

212

He'd already cancelled the next exhibition. The artist hadn't seemed that put out when he told her. Richard knew why; Catherine was poaching his artists. Kirsten had told him, even as she confessed to taking a contract herself. "It's better for me, Richard," she'd said over the phone, her voice sounding so far away. "There's going to be more money for art fairs and shit. What else can I do?"

Richard didn't go straight back to the gallery after the inquest. He stopped off at the Bacchus. He needed a drink to steady his nerves, and stayed for two, stepping outside for a cigarette between them. Of course it was a mistake. It didn't numb the pain enough and it didn't alter the direction of travel. The destination remained the same. Experience should have taught him that. Self-medication didn't fix things; it made them worse. When he got back to the gallery, he made a clumsy pass at Catherine and tried to kiss her. She slapped his face and pushed him away.

"You've blown it, Richard," she said. "You blew it a long time ago."

For some reason he made the pointless gesture of pulling off the tie he'd worn for the inquest, and tossed it onto the floor. Catherine laughed at him, and he slumped on to the sofa and fell back. He was tired and drifted off until the buzzer sounded as someone opened the front door of the gallery.

Getting up from the sofa, Richard went over to the glass wall of the office and peeped through the gap in the open blinds. Robson was in the gallery talking to Catherine; she had her hand on his arm and they were laughing.

Robson must have sensed they were being watched. He made his fingers into a pistol. Pointing it towards the office he pretended to fire it, jerking his hand to mimic the recoil. Richard twisted the plastic rod that controlled the blinds and they snapped shut.

Catherine came back into the office and started to put on her coat. Robson had found some premises he thought they could use for the new gallery, and he wanted her to go and look at them. Richard wanted to know what had happened to Rhiannon.

"Oh, she's fine," said Catherine. "Johnny's crazy about her, you know."

"So you're not sleeping with him?"

"You really are such a bloody fool," she said, pulling on a pair of black leather gloves.

"That's not much of an answer."

"It's the only one you're getting," she said.

"Are you coming back?" he said. "Or do you still need access to the database?"

"No to both," said Catherine. She stopped in the doorway and turned. "By the way, what happened at the inquest?"

"Death by misadventure."

"What does that mean?"

"She did it to herself."

"Let's hope that stops all the gossip," she said, and walked out into the gallery.

"Come on, Cat," said Robson.

So he has a pet name for her now, thought Richard. He parted the blinds with his fingers and watched them leave. Catherine slipped effortlessly into the passenger seat of Robson's Porsche and they drove away.

As the taxi pulled into the drive, Richard saw the Mercedes outside the house. His grandmother would be in the sitting room with Peter, having afternoon tea and planning trips. Or the two of them would be cackling over bridge club gossip. Life would have returned to normal.

Richard let himself in. He called out, and went straight into the sitting room out of habit. But there was no one there. No copy of the Daily Telegraph on the coffee table, no pot of tea with cups on a tray. There were still wine stains on the Persian rug and he found a scrap of blue and white police tape on the floor.

Peter came and told him that the sitting room was out of bounds.

"Jane can't stand to go in," he said and took him into the kitchen. "We're having a late lunch, come and join us."

They were having quiche, a potato salad and bread and cheese. They must have finished their lunch; their plates were pushed aside. But they were still drinking; there was an empty wine bottle on the table and another one on the go. Richard went to kiss his grandmother, and she offered him her cheek. It was the same cold, mechanical gesture as on the morning of the inquest.

Peter brought him a glass and asked him if he'd eaten. Richard shook his head and poured himself some wine. He ate some cheese and broke off a piece of French bread; suddenly he was ravenous. There was an awkward silence. They'd been talking about him, and now he was here they didn't know what to say.

"I could take a cloth and a bucket of water and clean up the wine stains on the Persian rug," he said.

"Don't bother," said his grandmother. "The rug's ruined."

She slammed her fist down on the table. Peter took her hand and squeezed it.

"The whole room is ruined," she said. "I shall have to have it redecorated. Refurnish it. Not that it'll do any good."

"What did that policewoman want with you?" said Peter. "She didn't seem to want to let you go."

"She said that they'd found the credit cards buried in the garden."

"Oh, yes. We knew that," said Jane.

"She thought it was odd."

"What was odd?"

"Amanda's fingerprints were on them."

"What nonsense," said his grandmother. "Don't speak ill of the dead, Richard. But then again you don't seem to be able to help yourself, do you? I'll always think you had a hand in it, you know. Always."

"It was death by misadventure," said Richard. "Which means she did it to herself."

"Well, you fooled the coroner, didn't you? You had to tell her about the accident. As if that excuses you of everything. I'm sick of hearing about that fucking deer. I really am."

That she was angry enough to swear sent his gut into spasms again. He'd wanted her to show him mercy. To put her arms around him, the way she had after his parents died, and tell him the world hadn't ended.

His chair fell over behind him as he stood up and rushed out of the kitchen. He went into the dining room, one of the places he'd sulked as a boy, thinking to crawl under the table and curl up into a ball. The afternoon light was fading. But he still noticed it; the slightly darker patch on the wall where the Verelst had hung.

25

Jane Waverley wanted Amanda's funeral to be perfect. She wanted a cortege of black limousines following the hearse. And as everyone gathered at the graveside, she wanted to step forward and throw a red rose into the grave.

Richard sat at the kitchen table, scribbling in a Moleskine notebook as his grandmother rambled on. Helping her to organise the funeral was his path to rehabilitation. He looked up as Peter passed him a cup of coffee, and saw the anxious look on his face.

The smell of paint and the sound of pop music drifted into the kitchen from across the hall. The decorators were in; the sitting room was being made new, ready for Amanda's wake.

"So how many cars, Nana?" said Richard, taking a sip of his coffee.

"How many are coming, Jane?" said Peter. "Have you made a list?"

"Well, I haven't counted. But everyone who knew her will be there."

"But who, exactly, Nana?"

"Well, everyone in the bridge club, for a start."

"How many is that?" said Peter.

One of the decorators knocked on the kitchen door. There was some question about the finish Jane wanted on the woodwork and she went to see to it. Peter changed seats, and sat next to Richard.

"This isn't good," he said. "The whole thing's going to be a disappointment for her. You know that Amanda hardly knew anyone. We'll get the bridge club, or at least most of them. But it'll just be a bunch of us old farts guzzling and gossiping about the same things we always gossip about. Jane's throwing herself into this. The idea's keeping her afloat. She'll crash. That's what I think. She'll just crash after this."

"Just you and me and the bridge club. There isn't really anybody else. Is there?"

"Doesn't exactly warrant a cortege, does it?" said Peter.

The police had finally returned Amanda's handbag. Richard took out her phone and scrolled through the contacts. There was a UK phone number and a woman's name, Nicole. Her friend from the gym? Surely, she would come to the funeral? He called the number and a woman answered. Yes, she knew Mandy from Pilates and Spin classes. They often lunched together.

"Too much Picpoul, sometimes," she said, and laughed. "Are you the cousin? Ohmigod. You were with her the night she died, weren't you? I read about it in the paper." Nicole paused. "We were just getting to know each other. I liked her."

Richard took his grandmother to view Amanda's body at the funeral directors. The Chapel of Rest was not a chapel at all. It was a suite of rooms on a corridor lined with pale oak doors, and carpet the colour of bleached sand. It had all the dull neutrality of a corporate office block and reminded him that death was business too.

A young woman in a black suit led the way. She stopped at one of the doors, opened it a few inches and gestured for them to enter. As they went into the room the door closed softly behind them.

There wasn't a coffin. Instead his grandmother had chosen an American casket, a mahogany hulk with chrome fittings. The top half of the lid was hinged and open; it was lined with white velvet. Amanda lay there in a black dress, hands on her lap, her dark hair framing her face. Her eyes were closed, her skin smooth and pale. Without her usual make up, the bright red lipstick and the sharp black mascara, Richard thought she looked like the girl he'd known in Toronto. But if there was ever any innocence or vulnerability about her, he didn't want to know about it now. She was dead and that was all there was to it.

Now he understood why Amanda had cremated her mother. It was always a problem for the killer, the disposal of the body. Something was always embedded in the corpse; evidence, memory, guilt. Burying it in the ground was one thing; out of sight was out of mind after all. But fire destroyed completely. The gas-fuelled incinerator at the crematorium was efficient, it turned everything to ash in double quick time. They should burn her, he thought, until there's nothing left.

The walls of the gallery were bare. Kirsten's paintings were covered in bubble wrap, stacked against the walls, waiting for Wolfgang to come and take them away. Richard was in the office packing. The front door buzzer sounded and he looked up. Walsh was standing at the window that looked on to the street, looking in with her hands cupped around her eyes. He knew she'd seen him, and went to let her in.

"I just came to tell you that there's no sign of your painting," she said. "I think Amanda destroyed it. Do you know why she would do that?"

"She liked to provoke people."

"When did you know she'd faked the burglary?"

"When you told me about the credit cards. Not until then."

"You didn't guess? She didn't brag about it? Let you know that she'd done it?"

"No," said Richard, folding a piece of bubble wrap around a stack of catalogues he wanted to keep.

"I'd say you're pulling out," said Walsh.

"I'm finished with it. Not just the gallery," he said. "I mean this bloody town. I'm going away. To Toronto."

"It's probably a good idea. People will always think you had something to do with Amanda's death. Even if you didn't. The coroner's verdict got you off the hook. Legally, I mean. But you know what people are like. Everyone likes to gossip."

"So, you think I'd get run out of town anyway," said Richard. "If I stayed?"

"Like I said, it's probably a good idea to get away. So what's in Toronto?"

"A woman. A girl I met when I was a teenager."

"I knew someone who met her teenage boyfriend again on Facebook. She went and left her husband and kids for him. So, who knows? You might strike lucky."

When Wolfgang came to take Kirsten's paintings away, his behaviour was strange, as if he was nervous. Richard helped him load the van, and thought he was embarrassed because of the part he'd played in the destruction of James' paintings. But then he remembered what Walsh had said.

After Wolfgang left, Richard called Lisa McKee. Her television was on. She was watching one of her cop shows. Well, he didn't mind that. He told her that he knew the date of the funeral now and was going to book a flight to Toronto.

"That's if you still want me to come," he said.

"Of course I do, darling," she said.

He said he was selling the house and the cottage and the lease on the gallery.

"Are you sure?" said Lisa. "You really are burning your bridges, aren't you?"

"There's nothing here for me anymore," he said. "I thought we could see what happens. One way or another."

He heard ice tinkling against glass. She was drinking. He tried to work out what time it was in Toronto. Was it too early to be drinking and watching cop shows on TV?

Richard had practiced his funeral expression in the bathroom mirror; shoulders slumped, face blank, and a little twitch at the corner of his mouth; a sad face smile. His grandmother, her arm through his, leaned against him on the long slow walk down the aisle as they followed behind the casket, and took their seats in the front row. Everyone turned to catch a glimpse of them as they passed.

He held the order of service in his lap, looking down at it, tracking each interminable moment of the ceremony, the vicar's guff, a hymn, a prayer, until he had to go up and deliver the eulogy. He said something about his teenage visit to Toronto. How, after the death of his parents, Amanda had given him love and affection in his darkest hour.

Of course that wasn't the end of it. The casket had to be carried out and lowered into the grave. Jane, in her long black coat and Edwardian velvet hat, threw the red rose in after it, and after that the others formed a line to toss in handfuls of dirt. Then the worst part began, the shaking of hands, fake embraces and kisses on cheeks. They all tried to look Richard in the eye while they pretended not to. He met each quizzical gaze with his sad, fake smile. To look away was as good as an admission of guilt. "He was shifty at the funeral." That's what they'd say.

From amongst the familiar, ageing faces of the bridge club, a blonde woman in an expensive black coat stepped towards him and took his hand. Then she kissed him on the cheek. She said she was sorry, so very, very sorry.

"I'm Nicole," she said. "Mandy's friend from the gym?"

He said that he was glad she could come. "My grandmother would really appreciate it if you came to the house afterwards. She'd love to talk to you." He directed her to where the limos were parked. "If you need a ride, I'm sure they can squeeze you in."

His grandmother had started walking away from the grave and back towards the cars, her arm through Peter's. Richard followed them back to the limousine and they rode to the house in silence. He wanted a drink. As soon as he got inside he grabbed a glass of wine and guzzled it. Then he thought to make himself useful, making sure everyone had a drink, or a plate of food. And then another quick glass for himself, and another to hold as he played out the final act. He thought he could handle it now, any funny business from the bridge club. But when he heard someone say "death by misadventure," he went out on to the patio for a cigarette.

Richard had to button up his jacket and turn the collar up against the cold. He heard the French door open and turned. It was Nicole. He'd noticed her bright presence in the room. She was as glamorous as Amanda had been. She still wore her long black coat, and looked comfortable, despite the chill, while he shivered a little as he smoked.

"I do all that stuff to get fit," she said. "And I still smoke. Stupid, isn't it?"

Richard noticed the unlit cigarette between her fingers. He flicked his lighter. As she cupped her hands around the flame to take a light, he noticed her long fingernails, glossy and red. She's a gym bunny, he thought, looking for something to do between glasses of Picpoul de Pinet.

"Mandy talked about you quite a lot, you know," said Nicole. "Said you used to have a crush on her. When you were teenagers."

"My cousin had a way of playing around with the truth."

"She said you weren't very nice to her at her mother's funeral. She was disappointed. After all she'd done for you."

"She used to tell lies," he said. "That was her thing. If you knew what she was really like, you wouldn't have been her friend."

"So she was right about something. She said you bore her a grudge for some reason."

"What reason could I have?" said Richard, turning towards Nicole, pushing his face into hers. "Did she say what reason? Did she tell you that?"

"So there was something."

"Yes," he said softly. "There was something." Tears stung his eyes.

"You're the only one who knows what happened to her. What happened that night, I mean."

"She died of a drug overdose. It's official. Death by misadventure."

"It's all anyone's talking about in there. Nobody knows what it really means."

"Why did you come?"

"I wanted to get a look at you. Because I liked her, I wanted to see what you had to say for yourself. There's a lot of anger in you, Richard. I think you had it in for her. I think you're the liar."

As he shuffled along, through the maze of Tensa-barriers towards baggage screening, Richard saw the armed police officers. Two of them holding assault rifles across their chests, watching over the slow-moving line of passengers. He noticed the suspicion in their eyes. And when he put his cabin baggage and his shoes onto a plastic tray and pushed it along the rollers towards the x-ray machine, he noticed the security officer give him a peculiar look.

The feeling of persecution didn't leave him. Not even when his plane took off for Heathrow. The cabin crew were Geordies, and he felt as if they knew who he was; that they'd read the papers, and thought he was guilty. Guilty of something, even if they didn't quite know what it was.

Even at Heathrow, far away from Tyneside and cruising aimlessly round the shops in Terminal Five, he couldn't relax. He realised that he needed to buy presents for Lisa McKee. In duty free he settled on a bottle of gin, a litre of Tanqueray, and a bottle of Veuve Clicquot. Then, because he saw the Christmas trees in the shop windows and in the concourse, he decided to buy her more presents; a pair of Versace sunglasses like the ones Rhiannon had worn, because they must have been fashionable, some Chanel Number 5 and a Hermes scarf.

Sitting on the flight to Toronto, waiting for take-off, he fell asleep. He had a dream; Walsh shouting at two uniformed officers to drag him off the plane. He jerked awake. At the same moment he'd dreamt of being yanked out of his seat, the steward shook him gently and told him to fasten his seatbelt.

It wasn't until the 747 was in the air that he relaxed. And after his first gin and tonic he started to believe he was on his way to Toronto again. It would be cold. He remembered what

Ray had said about spending the winters in Florida. But Lisa McKee had said she would buy him a parka.

She was going to meet him at the airport and then they would take a taxi, or perhaps she would drive her Hyundai Coupe, to her house in Rosedale. He would look at everything as if he had never seen it before; the American cars, the signs for strange burger chains, the wide boulevard that ran along the lakeshore, and the CN tower.

On Sundays they would go to the St Laurence market and buy food, take the ferry to the Islands and picnic on the little beach across the bay from the great glass towers of the city. When the money came through from the sale of his house and the cottage, he would open a gallery in the Old Distillery district. He would sell awful paintings and make money for the first time in his life. It dawned on him that he would never go back.

He wondered at what point in his past the trajectory of his life had been set. Of course, his parents' death was one thing. But now he knew his father had a hand in the way everything had turned out. Of course Amanda had something to do with it too, and he knew she'd been right; she'd owned him. That she'd still had some power over him after twenty years proved that. In some perverted way they were bound together, and neither of them had been given any choice in the matter.

Richard willed the aircraft on. The steward brought him another drink; a miniature bottle of Gordon's, a plastic glass with ice and a small can of Schweppes. Propped up against the edge of the fold down table he held a copy of Kirsten's catalogue. Not because he liked her paintings, which he did, but because it had been big enough to keep the fragment of the Verelst safe.

He studied the piece of canvas, putting on the overhead reading lamp to search out the butterfly. A Red Admiral, it hovered at the edge of the bouquet, as if trying to decide which flower to pollinate. But Verelst the painter had saved nature from itself. The butterfly had an eternity to choose.

Acknowledgments

Ailsa for everything. Literary and otherwise.

Special thanks to Jamie Warde-Aldam for reading numerous versions of this novel in progress without complaint. His close reading, advice, support and friendship have proved invaluable throughout.

I would also like to thank Tom Noble for helping me to publish this novel independently, and Tony Glover and Val Scully for their insight into the process.

Printed in Poland
by Amazon Fulfillment
Poland Sp. z o.o., Wrocław

49870040R00139